Additional Praise for Sandra Dallas

"As heartwarming as a homemade quilt."
—*USA Today* on *A Quilt for Christmas*

"The author's depiction of nineteenth-century Denver, especially its seedier side, is vividly authentic, while the nascent bond between Mick and Beret will have readers eagerly anticipating their next encounter."
—*Publishers Weekly* on *Fallen Women*

"A born storyteller, Dallas excels not only at plot but also at peopling her novels with memorable individuals."
—*Richmond Times-Dispatch* on *True Sisters*

"A tale of family, desire, vengeance, and betrayal that more than transcends the ordinary."
—*RT Book Reviews* on *The Bride's House*

"[Dallas's] sense of time and place is pitch-perfect and her affection for her characters infectious."
—*Kirkus Reviews* on *Whiter Than Snow*

"Putting down a Sandra Dallas novel is nearly impossible."
—*Daily Camera* (Boulder, Colorado) on *Prayers for Sale*

"An endearing story that depicts small-town eccentricities with affection and adds dazzle with some late-breaking surprises . . . Dallas hits all the right notes."
—*Publishers Weekly* on *The Persian Pickle Club*

ALSO BY SANDRA DALLAS

The Last Midwife
A Quilt for Christmas
Fallen Women
True Sisters
The Bride's House
Whiter Than Snow
Prayers for Sale
Tallgrass
New Mercies
The Chili Queen
Alice's Tulips
The Diary of Mattie Spenser
The Persian Pickle Club
Buster Midnight's Café

The PATCHWORK BRIDE

SANDRA DALLAS

ST. MARTIN'S GRIFFIN
NEW YORK

Published in the United States by
St. Martin's Griffin, an imprint of St. Martin's Publishing Group

THE PATCHWORK BRIDE. Copyright © 2018 by Sandra Dallas.
All rights reserved. Printed in the United States of America.
For information, address St. Martin's Publishing Group,
120 Broadway, New York, NY 10271.

www.stmartins.com

Designed by Devan Norman

The Library of Congress has cataloged the hardcover edition as follows:

Names: Dallas, Sandra, author.
Title: The patchwork bride / Sandra Dallas.
Description: First edition. | New York : St. Martin's Press, 2018.
Identifiers: LCCN 2017056739 | ISBN 9781250174031 (hardcover) |
    ISBN 9781250174055 (ebook)
Subjects: LCSH: Quilting—Fiction. | GSAFD: Love stories.
Classification: LCC PS3554.A434 P38 2018 | DDC 813/ .54—dc23
LC record available at https://lccn.loc.gov/2017056739

ISBN 978-1-250-17404-8 (trade paperback)

Our books may be purchased in bulk for promotional, educational, or business use. Please contact your local bookseller or the Macmillan Corporate and Premium Sales Department at 1-800-221-7945, extension 5442, or by email at MacmillanSpecialMarkets@macmillan.com.

First St. Martin's Griffin Edition: August 2019

10 9 8 7 6 5 4 3 2 1

To my grandmothers,
Hazel Mavity and Faye Dallas,
who taught me that love comes in tiny stitches

ACKNOWLEDGMENTS

Writing a novel is a little like quilting. Others contribute bits and pieces until the finished work becomes a collaborative effort. Thank you, Danielle Egan-Miller at Browne & Miller Literary Associates, for always having my back. You pulled me through a rough time. Thanks to agents Joanna MacKenzie and Clancey D'Isa, to editors Jennifer Enderlin and April Osborn at St. Martin's, for making this a better book, and to Arnie Grossman and Wick Downing for hanging in there with me. And especially thank you to my family—Bob, Dana, Kendal, Lloyd, and Forrest—for always being there for me.

CHAPTER ONE

The bright morning light that seeped through the attic window fell in streaks on the trunk which Ellen had opened. It was the third trunk she'd searched. She'd already gone through the contents in the barrel-back trunk and in the black metal one that had belonged to her grandmother. Now she looked through the leather trunk that she had brought with her when she'd gone to housekeeping on the ranch. She hadn't opened it in years. "At last," she muttered, pulling out a swath of white. She held out the fabric, slightly yellowed, then hugged it to her chest.

"What are you doing?"

Ellen whirled around. She hadn't heard him come up the stairs. "Looking for this," she replied, unfolding the garment. "Do you remember it?"

"You bet I do. You wore it when we were married. It's a dinger. You were, too." His eyes lit up.

Ellen smiled at him, surprised that such a little thing had stuck in his mind.

"What do you want that for?"

"For June's wedding quilt. The piecing's done, and I'm stitching it together. This morning I remembered it. I want it in the quilt. I'll cut a piece of it and tack it on."

"June's getting married?"

Ellen took a deep breath. She shouldn't have climbed the stairs. Her doctor had warned her, had said it wasn't good for her heart. She had taken the stairs slowly, resting on each landing, but still, she could feel the exertion. "June *is* getting married."

"Well, good for her. I hope he's worthy of her. She's the best of the bunch. When's the wedding?"

"You can ask her. She's downstairs in John's room, sleeping."

"June's here. Why didn't you tell me?"

Ellen clinched her fists, not at her husband but at fate. She *had* told him. In fact, he had gone into Durango with her the night before to meet June's plane. She had told him about the wedding, too, several times, and he had met their granddaughter's fiancé when the young man visited earlier in the year.

He turned his head to look out the window. "Maybe you did tell me. Maybe I just forgot," he said, sitting down on one of the trunks. "I forget an awful lot, don't I?"

"Your brain's just not big enough to cram everything into it. Some things have to get shoved out to make room for the new." She took his gnarled hand, the fingers twisted from where a devil horse had stepped on them, the skin mottled with scars and bumps, so many she had forgotten how he got them all. She loved his hands—gentle hands that caressed the horses, caressed her. She remembered those first years on the ranch, when he couldn't keep them off her, and even now, when he reached for her in the night, just to hold her, to know she was beside him. His hands remembered, even if he didn't.

He had forgotten so much. "It's age," the doctor had said, "age and being a rancher. How many times do you suppose he's been bucked off a horse?"

Ellen had shrugged. "I don't know. Too many to count. Surely there's something you can do. I won't have it. This just isn't fair."

There was nothing to be done, however. The confusion and the memory loss would only get worse, the doctor said.

"He mixes up things. He talks about something that happened forty years ago as if it were last week. And then he can't remember what he did yesterday."

"Old age is like that, Ellen. Just keep an eye on him so he doesn't wander off." He paused, then added that wouldn't be easy with her own health. She couldn't go gallivanting all over the countryside following him around. She and her husband would be better off living in town, finding a little house or better yet an apartment, so she wouldn't be tempted to overdo things. "I don't suppose old Ben would do that, would he?" he asked.

"We're not *that* old," Ellen replied. "Wild horses couldn't drag Ben into an apartment. He'd dry up if he couldn't be in his mountains. And I'll die before I let anybody take him away from the ranch. You just wait and see."

"You might do just that. With that heart of yours, you'd be better off in town, too. Think about it, Ellen."

The doctor was right. Another year on the ranch might kill both of them. Still, Ellen wasn't willing to give up, not yet, anyway. Oh, she had talked to a realtor. Prices for ranch land were good, and the ranch would sell quickly, but she wouldn't sign the papers. She'd wait until spring and see how things were. She wanted one more winter in front of the fireplace Ben had built out of rocks he'd collected, the two of them warm in her quilts spread over the solid wooden chairs. They would talk about their life together. What did it matter that Ben couldn't remember all of it? She would remember for both of them. Then the memories would die with her. Nobody cared about the stories of an old woman.

"Come on. Let's go downstairs," Ellen said, gripping her husband's hand as she stood up, the white fabric under her arm.

Ben looked confused. "I know I came up here for something, but I can't remember what."

"You came up here for me."

Later that morning, after Ben was gone, Ellen sat in the sunshine on the porch, sewing. The branches of the cottonwood tree sent shadows across the quilt top. Here and there, the sunlight seeped through the leaves, illuminating the swatches of silk and brocade, causing them to shimmer. Ellen stopped with half-drawn thread and smiled at the patches in the dappled light. She set down her needle and touched a scrap of the white stuff with the tip of her finger. It was as soft as butter and dear-bought because it was French and old even back then. She rubbed her finger against a bit of lace, now discolored with age, remembering. Then she slid her nail over the plain white piece of cotton she had rescued from the trunk, stitching it into place. It was still as sturdy as the day it was woven. As she flicked away a yellow cottonwood leaf that had fallen onto the quilt top, she lingered over a slip of brocade, still white as starlight. She had saved the scraps for years. They marked the moments in her life, her mother's and grandmother's lives, and the lives of friends. So many memories, she thought. She tucked under the raw edges of the tiny piece of white she had cut from the sash. It was plain cotton and didn't quite fit in with the other scraps, but it held memories—the best memories, she thought, knotting her thread. It should be part of June's wedding present. She took out a large-eyed needle and threaded it with embroidery floss.

"Is that my quilt?" June asked.

Ellen had been too lost in remembering to hear the girl approach. She looked up and nodded. "This will be the last one, the best one," she said, remembering that Ben had said just that morning that June was the best. She had made a quilt for each of her grandchildren when they married. June was the youngest, and now, with the girl's wedding set for the end of October, little more than a month away, before her fiancé was shipped out to fight in the war in Korea, June would get the last patchwork bride's quilt.

"It's beautiful, Granny, but it's not at all like the one you made for Elizabeth."

"No, it isn't." Ellen had quilted a blue-and-white Irish Chain for June's sister. That quilt and the others Ellen had made for her grandchildren had been pieced from cotton, with a mixture of ancient scraps of calico and new-bought percale from Penney's in Durango. Ellen wasn't sure why she had made a Crazy Quilt now, using cuttings of silk and satin and lace, with only here and there a bit of white cotton. She'd never liked the old-fashioned pattern. Crazy Quilts had always seemed indulgent and useless, too delicate for a ranch house. Many of the patches were irregular and wouldn't work for any other design. Besides, you couldn't piece a Lone Star or a Sunbonnet Sue or a Double Wedding Ring with such fragile fabrics.

She'd been a little shocked at herself for cutting up the old-fashioned dresses, although two of the garments were never finished. They had been stored in the cardboard box for too long. Some patches were foxed, others dark with age. The silk was split in places. It was foolish to cut apart the dresses, but what else would she do with them? They had been put away for fifty years, maybe a hundred. It was ridiculous to think anyone would ever wear them.

Besides, she thought, June was special. She deserved something unusual. June was the grandchild most like her, the one most like Ben, too. She loved the ranch, coming out from Chicago each year to spend her summer vacation with her grandparents. Those days would be over now that June was getting married. Ellen would miss her. Ben would, too. He had taught her to ride, had even given her one of the colts out of Little Texas. The other grandchildren had visited the ranch when they were small, but they had since gone on with their lives, sending postcards and thank-you notes for Christmas and birthday gifts, but they were too busy to visit. June was different. Instead of going to college in the East, like her brother and sister, she'd chosen the University of Denver, where she was closer to her grandparents and closer to the mountains she loved as much as Ellen did. When June couldn't visit, she wrote long letters to her grandmother, telling about college classes and boyfriends.

Ellen knew before June's mother did that June had fallen in love. In fact, she had met the young man even before June had taken him home to meet her parents in Chicago. David Proctor, his name was. June knew he was special or she wouldn't have brought him to the ranch that summer. He was a nice enough man, a little stiff, but maybe that was because he'd never ridden a horse before. Ben had taught him, and he'd taken to it. June liked the way he'd helped around the place and how he'd understood that Ben was slipping. Dave had been gentle with Ben, hadn't been annoyed when Ben forgot something or asked the same question three or four times. He told Ellen he wished he would one day know as much about ranching as Ben had forgotten.

"I was going to wake you, but I decided you needed your sleep. I'd thought you might want to go into Durango with your grandfather," Ellen told June. "He took Little Texas to the vet."

"Grandpa Ben still drives?"

"No, but he would if I didn't hide the truck keys." They'd argued over it, Ben demanding the keys and Ellen refusing to give them up. Ellen hated telling her husband he couldn't drive anymore, but she'd had to. He'd already gone into the ditch twice. Wesley, one of the ranch hands, took him, she explained.

"He's getting worse, isn't he?"

Ellen nodded, taking a stitch in the quilt. She was using creamy white floss to embroider designs along the seamlines of the quilt. Gold embroidery floss was traditional in Crazy Quilts, but Ellen had thought it too brassy. The white was more elegant, more appropriate for a bride. She had almost finished the embroidery when she'd remembered the white fabric in the attic and had gone to get it that morning.

"Will he get better?"

Ellen shook her head. "I suppose the time will come when he doesn't recognize even me. Frankly, I was a little surprised he knew who you were when you got off the plane. This morning, he didn't remember you were here." She paused. "The doctor says we should move into town."

"Leave the ranch? Oh, Granny, how could you?"

"I won't!" She paused long enough to settle down, then added, "I'll see how your grandfather is in the spring."

"And see how you are, too, Granny?"

Ellen didn't reply. If it weren't for her heart, she could

manage the ranch, but she was winded just walking down to the corral. She got palpitations when she made an error in the ranch's books, too. "Damn heart," she muttered.

"I'm sorry." June took Ellen's hand and stilled it for a moment.

Ellen looked down at their hands threaded together, just as she and Ben held hands sometimes. She had no reason to be angry. Theirs had been a wonderful life, the best she could imagine. She just had trouble accepting it. "If we move into town, well, I'll still have my memories."

"I want you to share them with me."

Ellen smiled then and brushed away a tear, embarrassed. She was a tough old bird and didn't cry often, not anymore. She patted the seat beside her on the swing and told June to sit down. "You tell me your story. Why are you here?"

"Isn't it enough that I wanted to see you?"

Ellen harrumphed. "You're getting married in a few weeks. You didn't just up and decide to visit your grandparents when you were in the middle of all those preparations. What's wrong?" She wrapped floss around her needle to make a herringbone stitch.

June shrugged.

"I imagine your mother has everything in order, down to the last detail. She's the most efficient woman I know," Ellen said about her daughter-in-law. She liked Evelyn, June's mother, although the woman could be a taskmaster.

"I know. She's arranged everything. All I have to do is show up."

"And will you?" Ellen glanced at her granddaughter out of the sides of her eyes, but June was not looking at her.

"That would be a memorable wedding, wouldn't it, if I didn't show up."

Ellen didn't say anything. She fastened her needle to one of the scraps and pushed the quilt top aside. She wondered if June was having second thoughts. Perhaps she wasn't ready to marry and Dave was pushing her, using the war as an excuse. Ellen understood that, understood it better than June could imagine. David would be shipped off to Korea and would want to know that June was waiting for him. It wasn't enough that they were engaged. June could always break an engagement, write him a Dear Dave letter. No, he would want the assurance that June was locked up, a wedding ring on her finger. June was strong-minded. She was Ellen's granddaughter, for heaven's sakes. Still, she was young and in love, and perhaps she didn't know what she wanted.

Ellen glanced at the girl and thought, again, that although they were separated by fifty years, the two of them were a great deal alike. Not that they looked alike. Ellen was tall and thin, with blue eyes and dark brown hair that was mostly gray now. June was shorter, with coppery hair and freckles that had come from Evelyn's side of the family. June had Ellen's hands, however. Her long fingers and long oval nails were just like Ellen's, too. Of course, June's hands were still sleek and pink, while Ellen's were brown and gnarled, toughened by the ranch work, the veins prominent, and the skin spotted from the sun that burned through the thin mountain air. Hands like Ben's. The two women's appearances were different, but inside, they were similar. June had Ellen's spirit, her sense of adventure, her love of the mountains.

"Do you have doubts?" Ellen asked.

"Maybe just a little."

"Of course all brides do, and with good reason. Marriage isn't easy."

"You had them, too?"

"Oh, my, yes." Ellen laughed. "I wouldn't have been human if I hadn't."

"But you and Grandpa Ben are so happy. Mom said once that the two of you beat with one heart."

Ellen smiled, thinking she was lucky to have a daughter-in-law who was so generous with her appraisal.

"You know, Granny, when I was little and came here in the summers, I thought you had the perfect marriage. I wanted mine to be just like yours."

"No marriage is perfect."

"I know. But I remember the way Grandpa Ben looked at you back then, the way his face lit up when you walked into the room. It still does, you know. I saw that last night. And you, Granny, your eyes follow him."

Ellen knew her granddaughter was right, and she felt fortunate. Theirs had indeed been a good marriage, the best she knew. They hadn't always agreed. Lord, no! She remembered the time she had wanted Ben to put a bathroom in the house, which back then was only three rooms. She was pregnant and wanted to take a bath without having to set up the tin tub in the kitchen and heat bathwater in a kettle on the stove. Ben said he was going to spend the money on a mare. Ellen had been so angry that she'd gone into town and withdrawn the cash from the bank to pay for the bathroom fixtures. Ben threatened to use the tub for a watering trough and didn't speak to her for a week. Once he got used to the indoor bathroom, however, he stopped complaining. They still had the tub, the porcelain cracked and nicked and stained orange from minerals in the water. It was in the old lean-to off the kitchen with the washing machine.

Remembering how silly that fight had been, Ellen turned her face back to the mountains. She could see the dark places where the clouds made shadows on the slopes, the horses running in the meadow, the snow in the crevices that had been there as long as she had lived on the ranch. "I'm a lucky woman," she told her granddaughter.

"I just want to know that fifty years from now, I made the right choice for my life, like you did. I don't want to end up sour like some of Mom's friends, sorry I ever let Dave pressure me into getting married."

Ellen studied the girl for a moment. "So you've run away, have you? That's why you came here."

June looked at her grandmother in surprise. "How did you know?"

"I just did."

June put her hands over her face. "It's awful of me, isn't it? After all the work Mom's put into making everything just right."

"Does she know you're here?"

"No." June brushed the tears off her cheeks. She'd called her parents in Chicago when she knew they wouldn't be home and left a message with the maid, saying that she didn't believe she could go through with the wedding, that she needed time to think things over and was going away. "I said I'd call later and explain things when I'd made a decision. I just couldn't talk to her then. How could I after everything she's done, all the work she's put in? I think Dad will be okay with it, but Mom will be furious."

"Oh, not so furious. Disappointed maybe."

"You won't tell her I'm here, will you? She might tell Dave."

"I won't lie to her if she asks, but no, I won't volunteer the information." Then Ellen asked about Dave.

June studied her hands for a moment. "That's the real question, isn't it?"

"Did you tell him you were running away?"

"Well, sure, I couldn't just leave him hanging, could I?" June stood and went to the edge of the porch and looked out. "I did it the coward's way, though. I didn't want to talk to him, so I left a letter at his place on the way to the airport, dropped it off when I knew he wouldn't be there. He'll have read it by now. I told him I just couldn't go through with the wedding. He'll be terribly hurt, won't he?"

"Probably." Ellen got up and stood beside her granddaughter, her arm around the girl's waist. "It's quite a view, isn't it? Those mountains soothe me when I'm troubled. They're so grand that they make what's bothering me seem small. They've been there for millions of years and make me realize my problems are temporary. Of course, they're my troubles, so they seem awful important." She squeezed June's waist. "I'm glad you came. This is the right place for you to think things through."

"Dave doesn't know I'm here either. Mom might guess, but I don't think Dave will. If he did, he'd show up on your doorstep. I don't want him to. I can't talk to him."

"You should."

"I know. It isn't fair to him."

"Do you want to tell me why you ran away?"

June turned and sat down on the porch swing, while Ellen returned to her stitching. "We had the worst fight, Granny." Getting married right away had been Dave's idea. She had wanted to wait. The night before June left, Dave had told her she'd be the perfect army wife. He'd said she'd be in a coffee klatch with the other wives and maybe do some kind of volunteer work at the base. "He went on and on, and I realized that as long as we were married, I wouldn't be me. I'd be a wife," June said. She had spent four years in college and wanted to do something with her life. That was why she had majored in business. She'd even been offered a job in a training program at a bank in Colorado Springs, an hour south of Denver, but of course, she'd turned it down since she was getting married. With Dave in the military, she couldn't count on staying in Colorado. "What Dave said made me look past the wedding. I'd feel buried. I wouldn't even have a name. I'd always be Mrs. David Proctor, an army wife. He referred to me as the little missus, and I just blew up. I told him I'd never settle for that. We were both so angry. I said he wanted to smother me, and he told me I didn't love him. Maybe I don't."

"It wouldn't be forever," Ellen said. "Dave will be discharged in a couple of years."

"That's just it. It *will* be forever. David plans to have a career in the military, like his father and his grandfather. Did you know he went to West Point? I should have thought this all through a long time ago."

"He could always change his mind," Ellen suggested.

June shook her head. "If he did, he'd resent me for it. The military's the only career he ever wanted. He'd blame me if he didn't stay in the army. That's not a very good basis for a marriage."

"So you ran away."

June gave a little smile. "Have you ever heard of such a thing?"

"Oh yes." Ellen ran her hand across the quilt top, then folded it and set it on a chair. There was coffee in the kitchen, she said. Maria, the cook and housekeeper, kept it on the stove in case Ben or one of the hands came in. She suggested June fetch coffee and Maria's bread, along with the apple butter the cook had made the day before. Then they could talk. "I'd like an excuse to do nothing but sit here in the sun," Ellen lied. The truth was, she didn't want to sit in the sun at all. She'd rather be on a horse, showing June the improvements she and Ben had made on the ranch since the last time June was there. But her riding days were over.

June got up and went inside, the screen door slamming behind her. Ellen watched her granddaughter disappear, then turned to study the horses as they raced across the meadow, the stallion in the lead. The sun shone on him, making his light brown coat appear almost white against the green mountains. He was descended from the stallion Ben had purchased years before. She was glad Ben had bought him, although she'd been angry enough at the time. She had wanted to remodel the kitchen, get rid of the old wooden Hoosier cupboard and put in cabinets, and they had quarreled. Then, perhaps remembering her defiance of a few years before when Ellen had spent their money on bathroom fixtures, Ben had gone ahead and bought the horse without her knowledge. She'd given him hell, but Ben hadn't backed down. The next year, however, he'd told her they ought to fix up the kitchen. He'd even insisted she get a gas range to replace the cookstove.

Ellen watched the horse as his tail swung in the sunlight. She loved the vista, had designed the porch for that side of the house so that they could sit there in the evening and watch the sun slip behind the San Juans. The mountains gave her a sense of calm, of peacefulness. She liked a God who had created mountains—and a husband who had given her a life among them. Of course, there would still be the mountains if they moved to Durango. They just wouldn't be at their doorstep, and there wouldn't be the ranch. No, by God, she'd have to find a way to stay here a little longer.

The screen's hinges squeaked again, and June set down a tray with slices of homemade bread, a crock of apple butter, and the coffee. The cups and saucers and plates were brown with ranch brands around the edges. The china had been manufactured after the Second World War, and everyone in the valley had it. Like Ellen, her neighbors had survived the bad years, the Depression and the war, and now that livestock was bringing good prices, the women felt entitled to splurge a little. June handed her grandmother a spoon and an opened can of PET milk.

Ellen poured milk into her coffee and stirred it, then sipped. She'd developed the habit of adding canned milk to her coffee years before, when the only coffee you could buy in cattle country was Arbuckle's and the only milk came in a can. She and Ben both preferred it to fresh milk. "What's your dress like?" she asked her granddaughter.

"White, of course. Silk with a chiffon train that's about as long as this porch. It would break Mom's heart if I didn't wear it. What do you do with a wedding dress if you don't wear it?"

"You could make it into a quilt. A Crazy Quilt."

June laughed. "That would be tragic, wouldn't it, cutting up all that expensive silk."

"Better than letting it rot away in a box."

"It would make a pretty quilt, at that." June reached over and picked up her grandmother's quilt and ran her hand over the patches. "A quilt like this."

Ellen nodded. "That's what it is. That patch there is from your great-grandmother's wedding gown."

"You cut it up?"

"There are several wedding dresses in here."

"Is one yours?"

Ellen nodded and pointed to the piece of white she had added to the edge just that morning.

June set aside the quilt and gave a brittle laugh. "Maybe you can cut up my wedding dress. That way, *you* at least will get some use out of it." She took a sip of her coffee. "I guess I'm a freak, aren't I?"

"No," Ellen replied as she traced one of the brands on her cup with her finger. "I know of a woman fifty years ago who ran away. She ran away three different times. The first was in 1898."

"Three times! From the same man?"

"No, three different men. Three different reasons. Do you want to hear her story?"

"I love your stories, Granny. If I were a writer I would put them into a book." June settled into the chair. It was her grand-father's chair, with a tattered old Indian rug for a cushion. "Were they good reasons?"

"Yes."

"You think she did the right thing?"

"She thought so at the time." Ellen shrugged. "But you tell me."

CHAPTER TWO

He called her Nellie Blue-Eyes, and she called him Buddy. Buddy wasn't his real name. But by the time Nell found that out, the name was so fixed in her mind that she wouldn't call him anything else.

Lucy had come outside to throw the dishwater on the flowers and said, "Why, I believe that's Buddy over there."

Nell stared at the cowboy as he dismounted and touched his hat to Lucy. He didn't pay attention to Nell until Lucy said, "This here's Nell. She's the new biscuit-shooter. She'll help with the cooking and so forth." Nell stepped out onto the warm stones of the portico, her hands wrapped in her apron.

"Ma'am," he said and touched the brim of his hat again. The thumb of his other hand was hooked in his belt. He smiled, and Nell could see he had all his teeth. Several of the cowboys didn't. He was tall and nice-looking and slightly bow-legged, and his eyes, well, they were the soft brown velvet of a doe's. "There's coffee," she said, thinking she wouldn't mind a bit if he came into the kitchen and bothered her. She expected him to since the other cowboys had done just that. They'd found excuses to go to the house, telling Lucy they had a terrible pain in their gullets or a hurting in their heads and needed to get out of the hot New Mexico sun.

"You got a pain, all right, and you want to give it to me, right where I sit down. Now go on with you," Lucy would tell them. "You'll meet the new girl soon enough, although I don't know why she'd want to meet you."

The new cowboy took off his hat, which had once been white but now was brown with the dust of the High Plains, and wiped his forehead with his sleeve. His face was tanned, although his forehead was pale where the brim of his hat had shaded it from the sun. The sun was so hot now that Nell reached up with the dish towel she was holding and dabbed at her face, embarrassed at its dampness.

"No thank you, Miss Nell," the cowboy said in reply to her offer of coffee, and she was surprised, disappointed. He was the only one of the hands who had turned her down. He was the only one she wished would accept.

"You have a good time up north, did you?" Lucy asked. She explained to Nell, "He was off to pick up a filly Mr. Archer's bought, been away two, three weeks, long enough for the filly to turn into a full-fledged mare."

"I was looking around some."

Lucy snorted. "Out looking at the world, I expect," she said.

"You were traveling?" Nell asked, hoping again that the man would stay. The screen door squeaked, and Lucy went back inside.

"Maybe," he replied, and she thought she had overstepped.

It wasn't any of her business what he did. She didn't want him to think she was nosy.

"Well, welcome back home," she said, putting one bare foot on the other. Her shoes were in the house, beside the door.

"Nice to meet you, ma'am," he replied, stepping past strings of bloodred chili peppers that hung from the *vigas* and pausing a moment in the shadow of the portico. He wiped his brow again with the sleeve of a shirt that had once been indigo but was now faded to the blue of the late-afternoon sky. "So long," he said. His fine eyes crinkled as he gathered the reins of his cow pony and turned around. He didn't jump onto the horse from behind or perform any of the tricks the other cowboys had done to impress Nell. He didn't even gallop off in a cloud of dust. He merely took the reins and walked his horse toward the corral.

"I thought he'd want a cup of coffee," Nell said after she went inside. She'd turned to watch the cowboy through the screen door.

"Oh, he's not like the others. He might look like the hottest thing since Texas chili, but he's awful high and mighty. Too much ambition for a cowboy. He reads books, that one. He's a knowin' man. Don't mind him."

"He can read?" Nell asked. Two of the cowboys had brought her their mail and asked her to read it to them. She hadn't been sure if they were illiterate or just wanted to spend a little time with her. This one, well, she hardly cared if he could read and write. She just wanted to sit and talk to him.

"He's had him some education," Lucy said by way of reply. "Some ambition, too."

Lucy left the kitchen door and went to check on her bread

dough. "It's raised," she said, punching down the dough. "You watch out for him. He seems square enough, but he's the worst practical joker on the place." That was saying something, since Nell already had learned how the other cowboys liked to play pranks.

"One time, he tied a string around the neck of a dead rattlesnake and coiled it up by the supper table. There was a new girl, and when she stepped beside him, he yanked on the string, and that head rose up, and the girl must have jumped ten feet and run out the door like the devil himself was chasing her. She was so mad, she quit the next day."

"I'm not afraid of snakes."

Lucy had been cutting hunks of the dough out of the wooden dough bowl, kneading them, then slapping them into pans. She stopped and turned around. "Well, you ought to be. Get bit by a rattler, and your leg'll turn black and swell up big as a flour barrel. It ain't the best way to die, although I don't know what is."

When Nell didn't reply, Lucy continued. "In case you're interested, you can forget about him. He sizes up pretty good. He don't drink, and he don't chew, but he's not the marrying kind, not with hired girls anyway. Some of the other girls that worked here, they already tried. So get that out of your head."

Nell stared through the screen, although Buddy had disappeared. The fire in the cookstove made the air hotter inside the house than out. She found a clean place on the roller towel and wiped her hands, then used her sleeve to wipe her forehead, the way Buddy had. "Grandma may think I came to New Mexico Territory to get married, Aunt Lucy, but I didn't."

In fact, she had. That wasn't the only reason she'd come to the ranch near Las Vegas, New Mexico Territory, that year of 1897, of course. She'd never been to the state before and had already spent a year teaching in the school in Harveyville, Kansas. She had kept company with a young man there, Lane Philips, but there had never been anything worth mentioning between them. Or between her and anybody else. She'd been restless. She'd lived on her grandparents' farm ever since her parents died when she was ten and thought she'd live in Kansas forever, although she didn't know with whom.

Then her aunt Lucy, her father's sister, had written from New Mexico, asking if he knew of a girl who'd like to work on the Rockin' A. It was a cattle spread, a big one, although not the biggest in the territory. Nell's grandmother fretted that at twenty-two, Nell was becoming an old maid. And Nell herself had begun to worry. There ought to be plenty of eligible young men in New Mexico, the two of them agreed. And Lucy would be there to chaperone her. Besides, being on a ranch with all those cowboys might be fun.

Lucy had grown up in Kansas, too, but she'd left twenty years before, when she married a homesteader. Her husband died before he could prove up the claim, and Lucy had worked for fifteen years as a housekeeper on the Rockin' A. The rancher, Mr. Archer, was a widower, and folks in Harveyville thought it wasn't proper for Lucy to live in the same house with him, since he didn't have a wife.

Perhaps that was why Nell's grandfather wasn't crazy about Nell moving to New Mexico. "Lucy will look out for her," Nell's grandmother had said.

"That's what I'm afraid of," he replied.

"Who's she going to settle down with in Kansas?" her grandmother asked. "She can do a sight better than Lane Philips. And Lucy is a decent woman."

After she arrived in New Mexico, Nell had thought her grandmother was right about that. Lucy had her own room, and she always called her employer Mr. Archer. He in turn referred to her as Mrs. Miller. There was never so much as an improper touch or even a glance between them, as far as Nell could tell. Then one day, Nell saw the dog hide a bone under Mr. Archer's bed, and when she pulled it out to toss into the yard, she discovered her aunt's slippers were under there, too.

Lucy had come into the room behind her and was aware Nell had seen the house shoes. "Nights get awful cold in the winter" was all Lucy said, although it was then summer and as hot outside as the cookstove.

Nell should have been shocked, but in fact, she was glad for her aunt. She understood why Lucy didn't want to be alone. And she understood why the woman loved the cracked earth of the High Plains with its rocky soil and sparse vegetation.

It hadn't taken Nell long to love it, too. Maybe a week—two at the most. The dry heat wasn't oppressive like the Kansas humidity. Nell liked looking east with nothing to block the view—she could almost see the earth curve—and west to the mountains that turned blue in the late afternoon. The big ranch house, made of mud bricks with jigsaw trim painted turquoise, kept out the summer heat, except in the kitchen when the wood-burning cookstove was fired up. The tile floors in the house were so cool that she and Lucy went about barefoot, their shoes beside the back door in case they had to go out. She loved the clouds that sent shadows a mile long across the prairie. Best of all were the sunrises and sunsets that spread from horizon to horizon with savage streaks of violet and crimson and gold. The colors seemed to fill the whole world.

Nell came to appreciate the men on the ranch, too, with their economy of words and their dry sense of humor. They were polite, sometimes overly polite, but they didn't patronize her. New Mexico Territory was still too raw to pamper ranch women. Females were not indulged but respected. The men expected everyone to work hard, to do their part. And the women did, without stinting. "Out here, it's a woman's job not to complain," Lucy told her.

Of course, Nell was new, and the men were still testing her. Just that morning, she'd said she'd take the breakfast scraps to the chickens and reached for her shoes. Lucy had warned her to turn them upside down before she put them on. Nell did just that, and a tiny cactus fell out.

"Those dang cowboys!" Lucy said. "Best to check your shoes anyway. You never know where a scorpion's going to take a nap." Then Lucy added, "You've been a good sport, Nell. The boys like that. Life ain't easy out here, and the cowboys respect a woman that can take it."

It wasn't more than a day or two after she met Buddy that Nell spotted the rattler curled up under the kitchen table, next to Buddy's boot. He hadn't said anything more to her than "Good morning," or a mumbled thank-you when she set a plate before him. She was disappointed, because she'd been drawn to him from the moment she met him. He was the only one of the cowboys who interested her, the only one who seemed a possibility. After a few weeks on the ranch, she had realized cowboys weren't much as marriage material. She'd given up on them and had decided she would view her job as a lark, an adventure, before she settled down back in Kansas or someplace more civilized.

Maybe Lane Philips was the best she could do. That was before Buddy came along, however. But he'd barely said more than hello. In fact, he seemed to have made a point of ignoring her.

She spied the snake out of the corner of her eye and thought she'd fix Buddy for thinking she was no more than a hired girl he could torment. She'd show him he couldn't fool her with a dead snake on a string. She'd been serving fried eggs from a heavy cast-iron skillet and slid three of them onto the cowboy's plate, her arm steady. Just as Buddy moved his hand in what Nell figured was his attempt to raise the reptile's head, she slammed the skillet on the snake, smashed it once, twice, and a third time for good measure. "Got it!" she said with no more emotion than if she'd swatted a fly.

"Cripes, Miss Nell!" Buddy said, jumping up and knocking over his chair. His plate with the eggs crashed to the floor. The other cowboys jumped up, too, and even Mr. Archer said, "Hell, woman, you sure put him out of business!"

"Anybody want more eggs?" Nell asked. The skillet held one perfectly good egg, although the yolk was broken.

"That's a damn rattler," Willy Burden said. He was a shy young fellow who was engaged to Martha, a girl in Albuquerque. He planned to marry her as soon as he saved up a hundred dollars. Another month or two, he'd told Nell, and he was quitting.

"Did you see the way she whacked it?. Ain't no woman I know could do that," another cowboy said.

"Man neither."

"It's just a snake," Nell said, thinking they were carrying the joke too far.

"You want the rattles?" Buddy asked. "Keep 'em in a jar." He opened his pocketknife and cut them off, then stood and handed the rattles to her. "Ma'am, I believe that snake would have bit me something bad. I reckon I owe you." He shook his head. "You were as calm as water in a horse trough."

She almost laughed to think he had cut off the rattles of his trick snake. Nell put the rattles in her pocket, as Buddy picked up the snake and said he'd take it to the chickens. He held it up by the tail so the cowboys could see how big it was. Nell looked for the string around the snake's neck, but there wasn't any. She glanced at Lucy, who was watching her wide-eyed. Slowly, Lucy shook her head, and Nell blanched. That snake had been alive. Nell put her hand over her mouth when she realized what she had done, but Lucy caught her eye and shook her head again.

Later, when the cowboys were gone, Nell asked, "That was a real snake, wasn't it?"

Lucy nodded.

"I thought they were playing a joke on me."

"Don't let them know that. Before the week's out, you'll be a legend around here."

The next afternoon, Buddy came up onto the portico with a bouquet of brown-eyed Susans. The flowers bloomed along the fence lines in the fall, alone with bright gold chamisa and purple asters. "I'd have brought roses, but they aren't to be had."

"Why, you didn't have to bring me anything."

"I reckon I owe you something for saving me from that snake. I never saw anybody as cool as you were." There was a touch of awe in his voice. Or was he teasing her?

"I guess I didn't know what I was doing. I just kind of, you know, did it."

"Maybe you thought there was a string around its neck."

Buddy knew she'd been told about his trick snake, but Nell wasn't about to admit it. "Sir?"

"I guess I would have smashed a snake with a skillet if I'd knowed it was already dead."

"It was alive. You saw it yourself. So did the other cowboys."

Buddy only grinned at her. "Well, you saved my leg anyhow. So I brought you a bouquet. It's pretty, but it doesn't smell like much."

Nell put the flowers to her nose, and as she did, a bee flew out of the bouquet and stung her. She threw the flowers at Buddy and said, "That was a mean trick."

"I didn't know that bee was there. I'm real sorry."

"Like hell you didn't!" Nell had picked up the expression from the cowboys.

"Ma'am, I swear—"

"Don't you swear at me, Buddy."

He blinked a couple of times at the name. "Ma'am, I mean to tell you—"

But Nell turned around and went inside, letting the screen slam.

"Ma'am, I'm not—"

Nell was furious. She'd dreamed about Buddy the night before and had awakened to thoughts of being with him under the night sky. Now she was embarrassed that she had presumed. "You're not welcome in this kitchen except at mealtimes, and even then I'd be obliged if you didn't speak. I mean that, Buddy."

"Don't call me Buddy," he said.

"I'll call you mud if I want to."

Two cowboys came around the edge of the house just in time

to hear the exchange. "Buddy?" one of them asked. "Did she call you Buddy?"

The other slapped his knee with his hat. "She called you Buddy. Well, I guess we know what she thinks of you."

Buddy waved his hat at the cowhand. "Now, you don't need to blab it around."

"Oh, I reckon I do," he said.

Nell slammed the inner door and went to the Hoosier cupboard for baking soda to put on her nose.

Lucy had heard the whole exchange. "I don't think he knew that bee was there," she said.

"Sure he did. You told me yourself he's a big practical joker." Nell touched her nose carefully. It had already begun to swell, and it hurt. "He's meaner than that snake." There were tears in her eyes at how foolish she'd been to think he might like her.

Lucy found the baking soda and made a paste with a little water and dabbed it on Nell's nose. "No, you're wrong about that. Cowboys love to play their jokes, but they're not mean, not these boys, anyway. I believe you hurt his feelings. I know you made a fool of him."

"Why, for getting mad?"

"For calling him Buddy."

"Well, that's his name, isn't it? I heard you call him that."

Lucy shook her head. "Buddy's the name of his horse."

CHAPTER THREE

After that, the cowboys razzed Buddy about Nell's name for him. He asked her to call him by his real name, but she refused. "You'll always be Buddy to me," she said.

"Cowboys have got a long memory. You watch out for him," Lucy warned. Days went by and then a week or two, and Buddy didn't retaliate. So Nell figured the practical jokes were done with, and she was glad. She'd all but forgiven him for the bee in the bouquet, and regretted banning him from the kitchen. Still, to Nell's disappointment, Buddy was polite but kept his distance, although one evening after supper, she came across him sitting on the porch of the adobe farmhouse, playing a song on a harmonica.

"That's the lonesomest music I ever heard," she said. In the dark, she didn't know who the cowboy was, and she sat down on a chair near him.

"It soothes the cattle," Buddy said. "Those old cattle drives, the boys used to play the mouth organ when the cows got the jitters."

Nell was surprised to hear Buddy's voice. But he had just as much right to sit on the porch as any other cowboy. "I guess it's easier to carry around a mouth organ than a fiddle, although I heard a fiddle the other night. Was that you, too?"

"That'd be Wendell. He's practicing up for a barbecue and dance over to the Iverson place on Saturday night. You heard about that?"

"I surely did," Nell said. She smiled in the darkness, thinking Buddy would ask to escort her. Maybe he really was interested.

"It'll be a real nice affair. Iversons got a piano, and there'll be one or two playing the squawk boxes."

"It sounds like a nice evening."

"I expect you'd like to go."

"I would." Nell all but grinned, thinking maybe she'd been right to dream about riding under the stars with Buddy.

He slapped the harmonica on his sleeve, then slipped it into his pocket. "Well, maybe if you're lucky, some cowpoke'll ask you." Buddy stood and walked toward the bunkhouse without a backward glance.

For a moment, Nell seethed at the insult. Then tears came into her eyes as she realized she had opened herself up, but Buddy didn't care.

A cowboy did invite Nell to the barbecue. In fact, two of them did, but Nell turned them down in favor of going with Lucy and Mr. Archer. The party was just for ranch folks, Lucy explained. No town rowdies or fancy girls. The Iversons barbecued a calf, roasted it in a pit, and served it up along with smoked venison. The guests brought pinto beans and baked beans and *frijoles,* potato salad and creamed potatoes, creamed onions, and green and red chili. And every woman in the valley brought her best cake or pie. Lucy and Nell together baked an apple cake, and each made a pie. Lucy's was raisin sour-cream, while Nell made lemon with meringue that stood four inches high. "Why, it looks like the Sangre de Cristos," Mr. Archer said when he came into the kitchen and saw it. One of the cowboys said it looked more like calf slobbers.

The cowboys came up to the ranch house to escort them. The men had washed and shaved and were feathered out in new shirts, their hair slicked down with bacon grease, and one or two smelled of barber oil. Nell promised each of them a dance, as she climbed into the carriage with Lucy and Mr. Archer. Buddy wasn't among the cowboys, and Nell wondered if he was staying behind, but not for anything would she ask. Maybe he'd gone on ahead with Wendell, she thought. Well, what did it matter? She had no intention of dancing with him. After the way he'd embarrassed her, he could dance with a cow. Then she thought, well, maybe if he asked nicely . . .

A moon as bright as a five-dollar gold piece hung in the sky, and the Iverson barn was decorated with a dozen lanterns. Mr. Archer helped the women out of the carriage and handed them the hamper with the cake and pies inside. Then he reached under the seat and took out a jug, which he gave to one of the hands, warning him not to get booze-blind.

Hands from the Rockin' A as well as the other ranches gathered around to offer to carry the hamper. Nell thought they wanted to see what the women had prepared, but Lucy snorted, "I guess the word's out we got a new girl at the ranch." She handed the basket to the cleanest cowboy while Nell glanced about, noticing that Buddy wasn't there. Lucy handed their wraps to one of the hands to take into the house, where the women's shawls and the men's coats were piled on a bed. She'd insisted Nell take a shawl with her because when they went home, the night would be cold.

Monty, one of the Rockin' A cowboys, took Nell's arm and asked if he could bring her a plate of barbecue. She nodded. Supper was already under way, and people were sitting on cotton-wood logs in the yard or perched on bales of hay in the barn, tin plates of food in their laps. Nell looked around, figuring there were only one or two women for every ten men. Wendell and the other musicians were already tuning up in the barn, and Monty hurried her through supper so that he could claim the first dance. She'd eat dessert later, she thought, although with the way the pies and cakes were disappearing, she wondered if there would be any left. She was pleased to see her lemon meringue pie plate was empty.

Monty followed her to the dance floor, then gripped her awk-wardly and began to dance. What he lacked in skill, he made up for in enthusiasm. All the cowpokes did. Willy Burden claimed her next, and he was just as lively as Monty. "I'm planning to dance at my wedding," he said. "I lack but a month's wages to reach that hundred dollars I need." Then he asked shyly, "Miss Nell, I would consider it a favor if you'd advise me on the pur-chase of a wedding ring." Nell agreed.

As soon as the dance with Willy was finished, a man stepped up to claim Nell for the next one, dragging her around the barn, stepping on her feet, even ripping the hem of her skirt—her best one. She was vain, so she'd worn a cream-colored skirt and starched white blouse, with a tight belt. Most of the cowboys had never seen her without an apron, which gave her a shape like a flour sack, and she wanted to show off her small waist. But she knew as soon as she arrived that she'd chosen the wrong outfit.

The skirt was already dirty from where it had scraped the barn floor, and the blouse was stained from the not-too-clean hands of her dance partners. There was even a streak of barbecue sauce where a cowboy had danced her too close to one of the tables. Nell knew she looked a mess, with her soiled dress, the blouse pulled out from her skirt in places, her hair falling out of her combs, but that didn't stop the cowboys from lining up to dance with her.

She had just finished a fast dance with a cowboy she suspected had never been on a dance floor in his life, and was hoping for a break, when Buddy took her arm. "I guess it'd be rude if I didn't ask for a dance with our hired girl," he said.

"Why, I thought I'd already danced with all the hired hands," she shot back at him. "I guess I was wrong."

He held out his arms, and they began to sway with the music. At least he didn't leap around the room and step on her feet. She felt his arms tight around her, and despite herself, she smiled at him.

Buddy smiled back, and she saw again that he had all his teeth in that warm smile. "You know, the boys say you have eyes as blue as the mountains at sunset."

Was he flirting with her? Or was he setting her up for something? "What do you say?" she asked.

"I'd say they look more like turquoise nuggets. I think I'll call you Miss Nellie Blue-Eyes."

Nell flushed. Maybe Buddy liked her at that. Maybe he'd just been cautious. Or shy. That was all right with her.

They finished the dance, and Nell said her feet hurt so much that she wasn't sure she'd ever walk again, so they went outside and sat down on a log.

"Is that what you'd call a harvest moon?" Buddy asked, looking up at the sky.

"That's what we called it in Kansas."

"Here we call it a Comanche moon and sometimes a spooning moon. I kind of like that one."

Nell flushed. "We didn't hit it off so good at first, did we?" she asked.

Now it was Buddy's turn to blush.

"I keep thinking you're going to play a mean joke on me," she said.

"You don't like them?"

"Not so much."

Buddy smiled and looked a little sheepish. "I never really played a joke on you yet, Miss Nell."

"I hope you're not thinking up one right now."

"Me?"

"Yes, you."

"Now, Miss Nellie Blue-Eyes, don't you think a fellow's got the right to a little fun?"

"Not at my expense."

Buddy kicked the log with the pointed toe of his boot. "You do not trust a person, do you?"

The music had stopped, and Wendell came out of the barn with his fiddle and went up to Buddy. "You taken care of—" He stopped when he saw Nell and said, "Well, howdy, Miss Nell."

"What were you saying?" she asked. "Don't mind me."

"I was just asking this ugly old cowpoke if he'd had a dance yet. He better hurry up, because folks are commencing to go home. Won't be long before we're playing 'Leaving Cheyenne.'" Lucy had told Nell that was the last song played at a cowboy dance.

The two men glanced toward the ranch house, where people were collecting their coats from the bedroom and gathering their baskets and pie plates and cake pans. Nell wondered if Wendell had been about to ask Buddy if he had a bottle. She'd noticed a number of the cowpokes stumbling around smelling of busthead.

"I think I ought to find Lucy and Mr. Archer," she said, standing up and brushing off her skirt. It was doubtful that she'd ever get it clean.

"I'll walk you back to the ranch house," Buddy said, but just as they started toward the building, a woman stopped in front of Nell and demanded, "Is this yours?" She held out a white handkerchief doused in cheap perfume. "I found it in my man's coat pocket. It has your initials on it. I don't know there's any other woman here with them initials."

Nell held out her hand, then turned away when she caught a whiff of the perfume, which smelled like something a sporting girl would wear. "It's certainly not my cologne," she said. She used only a little toilet water, and it had a rose scent. She held her breath and raised the handkerchief to her eyes to see it better in the dark. "But it is my handkerchief! I embroidered it myself. Where did you get it?"

"Like I say, it was in my husband's pocket." The woman gave Nell a stern look. "You better watch your step, miss. It won't do to go after a married man. He won't be stepping out with the likes of a gad-a-way like you."

The woman stomped off, her husband behind her, protesting, "Now, Mother, I don't know where that came from. I've never saw it before."

Nell hurried toward the ranch house, where she ran into Lucy. "The strangest thing happened. See that man over there," she began.

But just then, Mr. Archer put on his coat and reached into his pocket to take out his gloves. Instead, he pulled out a white handkerchief that stank of perfume. "What's this?" he asked.

"Oh, my lord!" Nell said, putting her hands to her face. "Somebody's put one of my handkerchiefs with that awful-smelling perfume into your pocket, too. The handkerchief is mine, but that's not my scent. I don't know how it got there."

Before they left, a third man approached Nell and said, "Miss Nell, is this yours? I am flattered as all get-out, but I'm thinking I'm too old for you." He held out a handkerchief.

"Looks like somebody's been pirooting around," Buddy said behind her. Nell turned and saw him exchanging a smirk with Wendell.

She grabbed the handkerchief from the man and threw it at Buddy. "You! I thought you weren't going to play any jokes," she fumed. "You took my handkerchiefs—you went into my room and stole them—and . . . and soaked them in that horrid perfume and put them into men's pockets."

"Why, I thought you'd be pleased. It's a real nice way to meet folks."

"To have them think I'm a fast woman, you mean. This is just awful. Awful!" Nell wasn't sure whether she was angry because of the joke or because she'd begun to think that Buddy was sweet on her.

She turned to Lucy, who glared at Buddy. It was Mr. Archer who spoke, however. "What did you think you were doing, son? Were you planning to spoil Miss Nell's reputation?" He turned. "And you, Wendell? I am surprised. You boys are a pair of crockheads."

The two hands looked down. "It was only a joke," Buddy said.

Lucy asked Nell how many handkerchiefs she had.

"Twelve."

"And you took all of them?" Lucy asked Buddy.

He gave a slight nod.

"I guess you two cowboys have some apologizing to do," Mr. Archer told them.

"Yes, sir," Buddy said. He glanced at Wendell, and the corners of his mouth went up a little. "I'm sorry, Miss Nell," he said. Wendell muttered a second apology.

Nell started to protest, but Lucy touched Nell's arm, and she fell silent. Later on, Lucy told her, "I know it's rotten, but it was a joke. And a pretty clever one at that. It reminds me of a little boy who dips a girl's braid into an inkwell to show he likes her. Maybe it's some special cowboy's way to get your attention. Whatever it is, if you want to get along out here, you have to learn to take it. The ranch needs cowboys more than it does a hired girl."

Over the next few days, half a dozen handkerchiefs turned up, all of them perfume-soaked. One man rode ten miles to call on Nell, and a woman in a store in Las Vegas all but slapped her before Nell explained that one of the Rockin' A hands had played a joke on her.

"Oh, well, I understand, then," the woman said. "Still, you keep away from my husband just the same."

Nell had recovered nine of the twelve handkerchiefs and wondered what had happened to the others. It was understood among the hands that this might have been the greatest practical joke Buddy had ever pulled.

Buddy tried to make it up to Nell, complimenting her on her cooking, opening the door for her when she carried the wash basket outside, even offering to help her hang the laundry, which Nell told her was a comedown for a cowboy. But she would have none of it.

"I believe he's stuck on you," Lucy said.

"What of it?" Nell was hurt that she had opened her heart to the cowboy and he had tricked her. "I don't like him," she told Lucy, who only rolled her eyes.

Nell did like Willy Burden, however. She liked that he was sweet on Martha, his girl in Albuquerque, and never seemed to mind that the other hands teased him about it. "After payday, I'll never see you buzzards again," he told them. Nell kept her promise, and one day when Wendell drove her into town for supplies, she went into the jewelry store with him to pick out a ring. "Solid gold," she told him. "You can buy cheaper, but fifty years from now, you don't want a ring that's got the gold worn off."

The ring cost seven dollars, more than he'd planned to spend, but Willy said that with his next pay, he'd still have more than the hundred dollars he needed to file for a homestead and set up housekeeping. Nell knew that Mr. Archer was going to give Willy an extra twenty-five dollars as a wedding present. She and Lucy had already presented him with a wedding shirt they'd made, and Nell had embroidered Willy's initials on the pocket. He'd tried it on for size and grinned and said he'd never felt so bugged up in his life.

A few days later, Willy was late for breakfast. When he came into the kitchen, he looked crestfallen. "I lost my wallet," he said. "I lost my wallet, and it had near a hundred dollars in it."

The cowboys stopped eating and stared. "You trying to get out of marrying, Willy?" one asked.

The others laughed a little, hoping this was a joke, for Willy was well liked.

"It ain't a joke. I went to get it this morning, and it's gone. I looked all through my trunk, even took out the bottom of it, and I gone through my clothes and everything, but it's gone."

This was a serious matter. "You think somebody took it?" Mr. Archer asked.

"No, sir, I can't say as I do. I think I must have lost it. Last time I remember it was when I went to town with Miss Nell."

The cowboys turned to Nell, who blanched, but Lucy stepped in. "You all know Miss Nell don't steal, so you can just forget about her."

"Is it in the wagon?" Nell asked.

"I looked all through it, and it ain't there neither."

"I'll check the groceries. Maybe it got caught in with the flour or the sugar."

Lucy took over the serving while Nell searched the larder. She and Willy spent an hour taking out all the cans and bags of potatoes and beans, sugar and flour. But the wallet wasn't to be found. "You must have left it at the store. Or maybe somebody found it in the street and turned it over to the sheriff," she said. "You want me to go into town and see if it's turned up?"

Willy said he'd go. He was away most of the day, and when Nell saw him ride into the corral later, she knew from the way his shoulders drooped he hadn't found his money.

She went to the corral and watched Willy unsaddle his horse. After a time, he glanced up at her and shook his head. "I guess I'm not getting married."

"She'll wait," Nell said. "She'll be disappointed, but she'll wait."

"Yes, ma'am," he said, but he didn't sound as if he believed it.

"There's another fellow been telling her I ain't the marrying type."

"If she loves you, she'll believe you. If you'd like, I'll write her a letter."

Willy looked up from the bridle in his hands. "Would you, ma'am? I'd sure appreciate that." But Nell could tell by the way he slunk off to the bunkhouse that he didn't believe a letter would do much good. She didn't either.

CHAPTER FOUR

Nell had gone to the chicken yard with a hatchet, to catch the old rooster. They would have chicken and dumplings for dinner. But as if the rooster knew what Nell had in mind, he took off, skittering across the yard toward the bunkhouse. The bunkhouse was all-male territory, but she had to catch that bird. The rooster scooted through the door ahead of Nell, and she stopped when she reached the doorway, not sure she should enter the cowboys' domain.

She hadn't been inside the bunkhouse before, and as she let her eyes adjust to the dim interior, she took in the row of bunk beds. Some were made up; the sugans, as the cowboys called their quilts, were smooth. Others were rumpled. She glanced around at prints of Indian fights and dogs playing poker and the magazine pictures of all-but-naked women, pinned to the walls. Scattered among them were *cartes de visite* of mothers and sweethearts, and provocative shots of scantily clad hookers. The prostitutes in Las Vegas sold such pictures to their clients. Tobacco sacks and decks of cards and dime novels were thrown about, along with one or two Bibles and what the cowboys themselves called bibles—packages of cigarette papers. Small trunks were shoved under the beds or placed against the ends of the bunks.

As she took a step into the bunkhouse, Nell spotted Buddy in the middle of the room, and she almost backed out. Would he think she'd seen him go into the bunkhouse and followed him? Her face burned at the idea, although Buddy hadn't seen her, because he was deep in conversation with another Rockin' A hand, Charlie Potter. She could slip back outside, and the men would never know she'd been there, but she had to get that rooster. Besides, she'd caught a few words between the two and was curious. Nell knew Charlie, of course, but not well. He generally gulped his food and left as soon as he was finished eating, barely exchanging a word with her or the other boys. He was surly and didn't seem to have friends among the cowboys. Now he was squatting beside an open locker, looking up at Buddy, red-eyed angry.

Neither man saw her.

"I asked what you're doing in here," Buddy said. "You were supposed to be with Gus, rounding up those cows over toward the mountains."

"I'm laid up. Must be something I ate."

"I ate the same thing you did, and I'm fine. You been on a spree, looks like to me."

"I reckon I was. Must have got hold of a bad batch of busthead."

"And you're still drinking it." Buddy pointed to a half-empty pint bottle lying on a nearby bunk. "Mr. Archer won't like it, you having liquor in here. Best you get rid of it before he finds out."

"Yeah, and who are you to tell me what to do? You think

you're the whole herd. I expect you're going to tell him, just 'cause you're sweet on that chippie."

Nell raised her chin a bit. What did she care that Buddy had a girl somewhere?

"You watch what you say about Miss Nell." Buddy raised a fist.

Nell's mouth dropped open. Were they talking about *her*? Was Buddy really sweet on *her*? Had Lucy been right when she'd said Buddy had played tricks on her just to get her attention?

"I seen you watching her, trying to get her to look kindly on you. She ain't much of nothing."

"You shut your mouth, cowboy. I'm not fooling around with Miss Nell. She's a lady. You take it—" Buddy stopped because he'd glanced at the floor. He looked up at Charlie. "I don't believe that's your trunk you're going through."

"No? Well, ain't that a dinger!"

"It appears it's Rafael's trunk, and you got his do-funny in your hand. That isn't yours either." The two men stared at a tiny silver statue of a saint that Charlie was holding. "Rafael sure would be sorry to lose that."

"Mind your business." Charlie spat a mouthful of tobacco juice on the floor, splattering it on Buddy's boot.

"Maybe somebody going through the wrong locker *is* my business. I had a silver pocket watch that disappeared. I never did understand it. Now that I think on it, there's other things that's got lost, too. I heard the boys complain about it. I wonder if maybe they'll turn up in your trunk."

"You accusing me of something, maybe saying I'm a thief?"

"Tell me something I don't know."

Charlie glared at Buddy. "I could kill you for that."

Nell wondered if she should sneak away. This was between the two men, and neither one would be pleased that she was eaves-dropping. She should tell Lucy what was going on. It would be up to Lucy whether to tell Mr. Archer. Still, she stayed where she was. She didn't want to leave Buddy to face Charlie by himself.

"I'm just asking for a look," Buddy said. "Be easy enough to settle if I just have a look in your trunk."

"Well, you can go to hell. I'll tell Mr. Archer myself, tell him you was going through my locker. Who's to say *you* aren't the thief."

"I believe he trusts me."

"Oh, so you do think you're something. I can talk a pretty good piece myself. There's nobody to speak up for you."

"I will," Nell blurted out, then put her hand over her mouth. She should have kept still. Now the two men knew she was there, and Buddy would think she'd been snooping. Nobody liked a snoop.

Charlie whirled around. "This is men's territory. Ladies ain't supposed to be in the bunkhouse. Mr. Archer won't like it. You get now."

"Roosters aren't supposed to be here either. I just came to fetch that old bird. I'll leave in a minute, but I'm kind of curious myself about what's in your trunk," Nell said, feeling brave as long as Buddy was there. Since the men knew she'd been listen-ing, she might as well find out if Charlie was a thief.

"Let's have a look, then," Buddy said.

"I ain't got the key."

"Then I'll shoot off the lock." While Charlie was talking to Nell, Buddy had removed his gun from his holster, and now he moved a little so that Charlie could see it.

Charlie shrugged. "You going to put me out of business, are you?"

"I intend to shoot that lock if you don't open it."

Charlie took a few steps toward Nell, Buddy behind him, and stopped at the unmade bed where the bottle of whiskey lay. The rooster had made itself at home next to it. Shoving the bird onto the floor, Charlie took a key out of his pocket and unlocked the trunk. He started to open it, but Buddy told him to step back. "Miss Nell, would you look inside? I kind of have a feeling there might be a gun in there somewheres."

Buddy was right. A loaded gun lay on top of a pile of dirty clothing. Nell took it out and set it on a bunk behind her, out of Charlie's reach. Then she removed the clothes, two dog-eared *Police Gazette*s, and a bunch of what Buddy had called do-funnies—trinkets. The trunk was empty, and she frowned. Something didn't seem right. She knelt down and peered into the locker, then felt the inside. "I think there's a false bottom," she said. She pried up a piece of cardboard that had been cut to fit inside the trunk. Beneath it lay a jackknife, a silver pocket watch, a lady's ring, a gold watch fob shaped like a bull, a collection of odds and ends, and a pair of woman's bloomers. Nell blushed when she saw the undergarment, glad it wasn't hers. She pushed it aside and discovered a wallet. "This is Willy's! I saw it at the mercantile when he bought his girl's ring," she said. She looked inside. "It's empty. Willy had almost a hundred dollars in it when he was at the store."

"I found it," Charlie said.

"Sure you did." Buddy glared at the cowboy. "And I just bet you'll say it was empty then, won't you? When were you going to give it back to Willy?"

"I forgot about it. You know I ain't much for remembering. You recollect that time—"

Buddy gestured at the items in the trunk with his gun. "You

forget to tell me you found my watch, too? And I believe you must have forgot to tell Wendell about his knife. You sure are something at disrememberin'."

"You know me—"

"Yeah, I know you. You're a thief, and a pretty low one to steal from your own pards."

The remark riled Charlie, who took a step forward, stopping only when Buddy aimed the gun at him. "You can't call me that. I've killed men for less."

"I bet you have, shot them in the back most likely."

"Where's Willy's money?" Nell spoke up.

"Yeah, I'd like to know that, too. Best turn out your pockets, Charlie."

Charlie did as he was told, but his pockets held only a few coins.

"There isn't any money in his trunk," Nell said. "Do you think he hid it?"

"Most likely, he gambled it away in some Las Vegas bucket of blood," Buddy told her. "He's got the reputation of a rotten gambler."

"You got a leaky mouth," Charlie said.

"And you got a lying one. Where'd you lose it?"

"I didn't have no chance. It was a fixed game. They was cheaters, all of 'em. They didn't leave me with even a cartwheel." Charlie suddenly brightened. "I didn't steal nothing. I was planning on doubling Willy's money for him. Now, wouldn't that have been a nice little surprise?"

"You damn fool! You think I believe that?" Buddy said. "Did you plan on doubling my watch, too, and Wendell's pocketknife?"

"I'll make it up to Willy. I'll pay him back."

"And how'll you do that?" Buddy sneered.

"Out of my wages. I swear."

"That'll be fine," Buddy said, and Nell wondered for a moment if he was going to let Charlie off. She'd heard about frontier justice where men, not the law, made decisions about how to punish criminals. Maybe if Charlie paid Willy back, everything would be all right.

"So we're okay on that. I sure do appreciate it," Charlie said.

"No, we're not okay," Buddy told him. "You can mail Willy's money to him. You get your bedroll now and your horse, and you get out. I want you gone right now."

"You can't do that. I don't work for you."

"You want me to get Mr. Archer?" Nell asked.

"That's up to you, Charlie," Buddy said.

The cowboy swore until Buddy told him to shut his mouth in front of a lady.

Charlie gave Buddy a surly look and muttered, "I'll get even for this."

"I expect you'll try, but I'm not worried," Buddy replied.

Charlie stared, until Buddy pointed with his gun at the bunk where Nell had dumped the clothes she'd taken from the trunk. With an angry motion, Charlie rolled up the clothing in a blanket. He reached for his gun, but Nell looked at Buddy, who shook his head. "I don't cotton to be shot in the back before he lights out," Buddy said. So Nell picked up the gun and held it behind her.

"Maybe Willy can get a dollar or two for it," Buddy added.

Charlie scowled. He kicked at the rooster, which was now hiding under the bunk, then strode out of the bunkhouse, and in a few minutes, Nell and Buddy saw him larrup up his horse and ride off.

"Now what?" Nell asked.

"Now we catch that rooster. That's why you're here, isn't it?"

"I mean about Willy's wallet. Are you going to give it to him?"

"I am."

"He'll be pretty broken up that it's empty."

Buddy sat down on a bunk near the door. Nell sat across from him. He reached over and took her hand, and she let him hold it. "Miss Nell, here's the thing of it. That wallet isn't going to be empty. It'll have almost a hundred dollars in it."

Nell was confused. "But I thought Charlie gambled away the money."

"He did."

"Then how . . . ?" She stopped. "You mean you're going to put your own money into it? You're giving Willy a hundred dollars?"

"You know of anything better I can do with my money? Willy's a real nice kid, and I don't believe his life ought to be ruined because a no-good like Charlie stole his money. That girl isn't going to wait forever."

"Why, that's the nicest thing I ever heard of. Willy will be indebted to you."

"It doesn't need mentioning." Buddy leaned forward until his face was close to Nell's. "Miss Nell, he's not to know it. He wouldn't take the money if he knew it came from me. I'll tell him I found the wallet. You tell him any different, and there's no end of jokes I'll play on you. I don't allow anybody to cross me."

Nell was taken aback by the threat and took her hand out of Buddy's. She knew he meant what he'd said. "Is that why you let Charlie go, so's you could give Willy a full wallet?"

Buddy nodded. "I could've told Mr. Archer, and maybe he'd have sent for the sheriff. Everybody would have known Charlie was a thief, but that wouldn't help Willy any."

"So you won't tell Mr. Archer?"

"Might be I'll have to, him wondering why Charlie lit out all of a sudden without asking for his wages. But Mr. Archer'll keep it a secret, and Miss Nell, as I said, I expect you to do the same. I don't want you speaking to Mr. Archer or to Miss Lucy about it either."

Nell understood and nodded. "Won't the other cowboys wonder why Charlie left?"

"Maybe, but he's not the likenest cowpuncher at the Rockin' A. Might be they'll think he's gone to Texas."

"Texas?" Nell asked.

"Oh, that's what we say when a man lights out ahead of trouble."

Nell thought a moment. Then she straightened up and looked Buddy in the eye. "I won't tell, but in exchange, you've got to promise me one thing."

Buddy frowned, and Nell realized he was stiff-necked. "What's that?"

"You've got to let me pay half of that hundred dollars."

Buddy scoffed. "Where'd you get that kind of money? Biscuit-shooters don't make much."

"Where did you? I know what ranch hands are paid."

For a moment, Buddy didn't answer. "Truth is I came out west with a little cash, fixing to buy a spread. But I had to learn the land out here first. You're not to tell that around either."

"And I got my teaching salary from last year all saved up. I don't intend to spend it on, what do you call them, do-funnies?" Nell didn't see any need to tell him she had inherited a little money from an aunt.

"I expect I have more than you, so I don't intend to let you pay."

"Then I'll have to tell Willy how his wallet came to be full of money."

"You wouldn't."

Nell put her hands on her hips. She could be as stubborn as Buddy when she thought she was right. "Lord, and why wouldn't I?"

Buddy glared at her, and she knew he was not a man to cross. But neither was she someone who gave in. Finally he said, "No wonder that rooster came in here. He knew once you had him by the neck, you'd never let go."

Nell didn't reply.

"All right. I guess you won. But don't think you can best me again."

She held out her hand, and they shook on it. Then Buddy grabbed the rooster and held it under his arm. "You going to give quarter to this old bird?"

"Not on your life."

As they reached the bunkhouse door, Buddy said, "You know what, Miss Nellie Blue-Eyes? This here's the best joke I ever done pulled, and nobody'll ever know it."

"*We*," Nell said. "*We* pulled it."

Buddy tipped his hat with his free hand. "We sure did, honey," he said. Then he added, "I'd have thrown him off the ranch just because he said something disrespectful about you. I wouldn't allow any man to do that." And then before Nell could react, he leaned over and kissed her. Nell not only let him kiss her, she kissed him back. The rooster squawked.

CHAPTER FIVE

Willy was too tickled at being handed his wallet full of money to question how it had been found. If the other cowboys were curious about it, they kept it to themselves. They did wonder why Charlie Potter had taken off, however. Not that they missed him. Buddy was right when he said that the other cowboys didn't like Charlie.

"He was cultus when he was full of busthead," Wendell said at the supper table the day Willy got his wallet back.

Nell blinked at Lucy, not understanding. "That means useless when he was drunk," Lucy told her.

"Which was most of the time," a cowboy added.

"I wouldn't play cards with him," Wendell added.

"He was the one-eyed man in the game, all right," Gus put in.

"How was it again you happened to find Willy's purse, Miss Nell?" Mr. Archer asked.

She nudged Buddy with her elbow as she made the rounds with the pot of chicken and dumplings that contained the remains of the rooster, spooning a helping into Mr. Archer's bowl.

"It was under the hen house. I found it when I was looking for eggs. I knew one of those hens was laying them where she wasn't supposed to."

Willy shook his head. "I wonder how it got there. I ain't been near the chicken house since I come here."

"Maybe that old rooster took it," Buddy said, suppressing a grin. "He might have found it and dragged it off."

"Well, if he did, we sure paid him back," Nell said, pointing with her spoon at the pot.

Wendell said, "Hey, I just thought of something. Wasn't you lucky, Willy, that Miss Nell found it instead of old Charlie? You'd never have seen it if he had."

Nell exchanged a glance with Buddy, then looked away so she wouldn't smile. Mr. Archer saw the look, however. After the cowboys filed out, he stayed behind, taking a seat among the red geraniums growing in coffee cans in the deep adobe window. "Kind of a coincidence Charlie taking off just about the time you found Willy's wallet, ain't it, Miss Nell?" Mr. Archer asked.

Nell was startled. She hadn't realized he was still in the room, because she was thinking about how Buddy had touched her finger as he left. It hadn't been an accident. She picked up a dish towel and began drying dishes. "Kind of," she replied.

"I guess I don't know everything that goes on at this ranch."

Nell kept silent.

"Here's another coincidence. Mrs. Miller, you remember that gold watch fob I had made a while back? It was of that prize bull I sold."

"You sure set store by that fob," Lucy replied.

"I was real careful with it, but I lost it. Looked everywhere for it, but I couldn't find it."

"I remember."

Nell continued wiping a plate, although it was dry. Buddy had recognized the watch fob among Charlie's loot, and Nell had sneaked it into Mr. Archer's room.

"I found it right on top of my dresser. Now, how do you suppose it got there?"

"Well, I didn't put it there," Lucy said.

"I did." Nell whirled around. "I found it outside and thought it must be yours."

"You sure are a whiz at finding things. I wonder, did you find Wendell's jackknife, too?"

Nell didn't answer. She put the plate in the cupboard and took up a cup to dry.

"Now, it looks to me like somebody found a whole cache of lost items and didn't care to have me to know. Maybe because whoever that was didn't want me to go to the sheriff to report a certain cowboy was a thief right here on the Rockin' A. Might be Willy'd have got suspicious about how that money come to still be in his wallet. Funny how Charlie Potter lit out like somebody'd give him a lucky break. I never knew a hand to leave without asking for his wages, especially one as tight-fisted as Charlie. I wonder what made him scoot like that."

Mr. Archer paused to take out a cigarette paper. He removed a pouch from his shirt pocket and sprinkled tobacco on the paper, then used his teeth to draw the yellow string, closing the pouch. He rolled up the cigarette, licked the edge, and put it into his mouth. Then he struck a kitchen match on his boot and lit the smoke. "Now, I can't help thinking, what if that wallet was empty when it got found, and somebody filled it up and didn't want Willy to know, being as how he wouldn't accept charity. There are some mighty nice folks around here." He stood and went to the door, peering out at the darkening sky. "Miss Nell, I'm proud you're working on the Rockin' A," he said before he left for the corral.

After he was gone, Lucy said, "Maybe I should have kept my mouth shut. I told him I saw you and a certain cowpoke leave the bunkhouse right after Charlie rode off, you with that wallet in your hand. Which one of you filled it up?"

"I promised I wouldn't tell."

"You went into your room before you showed it to me. I suspicion it was you."

Nell stared at her aunt a moment. She had promised Buddy to keep what they'd done a secret, but she couldn't let Lucy think she'd replaced *all* the money. Buddy ought to get the credit, even if Lucy was the only one who'd know. "We both did," she said.

"That's what I thought. You know, honey, you could do worse than that cowboy. There's not a finer man in the territory than your Buddy."

"He's not *my* Buddy," Nell muttered, although she was wondering if he might be.

"You seem to be the only one around here who doesn't know it." Lucy paused. "But I think you do. He surely does."

Nell blushed and turned away to put the cup into the cupboard. She reached for another wet dish but then had a thought. "You ever lose anything around here, Aunt Lucy?"

"I dropped my ring someplace, ruby and diamond it was. That sure did trouble me, since Mr. Archer gave it to me."

Nell set down the cup and reached into her pocket and held out the diamond-and-ruby ring she'd found in Charlie's trunk.

* * *

Buddy didn't play any more jokes after that. Now there were nice surprises. Nell found a branch of golden aspen on the table one day after Buddy had gone into the mountains looking for strays. Another time, someone put a hand-tooled leather belt in her bedroom, which was just off the kitchen. And on her birthday, when she stepped outside the kitchen door to ring the dinner bell, she discovered a package wrapped in newspaper with "Miss Nell" printed on it. She opened it to find a box made from tiny bits of wood. Those gifts were anonymous, although Nell knew they came from Buddy, and she treasured them. One day when she had been feeding the chickens and hurried back to the house unexpectedly, she discovered Buddy spreading a gray-and-red Navajo rug on the floor beside her bed. The design was a pattern of stripes and diamonds, and it was tightly woven. He'd been to Santa Fe that week, he explained when she caught him. "Those floors get awful cold in the winter," he said.

After dinner one afternoon, Buddy asked Lucy if she would give permission for Nell to leave for a few hours. "She might like to see that pretty land over toward the mountains."

Lucy eyed him. "I guess I could spare her if she's back in time to dish up supper. Are you planning on saddling Sky High for her?" Sky High was a devil horse that few of the cowboys would ride.

"Why, no, ma'am," Buddy said, surprised. "That bronco wouldn't do. I'll fetch Bean for her." Bean was a gentle old dun, and riding her was like sitting in a rocking chair.

"You think she can ride that horse without falling off?"

"I'll make sure she can. Does she know how to ride?"

Lucy shrugged.

"You think she'll go with me?"

"She will unless she wants to stay here and black the stove."

"You give your permission, then?"

"It's all right with me—if it's all right with Nell."

Nell didn't like them talking about her as if she weren't there, the two of them deciding between them whether she should go riding. But then she wondered if Buddy was shy about asking her, afraid she might turn him down. That was why he'd asked Lucy instead. "She might go if you'll ask her direct," Nell told him.

"Yes, ma'am. I sure would be pleased if you'd ride out with me."

"Why, I'd like that," she said.

"Such foolishness," Lucy observed after Buddy left and she had gone to her room for a pair of pants for Nell. Ranch women didn't ride sidesaddle anymore.

In a few minutes, Buddy was at the portico, sitting on his horse and leading the dun. He dismounted and held Bean's stirrup for Nell. "Now you mount up on the left side," he explained.

Nell frowned. Where had Buddy gotten the idea she didn't know how to ride a horse? She'd ridden the horses on her grandparents' farm, ridden them bareback. Nell put her foot into the stirrup and swung onto Bean. They rode out of the ranch yard at a slow pace, Buddy explaining how to hold the reins, how to sit in the saddle. Once past the corral, Nell kicked the horse into a trot, and then she spurred him into a gallop. Buddy, caught off guard, hurried to catch up with her. When he did, she yelled, "Race you to the poplars," and kicked Bean with her heels.

Buddy grinned and spurred his horse, reaching the trees just ahead of Nell. "Beat you!" he yelled, when she stopped beside him.

"Only because you gave me this tired old horse."

"Next time, you can ride my horse, unless you want to try Sky High," he told her. "But you won't beat me. No woman can best me at horses." Then he grinned at her with a look of appraisal. "You sure are some horsewoman, Miss Nellie Blue-Eyes."

He trotted his horse off toward the mountains, Nell behind him. He liked that she knew how to ride a horse, she decided, and she glowed at his approval. Still, she wondered what his reaction would have been if she really had beaten him. He wouldn't like it, she thought. Maybe she'd better not challenge him.

The fall was a happy time for Nell. She was having fun, and she was crazy about Buddy. He seemed to feel the same way about her. Sometimes in the evenings, Nell sat in a chair outside on the porch with her piecing while Buddy leaned against a porch post or sat on the steps, playing his harmonica or talking. Nell thought she would make a quilt for him since his sugan, like the others in the bunkhouse, was dark and poorly made. She was afraid the other cowboys would tease him about it, however. One of Nell's quilts, even a string quilt made from random bits of leftover fabric, would stand out as much as a lace spread. She pondered what she could make for Buddy but gave up. He wouldn't want an embroidered pillow sham, and it wouldn't be proper to sew him a shirt. Finally she decided she would buy him a silk handkerchief that she had seen in the mercantile in Las Vegas. It was bright red, Buddy's favorite color, and had fringe on the ends and was very fine. It cost two dollars. She'd find a way to sneak it into his trunk or maybe under the blanket in his bunk.

"You make a real pretty picture, Miss Nell," Buddy said, watching her as she bent over her sewing one evening after supper.

He was sitting on the steps. "A person would never know you had a temper."

Nell laughed. "And you, Buddy, sitting there playing your mouth organ. Who'd know you came up with the meanest practical jokes ever invented."

"They weren't so mean."

"Last week, I got one of my handkerchiefs returned in the mail. It stank up the envelope. I don't know who sent it." By now, the story of Nell's perfumed handkerchiefs was known across New Mexico Territory. "I bet some people still think I'm a loose woman."

"How many you got back?"

"Ten. Two are still missing."

"One," Buddy said. He reached into his pocket and pulled out a white square.

"You've been carrying it around with perfume sprayed all over it?"

"This one doesn't have perfume."

Nell considered that handkerchief. She hadn't been at the ranch long when Buddy took the handkerchiefs. Had he cared about her from the beginning, and that was why he'd kept one for himself? Had he been as attracted to her that first day as she was to him? She thought to hold out her hand for the square of cloth, but she liked the idea of Buddy carrying it like some favor given to a knight, and she smiled. Buddy put the handkerchief back into his pocket.

The wind came up, and Nell tightened the shawl around her shoulders. It was almost too cold to sit outside, but she relished those evenings with Buddy. "You want my coat?" Buddy asked, taking off his denim jacket.

"I'm fine," Nell said.

"It's getting cold."

"I don't need it."

"Best you put it on." Before she could object again, Buddy had placed the jacket around her, grasping her shoulders a little too long. She liked the gesture, but she didn't want the jacket. It weighed down her arms and made it awkward to sew, but when Buddy thought a thing was right, he didn't allow disagreement. It was a little thing, Nell thought. Besides, most men she'd known were that way. Still, after a few minutes, she let the jacket slide off onto her chair.

"There's a shindig going on at the Mackintosh house in Las Vegas come Saturday. You going to let me take you?"

"I heard about it. I was thinking of riding there with Lucy and Mr. Archer."

"Might be they'll want to be alone."

Nell glanced up from her stitching. Her aunt and her boss were so circumspect that she believed she was the only one who knew what went on between them. "I wouldn't mind being alone with you either," he added.

She stared at Buddy a long time, until he dipped his chin and looked down at his harmonica. "We could ride horseback if there'll be a moon. I wouldn't want to ride if it was total dark," she said.

"I was thinking that myself. I promise a moon, a spooning moon," Buddy told her. "I'll saddle Bean for you."

"I can saddle her," Nell said.

"No," Buddy said. "It wouldn't be right, me inviting you to go with me and you saddling your horse. It's not proper."

Nell didn't see anything wrong with it, but she'd learned not to object when Buddy put his foot down. It didn't matter.

What mattered was riding across the plains with Buddy under a spooning moon.

"Your cowboy was sweet once on Alice Mackintosh," Lucy said, after Nell told her she'd be going to the party with Buddy. "We all thought he was going to marry her. Maybe he would have if you hadn't come along."

Nell was taken aback. She'd never thought about Buddy having a girl before she arrived at the Rockin' A. Lucy had said he hadn't taken a shine to any of the other hired girls, but she hadn't said a word about town girls. Suddenly Alice Mackintosh made her uneasy. Maybe Buddy wasn't *her* cowboy after all.

CHAPTER SIX

*Nell had only two outfits suitable for a party. She'd worn the cream-*colored skirt and white blouse to the shindig at the Iverson ranch, so she decided on the other, a red dress, for the Mackintosh event. She wanted to look nice, especially if Buddy was going to compare her to Alice Mackintosh. She wondered why Lucy hadn't mentioned anything about the girl before then.

Alice had not attended the affair at the Iversons'. She had been away at school in the East and then had gone to New York for the season. The party was a welcome home for her.

"She's pretty, just like a china doll," Lucy said when Nell asked about Alice. "She's a gad-a-way. Buddy wasn't the only cowboy she had on her string, but she liked him best, and I expect she thinks he's been waiting for her. Alice is quite a catch. Her father's a banker in Las Vegas and owns half the town. She and her brother will inherit it all. She usually gets what she wants."

"Do you like her?" Nell asked.

Lucy had been kneading dough in a wooden bowl and stopped

and dusted the flour off her hands. "Like Alice Mackintosh?" Lucy laughed. "I like her almost as much as that rattlesnake you killed with the skillet."

"Really?" Nell was surprised. "What's wrong with her?"

"Her nose is so high she'd drown in a rainstorm. Stuck up, vicious as a badger." Lucy began kneading the dough with a vengeance. "I'll tell you, Nell, if you fancy your cowpoke, you just might have a fight on your hands, now that she's back. I never mentioned her before, because I didn't know she was coming home. And I hoped she wouldn't. I thought she'd marry some fellow back there. Even if she doesn't want your Buddy, she's likely to go after him just to spite you."

"I doubt she'll take much notice of me."

"Oh, I wouldn't bet on it. My guess is she already knows everything there is to know about you. Don't underestimate her. The other girls around here know better than to tangle with her. She's not much liked by the women. She thinks she's cut finer than frog hair." Lucy laughed again. "Men's another thing. They don't seem to notice how unpleasant a woman can be until it's too late. My advice is steer clear of Alice Mackintosh and keep that cowboy away from her if you can." Lucy slapped the bread dough onto the table and began cutting off loaf-size sections with a butcher knife and shoving them into pans. "But I don't suppose there's anybody that can keep a man away from Alice Mackintosh once she sets her cap for him."

The afternoon of the Mackintosh party, Nell took extra care with her appearance. She'd washed her hair that morning, and before she dressed, she arranged it on top of her head and put rouge on her cheeks, which she knew were too tan from riding in the sun.

She rouged her lips, too, then glanced into the mirror and decided she looked like a chippie and rubbed off the color. Finally she put on the red dress and asked Lucy to button the back.

"How're you going to ride Bean in this dress?" Lucy asked.

Nell hadn't thought about that. She'd have to push the dress up to her waist if she rode astride, and that wouldn't do.

"Best you ride in the carriage with Mr. Archer and me."

Nell wanted to ride with Buddy, however, wanted to ride with him under that moon he'd promised, and she thought it was a good idea to show up at the party with him, just in case Alice claimed Buddy. So she changed into a divided skirt that she had ordered from the wish book, pairing it with a white shirt and black boots. The skirt came well above her ankles, and Nell wasn't sure that was proper, but Lucy told her she looked up-to-date, just like a picture in a ladies' magazine.

Buddy's rich brown eyes lit up when he saw her, and he muttered, "Pretty as daybreak." He had shaved and had put on a new flannel shirt, Nell judged from the fold lines still in the garment. He had polished his boots and brushed his hat, and wore what must have been his good coat. Nell had never seen it before. He'd knotted the red silk handkerchief around his neck, too—the one Nell had bought and sneaked into the bunkhouse and put into his trunk. He'd never mentioned it, perhaps because he didn't know it had come from her. Buddy looked handsome as a dime-novel hero in all his finery, and Nell thought perhaps he'd wanted to impress her. Or maybe it was Alice.

Lucy looked at him, hands on her hips. "You got your low-neck clothes on," she observed. "Well, you ought to wear your Sunday best if you're taking our Nell here to the party."

"I sure wouldn't want her to be ashamed of me," he said.

"I hear Alice is back," Lucy said.

Nell looked away. She wished Lucy hadn't brought up Alice, but then, maybe she ought to know what she was up against—if she *was* up against Alice. Were they rivals? Buddy hadn't mentioned a word about Alice, and of course, in the past weeks, he'd acted as if he was stuck on Nell. Perhaps she'd just been a diversion. Maybe he'd been stringing her along hoping Alice would return. Nell didn't want to think he was like that, but she couldn't be sure.

"So I hear. I hope she hasn't got too full of herself back at that school."

"She was always too proud," Lucy replied.

"Now, Miss Lucy, I don't know why you gals are so down on Miss Alice. I always thought she was mighty nice." He considered the remark. "Almost as nice as Miss Nell here."

Nell hoped he meant that, but perhaps it was an afterthought. She felt unsure of herself and was apprehensive about meeting Alice.

"Well, just don't get your spurs tangled, cowboy," Lucy said as she and Nell went back into the house to carry out the pies. Lucy had baked a dried apple pie with raisins and cinnamon, while Nell had made her lemon meringue. It had received so many compliments at the Iverson party that Nell had baked it again, this time using even more egg whites so that the meringue rose up like a blizzard on a mountain.

Buddy helped Nell mount Bean, then climbed onto his own horse. Nell thought to race him to the gate, but she found herself wondering if Alice would do that. Probably no—not if the girl had been in New York attending debutante parties. Besides, Nell didn't want to arrive at the Mackintoshes' sweaty and windblown. It was bad enough she wore a riding outfit instead of a party dress.

"Have you seen Miss Mackintosh since she came back from New York?" Nell asked, as they trotted across the prairie, side by side. It was the tail end of daylight, with no sign yet of a moon. The earth was brown, covered with sage and chamisa and clumps of buffalo grass. They could see a long way off east, where there was nothing but a few cottonwoods to block the view. To the west, the mountains were a blur of blue in the darkening sky. A hawk flew high above them, then dropped suddenly as it spied a rabbit. As it rose, it clutched the animal in its talons and flew into the dying sun. Far off, the cattle were lowing, and Nell heard the rattle of a wagon, or perhaps Mr. Archer's carriage, in the clear air, where sound traveled for miles. The world seemed enormous to Nell.

"Nope," Buddy answered.

"I imagine you're old friends."

"That's right."

"Then I'm sure she'll be glad to see you."

"Hope so."

Buddy didn't seem inclined to talk, and Nell didn't want to sound nosy or—worse—jealous. So she was silent as she rode beside him, the only sounds now the horses moving through the underbrush, crushing the sage, which sent up its sharp smell. They passed the remains of a wagon, its wheels broken, its bed sagging into the ground.

Then Buddy asked, "You got anybody you're sweet on back in Kansas?"

Nell turned to him in surprise. She almost said no, but something told her not to be so quick to dismiss the idea. She wasn't sure about Buddy and Alice. It might be a good thing if he thought he wasn't the only one on *her* string. "There's a fellow. Lane Philips is his name. But I didn't . . ." She shrugged and did not finish, and Buddy asked no more questions.

As they approached Las Vegas, Buddy adjusted the handkerchief and said, "You didn't say anything about my neckwear."

"It's handsome," Nell replied.

"Funny thing it showing up in my trunk the way it did. Kind of a present. I wonder who put it there. Maybe it was from somebody that admires me."

"Maybe." Nell couldn't quite bring herself to admit it. "Or maybe from somebody thinking you needed some low-neck clothes."

"You think so?" He chuckled. "Well, I sure do thank that person. If I knew who she was, I'd give her a kiss and an old white handkerchief."

"Then maybe she'll tell you who she is."

The two of them grinned at each other. Then suddenly Buddy reined in his horse and jumped off to pluck a dried yellow flower from a chamisa bush. He presented it to Nell with a bow, and she tucked it into the buttonhole of her shirt.

They arrived ahead of Lucy and Mr. Archer. The other Rockin' A cowboys had not been invited, since this was a formal party in town, not like the event at the Iverson ranch, which had been open to the cowhands as well as the ranchers. They rode past low mud-daubed buildings and fussy frame houses. Then Buddy reined in at a black iron fence in front of a large Victorian house with a tower and a mansard roof, a cast-iron fountain in the yard. The house seemed overbuilt, and Nell preferred the Rockin' A ranch house with its soft adobe walls, which seemed at one with the earth. She found the Mackintosh mansion too showy.

Alice Mackintosh was standing on the porch steps. She had

to be Alice, Nell thought, because who else in New Mexico Territory would be wearing a low-cut white satin gown with jet beading, and a hothouse corsage pinned to her shoulder? With her blond hair artfully arranged on top of her head and a complexion as pale as cream, Alice was the prettiest girl in Las Vegas. Certainly prettier than Nell was with her tanned face and sun-bleached hair, Nell thought. Who could blame Buddy for wanting to see her?

Alice's face lit up as she spotted Buddy. She did not rush to meet him but waited like royalty on the steps of the mansion for Buddy to dismount, tie his horse to the fence, and go to her, taking her hands. He seemed to have forgotten Nell, who dismounted on her own and walked up beside him.

"My dearest old friend, what a pleasure to greet you." Alice held on to Buddy's hands a little too long.

"Welcome home, Miss Alice."

"*Miss* Alice indeed. We mean far too much to each other for such formality." Alice started to say more but became aware of Nell, who was standing next to Buddy. "Oh, do forgive me. I thought you were one of the hands, dressed that way."

"This is Nell, Miss Lucy's niece," Buddy said.

"Oh, yes, I've heard the Rockin' A had a new hired girl. How thoughtful of you to bring her along." Alice smiled to take the sting out of her words, but the insult was there all the same. Then, without releasing Buddy's hands, Alice asked Nell to excuse them because they had so much to talk about. "The kitchen is over there," she told Nell, with a wave of her hand.

"Buddy—" Nell began.

Alice cut her off. "Buddy?" she said. "You call him Buddy? Why would you do that? That's the name of his horse." Alice laughed, a sound like the tinkling of bells. She took Buddy's arm and led him inside the house, and Nell heard her say again, "*Buddy!* Isn't that the oddest thing? Is she addled?"

Buddy didn't give Nell a backward glance as he went through the door. Nell stood frozen, humiliated, as she watched the other guests arrive. Although the women were not as finely dressed as Alice, none of them wore riding clothes, and Nell realized she should have put on the red dress, even if it meant riding with Lucy and Mr. Archer. She straightened the collar of her shirtwaist and touched the tiny chamisa flower. It looked silly compared to the flower pinned to Alice's dress, but still, Nell wouldn't have traded corsages for anything.

Nell stood by the steps and waited for her aunt and Mr. Archer. When the couple arrived, Lucy handed down the pies. "I suppose for a party as fancy as this, we didn't have to bring anything, but I'd rather err on the side of being neighborly."

"I know where the kitchen is," Nell said.

"How's that?" Lucy raised an eyebrow.

"Alice told me."

Lucy laughed. "I just bet she did. You crossed spurs with her already, then? Where's your escort?"

"He left me behind." She stamped her boot in frustration.

"Now you're acting the way she wants you to, and just girly enough to make Buddy think you're silly," Lucy warned.

The two women walked through the front door and back to the kitchen, where Mrs. Mackintosh was checking the food preparations. Unlike her daughter, she was plump and disheveled, and she fluttered about like a prairie chicken. When she saw Lucy, she threw up her hands. "I should have taken you up on your offer to help. I thought Alice and me . . ." She rolled her eyes as she mentioned her daughter. "Alice spent more time getting dressed than she did in the kitchen. All to make an impression on that cowboy."

"Mildred, you haven't met my niece, Nell," Lucy said quickly.

"No, but I sure heard about you."

Nell looked confused.

"You know, those perfumed hankies." She laughed. "What a trick. Well, I heard the cowboys admire that you can laugh at yourself. Now, which one of you made that momentous meringue pie?"

"Nell did," Lucy said.

"I imagine it will be the first thing to go." She looked up and said, "There she is now. Alice, look at this pie Lucy's niece baked. Ain't it a beauty?"

Alice leaned over the pie. "If you like pie." She turned to Buddy. She was holding his hand. "I made your favorite chocolate cake, dear."

Alice led him to the dining room where the desserts were waiting: pies and cakes and cobblers, chocolate pudding, lemon pudding, and what the cowboys called frog-eye pudding—tapioca. Alice's mother shook her head and said in a low voice, "That one can bake a chocolate cake about as well as I can ride a bronco. I should have sent her to cooking school instead of to that fancy eastern female seminary." Still, she smiled as she glanced into the next room at her daughter. "But I don't expect any cowboy to care how well she can cook. Not that cowboy, anyway." Mildred Mackintosh apparently had not heard that Buddy had been riding out with Nell.

"She's a very beautiful girl," Nell said, determined to take Lucy's advice and not appear jealous.

"Yes. I thought she'd find a young man in the East. But she

didn't. There must be something about cowboys." She grinned at Lucy. "Me and you both know about that, don't we, Luce? Maybe Alice does, too."

Mrs. Mackintosh touched Nell's arm and said, "I hope you'll be a friend to Alice. There's some that think she's too stuck on herself, but deep down, she's a nice girl." She added to herself, "I hope she is."

"I shouldn't have come," Nell whispered to Lucy when Mrs. Mackintosh turned to the stove. "Maybe I should say I'm not feeling well and go on back home."

"Now, don't try to alibi your way out of it. Nothing would please Alice more. You just stay here and enjoy yourself. Why, you'll turn out to be the belle of the ball."

Nell looked down at her riding skirt and shook her head. "Not with Alice Mackintosh around."

Nell stayed in the kitchen with Lucy and Mrs. Mackintosh, dishing up food and taking it to the dining room table, which was as big as half a dozen bunkhouse beds shoved together. Alice came into the kitchen again and carried out the desserts, placing her cake at the front on the dessert table. Nell's pie was on the side. Buddy, standing with the men around the bottles Mr. Mackintosh had set out, watched her. When the tables were loaded with food, Mrs. Mackintosh rang a little bell, and everyone trooped into the dining room and picked up plates—china, not tin, Nell noted. The Mackintoshes had enough china plates for dozens of guests.

Alice, with Buddy in tow, led the others, and they helped themselves to the food spread out before them. "Now, save room for my cake," Alice said, moving to the dessert table. She cut a sizable piece of the chocolate cake and set it on Buddy's plate. As she did, Buddy stepped backward and tripped, righting himself by grabbing hold of the table, pushing Nell's lemon meringue pie onto the floor. It landed meringue side down.

"Oh, look what I've done. I've spoiled it," he said, searching for Nell, and when he spotted her, he gave a mournful look.

"You sure did," Lucy muttered. "Almost on purpose, looks like."

Alice laughed. "Oh, there's plenty more, and I'm sure it wasn't much anyway." She called to Nell, "There's a rag in the kitchen to clean it up."

Nell glared at her, but Alice only laughed and turned away, and, mortified, Nell went into the kitchen for something to wipe up the spilled pie. Why would Buddy have done such a thing, she wondered, and was it really an accident? After she had cleaned up the mess, Nell didn't care to eat. "Now I really am sick. I can find my way home by myself."

"You'll do no such thing," Lucy told her. "Don't you dare let Alice Mackintosh drive you away. And don't turn moody. You're going to stay and have a good time. And you'll dance every dance, even if you have to dance with *me*." The two had taken their plates to a nook in one of the parlors. Lucy glanced at a man nearby, then said, "Why, Owen, you haven't met our Nell. Owen Mackintosh is Alice's brother."

Owen smiled. "I was wondering who the girl was who refused to ride a horse all gussied up in a satin dress." He bowed a little. "I saw her from the window, and I would be honored to claim the first dance with her." He stood and held out his arm. "I think I hear the musicians now. Would you do me the honor—unless you want some of my sister's wretched cake."

Lucy shoved at Nell, who stood and took Owen's arm. "I

would be pleased," she said, but she wasn't. She would rather dance with Buddy, although she allowed Owen to lead her upstairs to the ballroom.

Owen was a good dancer, but he was only one of the men who claimed Nell. As soon as a dance ended, another man took her arm, and when that dance was finished, Owen was back again. Once Buddy stepped up and asked her to dance, but as soon as he did, Alice said, "Why, I believe I promised you this one." She smiled at Nell, "Honestly, don't you think we ought to have dance cards? I just can't keep all the men straight." She pouted as she added to Buddy, "Of course, you'd fill up my card and wouldn't let anyone else dance with me."

About midnight, Lucy told Nell that she and Mr. Archer were leaving. "You can come with us, if you're tired," she said, glancing at Buddy, who was dancing with Alice again. "Might be safer since it looks like snow."

Buddy saw them, however, and left Alice to say it was time he, too, went home. "That is, if you're ready, Miss Nell."

"I can ride home with Lucy," she said.

Buddy frowned. "I invited you, and I'll take you home. Wouldn't be right not to." He was firm.

"Oh, you can't leave already," Alice said, but Buddy told her he had chores in the morning.

"Maybe we can go riding."

"I thought you didn't like to ride," Buddy said.

Alice linked her arm through his. "I do with you. Perhaps we can invite Owen and—Nellie, is it?"

"Nell," Nell told her.

"If you can get away from the kitchen," Alice added.

They said their good-byes, and Buddy helped Nell mount Bean. Then, instead of following the carriage on the road to the ranch, he led Nell through town and took off across the High Plains, just as flakes of snow began to fall. They floated down, leaving patches of white on the sage and chamisa. After a mile, Buddy slowed his horse, and Nell came up beside him.

"Did you have a good time?" he asked.

"Mmm."

"You sure were pirooting around with Owen Mackintosh."

Nell flared. "I wasn't fooling around with anybody."

"He's cultus, doesn't know a thing that's useful. He's been off to college in the East," Buddy said.

"So has Alice."

"It's different with a girl."

"Why's that?"

Buddy thought that over and didn't reply. "I just wanted to warn you. Don't go thinking he's anything special."

"Not like Alice."

"He's all but engaged to a girl in New York or someplace like that. Alice told me."

"I'm not out to marry him. I just wanted somebody to dance with since the fellow who brought me to the party was busy with another girl." There, she'd said it. Nell wasn't sure she should have. But she was hurt. Buddy had treated her shabbily. Her eyes watered, and she wiped them with the sleeve of her jacket. She'd been so foolish. How could a hired girl dressed in a rough riding costume think to compete against Alice Mackintosh with her satin dress and skin as pale as the snowflakes? No wonder Nell could hardly keep from crying. She turned away so that Buddy wouldn't see the tears.

Buddy reined in his horse and stared at her. The moon he had promised wasn't visible, but it sent just enough light through the snow that he could see her face. "You think I went over there to see Alice?"

"Looks like it to me, but what do I care? You're free to do anything you like. Only next time, don't invite me to go with you." Nell tossed her head and kicked Bean, but Buddy grabbed her reins.

"I didn't have any choice. I tried to eat supper with you, but you were in the kitchen, and Alice kept ahold of me. I couldn't shake her, and that's the truth. Every time I tried to dance with you, you were with Owen, and then Alice would tell me I'd promised that dance to her. It just all got too confusing."

"Is that why you knocked over my pie?"

"It was an accident."

"Didn't look like it to me."

Buddy turned away, then looked back at Nell. "It wasn't."

"You did it on purpose? I thought you were done with practical jokes." Her voice was choked, and she dabbed at her eyes again. This was supposed to have been a wonderful evening with Buddy, but it hadn't turned out that way. Even the moon he had promised was obscured. Nell grabbed her reins from Buddy and was ready to ride off.

"'Course I did it on purpose. Maybe you didn't see her shake salt all over the top of it."

Nell stared at him, a frown on her face. "What?"

Buddy nodded. "Anybody ate your pie was in for a bad surprise. I already spoiled your reputation with those handkerchiefs. I didn't want folks talking you couldn't bake a pie."

"Is that the truth? You did that? For me?"

"Well, sure I did. Alice has got it in for you, and I don't know why."

Nell blinked. Was it possible he really didn't know why Alice would go after her?

Then Buddy said, "I wouldn't do anything to hurt you. I got feelings aplenty for you, Nell. I like you awful well." It was the first time he hadn't called her *Miss* Nell. "And I was kind of hoping you had them for me. I was thinking that was why you bought me this red handkerchief."

Nell couldn't say anything.

"Am I right?"

She stared at him in the moonlight, brushing off the flakes of snow that had fallen on her hair. Why hadn't she brought a scarf or a hat?

"I said if I found out who gave it to me, I'd give her a kiss and a white handkerchief. Well, I lied about that. I'm keeping the handkerchief." Buddy reached over and touched her hair, which was damp from the snow. Then he took off his big white hat. As he leaned over to put it on Nell's head, he kissed her. Harder and longer this time.

CHAPTER SEVEN

Nell loved the snow that fell on the High Plains. She liked standing in the doorway and looking out at the sweep of white, the far mountain peaks shimmering. When she rode out across the prairie with Buddy, she saw the footprints of rabbits and deer, and sometimes she caught sight of the brown antelope with their white rumps that were almost invisible against the snowy land. Buddy told her they were curious, and once they tied their horses in an arroyo and crept along so they were close to the animals. Buddy tied his bandana to a stick and raised it up, and the antelope came over to investigate.

The New Mexico snow was dry, and unlike the heavy midwestern snows that Nell was used to, it didn't stay on the ground all winter but melted away as soon as the storm ended and the sun came out. Of course, it was too cold to sit on the porch on winter evenings, but Nell and Buddy found ways to see each other. Nell waited until Buddy was in the corral before she went out to feed the chickens. She loved the chickens, each one with a different personality. The blue one missing feathers on one side was mean, always pecking at the others, while the chicken with the brown feathers, the tips red as a rooster comb, was cheeky, the white one a worrier. Sometimes Nell and Buddy sat on the corral fence and watched them, throwing corn or food scraps to their favorites.

Buddy found reasons to come to the ranch house at night. He chopped stovewood and brought it into the kitchen. Then he sat among the geraniums in the window ledge in the light of a kerosene lamp, patching a bridle or oiling his boots, while Nell pieced her quilts. He found excuses to come into the kitchen during the daytime, too, watching Nell and Lucy cook, paring potatoes for them or carrying out scraps to the chickens. He even helped Nell hang up the laundry, handing her wooden clothespins while she pinned the sheets and shirts to the line to dry as hard as fence posts in the stiff winter wind. Once he brought his woolies—angora chaps—to Nell and asked her to help wash them.

"Makes the house smell like sheep dip," Lucy muttered. "That's not a good thing for a cattle ranch." But Lucy liked Buddy and approved of the courtship.

When their work was done, Buddy took Nell riding, often over snowy trails toward the mountains. Sometimes they checked on the cattle, or Nell helped Buddy repair a fence. She wore heavy gloves lined with rabbit fur, but even then, her hands got cold, and Buddy would take off their gloves and hold their hands together inside his coat.

Often as they rode along, side by side, Buddy talked about the future. "I'm not always going to be a hired hand. I plan on having my own ranch," he told her.

"Doesn't that take an awful lot of money?" Nell asked.

"I've got a bit saved up. More than a bit."

Nell knew what a cowboy's wages were and said, "You'd have to work a long time to save enough to buy a ranch." And then she realized that Buddy could marry someone who had enough money to buy a ranch—Alice.

"Oh, like I told you before, I had a dab of money before I came here. I'll need more to swing it, but I got enough for a down payment," Buddy said, as if he knew what she was thinking. He explained that he had inherited his parents' farm in Iowa and sold it. "I didn't want to be a granger all my life. I came out here to learn the cattle business, and I guess I know enough now to make a ranch."

"So you're leaving the Rockin' A?" Nell tried to keep her concern out of her voice. Maybe Buddy had just been trifling with her. She knew he liked her, but he'd never declared himself.

"Not just yet, but before too long. I got a place in mind." He was quiet, and Nell didn't push him.

She learned a great deal about Buddy on those outings. He was kind and compassionate. He didn't like to hurt animals, and if he found a bird with a broken wing, he'd take it back to the barn and try to doctor it. While the other cowboys tossed the bunkhouse mice they caught into the stove, Buddy took them outside and let them go. He hunted antelope and deer, but that was for food, not for the joy of killing.

Buddy was patient. He would sit and think through a problem before he tried to solve it. And once he made up his mind, he never deviated. He was stubborn that way, too stubborn, Nell thought, although she understood it, because she was stubborn, too. He expected once he'd made up his mind about a thing, she should go along with it. Nell didn't always agree, particularly when it came to what he expected of *her*.

There was one other thing: He was jealous.

Owen Mackintosh showed up at the Rockin' A in a buggy one Sunday after Christmas and invited Nell to have lunch with him at the Plaza Hotel in Las Vegas. Buddy, sitting in the kitchen when Owen arrived, seethed, but he hadn't any right to tell her not to go. Nell wore her red dress and had a grand time. Owen was polished, a fine talker, and he ordered a good meal. She even let him buy her cowboy coffee—whiskey neat—and on the way home, warm under a fur robe, the two sang college songs. Buddy was in the corral when they rode past. Except for meals, Buddy didn't come to the ranch house for two or three days.

Not long after that, Owen rode out to the ranch, arriving just at dinnertime. Mr. Archer invited him to sit down with the cowboys. Nell thought the hands might find Owen high-headed, maybe play jokes on him, but Owen fit right in. He knew enough about ranching to join in the conversation, and when he failed to understand a thing, he didn't try to bluff. Instead, he asked outright what was meant. The hands liked that, all but Buddy. He glared at Owen until Lucy asked Buddy if he was off his feed. When the other cowboys went back to work, Buddy stayed in the kitchen, watching.

Owen didn't seem to mind him. In fact, he told Buddy he was glad for his company, because, he said, "I have a grand idea. There's a winter carnival with ice skating in town on Saturday night, and Alice is dying to have you escort her. I could take Nell. We thought the two of you could ride into town together, and we'd meet you there."

Nell wasn't sure it was such a grand idea. She wouldn't mind attending with Owen, but she didn't like the idea of Buddy taking Alice.

Lucy, who was washing the dishes, spoke up. "You go on, Nell. I can handle supper for the boys."

Nell glanced at Buddy, who had been watching her. He grinned slyly. "Why, that's a fine idea."

Nell stiffened. Maybe Buddy wanted to be with Alice.

"Capital!" Owen said. "Alice says she thinks you've deserted her. She'll be delighted." He winked at Buddy. "Wait until you see the cunning little skating outfit she's going to wear."

"Do you know how to skate?" Nell asked Buddy.

"I guess I can manage."

After the men left, Nell told Lucy, "You should have said I couldn't go."

"Don't be so glum. Buddy's only trying to make you jealous. You go and have a good time with Owen. That'll be the best revenge."

Nell wasn't so sure.

The two of them rode their horses into town the afternoon of the carnival. The sky was clear, but Buddy said you never knew when it might snow, and if it did, they would be better on horseback than in a buggy. When they arrived, Alice and Owen were already at the skating rink, Alice surrounded by young men. She was indeed ragged out, in a white skating outfit with a little fur muff. Nell had worn her divided skirt and a wool coat of Lucy's, cut from a trapper blanket, and thought she looked fine when she viewed herself in a mirror at the ranch. Compared to Alice, however, Nell felt dowdy.

"Alice is likely to freeze to death. You're dressed just exactly right," Owen told her, taking her arm and leading her to a booth that rented skates. He turned to Buddy. "Alice brought your skates from the house."

"I wouldn't think a cowboy would know how to skate," Nell said.

"Oh, he didn't. Alice taught him last winter. She even bought him skates for a Christmas present. The cowboys teased him something awful, but in fact, he's quite good."

Nell was a competent ice skater, but nothing like Alice, who flitted back and forth across the ice, twirling around, her skirt billowing about her. Sometimes she skated by herself, but most of the time she held hands with Buddy.

"They're very good together, don't you think?" Owen asked, and Nell had to grit her teeth and agree. "I guess it's plain she's stuck on him," Owen added.

Once, the two couples exchanged partners. "Alice is awfully good on skates," Nell repeated, determined not to let Buddy know she despised the girl.

"If you like ice skating, I guess."

"Don't you?"

"I'm a cowpuncher. I'll get teased like the devil if the boys find out I went ice skating again."

"Then why did you come?"

"Why did you?"

"I wanted to have a good time. Isn't that why you're here?"

Buddy nodded. "Well, somebody had to protect you from Owen."

Nell should have been pleased by the remark, but instead, she flared. Buddy was presumptuous. "I can take care of myself.

I don't need some self-appointed rescuer. Besides, Owen's a gen-tleman."

"You mean he's no cowpuncher."

"I didn't say that. And you know I don't believe any such thing."

The scratchy gramophone music ended, and the couples changed partners again. Owen suggested they get cocoa, and the four skated over to a concession stand. Owen pulled out a flask and poured a slug of whiskey into Alice's cup and then his own. He held out the flask to Nell, who poured a small amount into her cocoa. Buddy shook his head. Then Owen proposed they take off their skates and sit in the stand to watch fire-works, but Nell said she had to leave. "I get up early to help with breakfast," she told them.

"Oh, I forget you're the hired girl," Alice said. "I suppose you expect Buddy to take you home."

"I can ride out with her," Owen said. "I'll just get my horse."

Buddy put his hand on Owen's arm. "I brought Miss Nell, and I'll see her home," he said in a firm voice.

Alice pouted. "We haven't been together in over a year, and you're leaving already. I am entirely hurt," she said, then kissed Buddy on the cheek—and would have kissed him on the mouth if they'd been alone, Nell thought.

The night was bright with stars, millions of tiny white lights sparkling from horizon to horizon, and lit by the moon. The prai-rie was vast and silent, and it seemed they were the only ones out. Nell and Buddy rode in silence, but it was a comfortable silence, as if neither wanted to spoil the majesty of the night by talking. In fact, it would have been a perfect night if it hadn't been for Alice, Nell thought. But she didn't say anything about her, and Buddy didn't comment on Owen. As they neared the ranch house, Buddy said, "I'd appreciate it if you didn't tell anyone that I went ice skating."

Both of them overlooked their jealousy at the ice-skating party and fell into their familiar ways again. Buddy came to the ranch house in the evenings, and Nell found chores to do outside when Buddy was around. Sometimes, after Lucy and Mr. Archer retired for the night, Buddy sat next to Nell in front of the adobe fireplace in the kitchen and held her hand, or tucked her head under his chin and put his arm around her. He hadn't said anything about the future, and Nell knew she couldn't hurry him.

One day, Owen sent a note to the Rockin' A, inviting Nell to go into town with him to see a play. She could stay all night with Alice at the Mackintosh house. Nell talked it over with Lucy. Buddy overheard and told her that sleeping at the Mackintosh house when Owen was there wasn't proper. He said people would talk and she wasn't to go, not if she cared about her reputation.

"You didn't mind what people thought when you gave out my handkerchiefs," she flared, but Buddy told her that was different. Nell didn't see much difference.

"I won't allow it," he said.

"*You* won't allow it," Nell flared. She had been ironing, and she held the sad iron in the air as if it were a weapon. "*You* don't have any right to tell me what to do."

Buddy looked sheepish. "No, ma'am, I do not. I was only advising you."

Nell thought it over and eventually told Owen no. She said she was needed at the ranch, but that wasn't the reason. While she chafed at Buddy's presumption, thinking he hadn't the right to interfere, and she was disappointed that Buddy's affection hadn't gone beyond a few hugs and kisses, Nell turned down Owen's invitation because she didn't want to stay in the same house with Alice. She liked Buddy too much. In fact, Nell loved him. She hadn't told Lucy—or Buddy, of course. She'd barely told herself. She'd never feel that way about Owen, and it would be wrong to lead him on. Besides, making Buddy jealous, she realized, only led to trouble.

"I'm glad you didn't go to that play in town," Buddy told her one afternoon in late winter when they had ridden out to check on a windmill that had stopped working.

Nell was silent. She didn't tell Buddy that Owen had asked her out twice more and she'd turned him down.

"I never had a liking for him. He's too high-hat for the rest of us," Buddy continued.

And Alice isn't? Nell wanted to reply, but kept the retort to herself.

"He flaps his mouth too much, just like that windmill—at least, when it's working," Buddy said, when they stopped at the watering tank and looked up at the blades. "I guess I'll have Wendell to fix it."

"Why can't you do it?" Nell asked. She was surprised because Buddy seemed to be able to fix anything.

"I expect I could, but I'm not going up there."

"Why not?"

Buddy turned red and looked away.

"I thought the cattle needed the water."

"Yep. But the truth is I'm scared to death to climb up there."

"You?" Nell had seen Buddy ride bucking broncos and go out in a blizzard to check the cattle. He'd stomped on a rattlesnake that had coiled itself around the clothesline pole, and he'd distracted an angry bull from Monty, who'd been bucked off his horse near the animal.

"I can't get more than five feet off the ground without my hands sweat and I get all light in the head. It's a failing I have, and it shames me."

Nell thought that over. "I could do it. I could climb up there."

"It's too dangerous," Buddy told her.

"I've climbed trees higher than that."

"It wouldn't be right, a lady like you climbing that windmill."

Nell didn't argue. Instead, before Buddy could stop her, she grabbed a coiled rope, put it over her shoulder, and began climbing the windmill. She didn't stop until she was at the top. "I can see right here how it's broken," she said. "Send up those do-funnies you brought along. Put them in the bucket that's over next to the tank." She tied one end of the rope to the windmill and tossed the other end to the ground. "You send them up, and I'll fix it."

Buddy put the items into the bucket and tied the rope to the bucket handle, and Nell pulled it up. Within minutes she had completed the repair and was back down on the ground.

"Where'd you learn to fix windmills?" Buddy asked.

"My grandparents' farm. Grandpa had rheumatism and couldn't climb, so he sent me up when anything went wrong with the windmill."

"Well, I never saw a lady that could do that before."

"Oh, I can do plenty of things," Nell said, basking in Buddy's approval. Then she added, "And some of them aren't so ladylike."

"Well, I like a girl that can do for herself," Buddy said.

Nell thought of Alice and preened a little.

"That's the kind of girl I'd like to have on my ranch one day."

Nell's heart thumped as she glanced at Buddy, not sure what he was getting at.

"You think I could hire you as one of my hands?"

Oh, Nell thought. That was all. He was joking. "Not if I have to sleep in a bunkhouse."

"I mean . . ." Buddy cleared his throat. "I mean sleep in my bed."

Nell was so startled that she dropped the bucket. "What!" she said. There was anger in her voice.

Buddy turned red and shook his head. "I didn't mean it like that." He paused. "I didn't plan to ask you until everything was ready. But I guess now's as good a time as any, since I've just got myself into a nest of rattlesnakes here. That ranch I got my eye on, I'll own it before the year's out. It's a fine place, good water and grass. A little cabin, too, and I plan to buy a real bed, no tick stuffed with straw. And a cookstove. It's everything I ever wanted, but I don't care to live there alone. A ranch can get awful lonesome if you're by yourself." He paused and looked down at his hands. "I think you like me, and Lord knows I like you, and . . . Oh, hell, Nell, will you marry me?"

For a moment, Nell was speechless. She had dreamed of this, but she was startled. She'd never thought Buddy would propose at a water tank. Finally she murmured, "You want me to marry you?"

"I think I just said that."

"You mean this is a proposal of marriage."

"I'd get down on one knee, but the ground is awful muddy."

"I just—"

"You can say yes, or you can say no, but don't tell me you got to think it over."

Nell took a deep breath and looked into Buddy's eyes, which at that moment were the exact color of the earth. "Of course I'll marry you."

Buddy took her in his arms and swung her around and around, until he slipped and they both fell into the mud. Nell landed on her back, Buddy on top of her, and they lay like that for a long time, Buddy pinning her down and kissing her.

CHAPTER EIGHT

One spring morning as Nell was clearing the dinner dishes, Buddy asked her to ride with him to the mountains to search for cattle that had wandered off. Wendell was laid up with a bad back, Monty and two other cowboys were in the north range, and Mr. Archer hadn't yet replaced Charlie or Willy, who had gone to Albuquerque and married his Martha.

Nell wasn't sure she should go. She had to help Lucy with three meals a day, seven days a week, and she'd already taken too many opportunities to be alone with Buddy. They had been engaged for a month, but they hadn't told anyone. Nell hadn't written her grandparents either. They would announce their engagement in the fall and marry in the new year, after Buddy had his ranch in order. That way they'd avoid the teasing and practical jokes as long as possible. Nell didn't care about the teasing for herself, but she knew the cowboys would be merciless with Buddy, especially since most had been victims of his practical jokes.

Nell had just put her bread in the oven, and the yeasty smell filled the kitchen. If she waited for the loaves to be done, she could leave with Buddy, she said. Lucy told her to go ahead, however; she'd take care of the bread. "You'll be cowboying—and paid a lot less for it than the hands," Lucy said. "Be sure and take a heavy coat and a bedroll. You never know when it's going to snow."

Nell scoffed at that. It was the prettiest kind of day, the sky sapphire blue without a single cloud. And as for a bedroll—the idea made Nell blush. If bad weather rolled in, she and Buddy would just head back to the ranch. Still, she followed Lucy's advice.

Buddy had Bean saddled and ready to go when Nell emerged from the ranch house, a rolled-up blanket in her arms. She carried the coat, too, because the day was too warm to wear it. While she tied them to her saddle, Buddy stuffed a sack of food Nell had prepared into his saddlebags. It was their dinner and maybe supper, too, because they might not get home until late.

While she had lived on the ranch for six months, Nell had never gone into the mountains, and she was excited about the ride. The two of them loped past the poplars that shaded the ranch, across the plains, through the chaparral and the buffalo grass, dead and brown now. Sagebrush, its leaves glinting silver in the sunlight, scented the air. When she had arrived at the ranch, Nell thought the prairie was flat, but she'd learned it had gentle rises and was cut by arroyos where deer hid. Far off, she saw a herd of antelope, and as they rode along, she heard the sound of a meadowlark and saw hawks dip out of the sky in search of mice and rabbits. Once Buddy pointed out an eagle high above them. Buddy led her up a trail that was lined with piñons and scrub oak and chamisa. In the fall, the chamisa had turned yellow, giving the land a dusting of gold, but the flowers that remained were a dull gold now—just like the chamisa "corsage" Buddy had given her before Alice Mackintosh's party. Nell had pressed it in her Bible.

"There's a couple of mama cows that like to sneak off and come up here," Buddy said. "We'll find them and drive them down. Only hard thing is figuring out where they are."

The trail was steep, with sharp drop-offs on one side. They didn't bother Nell, but she wondered if Buddy was afraid of them. He'd admitted he was scared of heights. She didn't ask, however. Instead, she looked out over the sweep of land. Clouds had gathered far to the north, and they sent blue shadows across the prairie, which was vast and brown and silent. She'd never seen a country so empty. From the high trail, she tried to spot the ranch house, but it was too far away. Above her were giant pine trees and patches of aspen. She remembered in the fall when the aspen had been swaths of gold against the dark mountains, but now the branches were bare and stood out like old gray bones.

Buddy dismounted and squatted on the trail, studying the dirt. "The cows have been along here, all right. See the tracks," he said. "They hit out for the darndest places." He mounted his horse and started off, the horse kicking loose a rock that clattered down the side of the mountain. Nell thought again how steep the trail was, and she was glad they were riding it in sunlight. Well, mostly sunlight, she thought, glancing up at the sky. There were a few more clouds, but they were still a long way off.

Buddy pulled off into a small valley, and they looked for the cattle. There were signs of cows, but they must have wandered away, maybe gone into some gully, Buddy said. He glanced up at the sky. "We should have checked the meadow first. It's farther on. Most likely that's where they are. We wasted time here." They went back to the trail, and after a time, they came to a clearing where meadow grass was just greening. A stream ran through the open area, and on one side was a log cabin.

"Does somebody live here?" Nell asked.

"Not now. They did once. Maybe a trapper or a prospector, although there's no gold hereabout. It might even have been an outlaw. Whoever it was is long gone. Cowboys use it sometimes. See that wood by the door?" He pointed to a woodpile near the cabin. "Out here, you're welcome to stay at a place, but you got to replace what you take. Looks like somebody's been here, all right, but I couldn't say when."

"An outlaw?" Nell shivered, either from the idea that a bad man might have been in the meadow or from the cold that was blowing in.

"Most of them are gone. But it could have been a rustler. We get them on the range sometimes."

"Do you think Charlie was here?" She remembered that Charlie had threatened Buddy.

He shrugged. "Maybe. But he's gone. I don't see any sign of a horse." While he talked, Buddy searched the meadow, and he held up his hand and nodded with his chin. "Over there, in the trees."

"Charlie?" Nell wondered if Buddy had brought a gun.

Buddy laughed. "No, our cows."

Nell narrowed her eyes until she saw them, dark shapes among dark trees under a darkening sky. She felt foolish about Charlie.

"They're a wild bunch, and they won't want to come. We'll get behind them and holler so they'll head for the trail. You ride to that side, and I'll go to the other. When I yell, you wave your hat and yell, too. That'll get them going." Buddy was about to kick his horse into a run, but he paused. "You think you can do that? Those cows can stampede out of here if they get riled. If they scare you, I'll do this by myself, honey."

Nell smiled at the word "honey." "I came up here to help. I'll be all right," Nell said. She was less afraid of the cattle than she was of doing something wrong and letting the cows run farther into the mountains. She'd be mortified if she caused the cattle to scatter and make more work for Buddy. "Wait till I put on my coat. It's turned cold." She dismounted to untie her coat, and as she did, she felt something cold and wet on her hand—snow. She looked up into the sky, wondering how the clouds had covered it so fast. There hadn't been a single one when they left the ranch. Now they rolled across the sky with a fury, and the sky was turning black. Still, she wasn't worried. It was spring. There wouldn't be much snow, would there?

Buddy looked up, too. "I don't like the looks of this," he said.

"Oh, I bet it blows over," Nell told him.

Buddy studied the sky, then looked at the snow that had begun accumulating on the ground. "Maybe we ought to forget the cows and go on back."

"Oh, honey. It's only a little snow." She hoped Buddy was as pleased with the term of endearment as she had been.

He didn't seem to catch it, however. "It's a spring blizzard, Nell. We could get four, five feet before it stops. Maybe more. Anything happens to you, Lucy'll snatch me bald-headed. The boys, too. Let's go on back. We can get the cows another day."

"Why don't we round up the cattle first."

"Let's go. Get on your horse. We got to pound leather."

Buddy had been so gentle with her, so sweet, after they became engaged. But now he spoke in a voice that made it clear he was not to be crossed. She didn't like it, and she said, "I don't understand why we can't take the cattle." She took her time untying her coat.

"I don't want to ride that trail when I can't see it. We could go over the side. Let's quit here." Buddy sounded almost angry.

"All right." Nell's coat was wadded up, and she flapped it to straighten it out before she put it on. The movement startled Bean, and he shied. And then suddenly he took off, heading into the swirling snow, toward the cattle. "Bean!" Nell called, but the horse disappeared. She turned to Buddy, and suddenly she was scared. "What do we do now?" She added, "I'm sorry, Buddy."

"It's all right," he said, his voice soft again. "My horse could carry us both if it wasn't for the snow. It's not a good idea to ride double down that trail when we can't see where the edge is. Fact is, it's not a good idea to ride down that trail at all in this weather. I guess we'll find out what that cabin looks like inside." Buddy reached down and hauled Nell up behind him.

"What about Bean?" she asked over the sound of the wind, which was blowing hard now.

"There's no way to catch him, but he'll be all right. We'll find him when the storm's over. Or maybe he'll make his way back to the ranch. He's a smart horse."

Smarter than she was. Nell hoped Buddy didn't think she was too stupid to be a ranch wife.

The snow was all around them now, and Nell didn't know how Buddy could find the cabin. She thought it was the other way. She had lost her sense of direction. But then, she had never seen a storm come on that quickly. It hadn't been five minutes since the snow started, and now it was so thick that she couldn't see five feet in front of them. She held tight to Buddy's waist. At least she had faith that he knew where he was going.

And he did. In a few minutes, they were at the cabin. Buddy

tied his horse to a post near the door, then led Nell inside, walking about the cabin for a moment, his spurs trailing along the splintered board floor, as he checked for creatures that might have made their home there. He went back to unsaddle his horse and bring in his blanket and saddlebags. "Good thing we put the feed in mine," he said, setting down the bags and removing his sheepskin gloves. Nell, shivering, kept hers on. She took out the lunch she'd packed and set it on the table.

"We better wait," Buddy said. "We could be here a day or three."

"Three days!" Nell said.

Buddy shrugged. "Maybe." He looked around the cabin. "It's not so bad. Roof's tight. Somebody even set a fire."

"Maybe he's coming back."

"Not from the looks of it. This fire's been here awhile."

Nell swiped at the dust on a broken chair. Judging from the dust and the spiderwebs, Nell thought whoever had been there last had indeed left a long time before. The magazine pictures pinned to the walls were water-stained and tattered, and the tin cans strewn across the floor, cans that had once held sardines and potted meat, were rusted. She found a rag of a shirt and dusted off the table and chairs. Then she used a broken broom to destroy the spiderwebs and sweep up the rodent droppings and the chinking that had fallen out of the log walls. When she opened the door to sweep out the refuse, the wind grabbed the sweepings from her and scattered them back into the cabin.

"Stay inside," Buddy said as he stepped past her with a bucket in his hands. In a few minutes he was back, the bucket filled with snow. He set it beside the fireplace, then lit the fire, watching it carefully to make sure the smoke didn't back up. "This snow'll melt, and we'll have drinking water," he said, going back outside to bring in more wood. "I wish we had us some canned tomatoes. They're as good as water when you're thirsty, better sometimes."

Nell followed. She could carry the kindling, too. But Buddy told her to go back inside before she took a wrong step and disappeared in the whiteout. Nell thought she wouldn't do that, but after the mistakes she'd made that day, she didn't argue. She stared at Buddy's broad back as he went into the snow, thinking how glad she was he would take care of her, thinking how much she loved him.

After Buddy stacked the wood, he checked the fire again and said he thought the chimney was good. "A bird'll built its nest on a chimney top, and that'll cause the smoke to back up," he explained. "I'd sure hate to have to climb up there and to knock it off."

"Maybe I'd do it," Nell said, giving Buddy a sly look.

Buddy caught her meaning and laughed. "Maybe in all this snow, I couldn't see how high up I was."

The fire was warm now, and Nell moved away from it to a broken stool. Buddy unrolled his bedroll and made a cushion for her, and she sat down.

"My blanket!" she said suddenly. "My blanket was on Bean. What am I going to do?"

"I reckon you can use mine."

"That wouldn't be fair. It's my fault. I spooked Bean."

"Maybe he'll come back."

Maybe, Nell thought, but it wasn't likely. She sat staring into the fire for a long time, not knowing how late it was, although she thought it might be close to evening. When Buddy went outside to fill the water bucket with more snow, she saw blackness through the doorway, but that could have been the storm.

"Are you hungry?" Buddy asked. He went to the table, where he had placed the sack of food. Nell had packed cookies and apples, along with half a dozen sandwiches, one of which he removed and broke in two, handing half to her. "We better go easy on eating since we don't know how long we'll be here," he said. He returned the food to his saddlebags so the mice wouldn't get it.

They ate their sandwiches slowly, making them last, and drank water from a tin cup Buddy found on a shelf.

"If I'd brought a guitar, I could have played it for you—that is, if I knew how to play a guitar," Buddy said with a laugh.

"Can you sing?"

"Every cowboy can sing. We sing to the cattle. It's just that most of the boys can't hold a tune."

"Can you?"

Instead of answering, Buddy began to sing "The Cowboy's Lament." His voice was soft, but it was clear, and he hit the right notes. After the first verse, Nell joined in. She had a strong voice.

"Where'd you learn that song, Miss Nell?"

"Oh, I heard some cowboy singing it in the bunkhouse."

"Probably Wendell."

"More likely you."

"Do you know this one?" He began "There'll Be a Hot Time in the Old Town Tonight," then sang it alone, because Nell had not heard it before.

When Buddy was finished, he unfolded his blanket and spread it before the fire, and the two sat down on it. "How about 'Lorena'?" she asked. "Everybody knows that one." And the two began singing it together, Nell doing the harmony. For a long time they sang hymns and popular songs.

"This is what it'll be like when we're married," Buddy said, and he put his arms around Nell.

She snuggled up beside him. "Only we'll have a cookstove. And a bed." She yawned, and Buddy said he reckoned it was time to sleep.

Where? Nell wondered. She had put the idea of bedding down with him in the cabin out of her mind, but now she wondered just what their arrangement would be. They'd have to share the room, of course. Buddy had kissed her—kissed her often and held her close—but he'd never done anything more than that. Nothing would happen until they were married. They hadn't talked about that, but it was understood—at least on her part. She supposed Buddy could hang his blanket across the room for privacy, but it was cold, and there was only one blanket. So that wouldn't make sense.

"I guess you'll be wanting the blanket over you," he said.

"It's not my blanket," she told him.

"Well, I'm not going to let you freeze. You put your coat under you, and cover up with the blanket."

"What will you do?"

"I guess I've slept in my coat before."

Nell knew she should protest, but she was cold. The fire was still blazing, but wind blew through the cabin where the chinking had fallen out, and snow had sifted through the cracks. "Maybe we should share the blanket," she said at last.

"It makes sense," he said. "I reckon if it was Wendell, I'd share it with him." He chuckled. "I'm sure glad it's not Wendell." He spread their coats on the floor, and they lay down, their backs against each other, the blanket over them. Buddy had built up the fire, but even so, Nell was cold, and she couldn't sleep. She lay there a long time, her teeth chattering, moving around to get warm. And then she felt Buddy turn and put his arms around her, holding her tight. She relaxed a little, warming her body against his, and in a little while, he turned her toward him so that she nestled in his arms. Her face was against his, and she felt his lips on her forehead and then on her eyes and finally on her mouth.

His arms moved over her, touching her. She should push him away, Nell thought. They weren't married yet. They should wait. But she didn't want him to stop. She wasn't cold any longer, and she wanted him, wanted him in a way she knew wasn't right, but she didn't care. She helped him remove her clothes, and then he stripped off his, and he held her close, murmuring so softly that she didn't understand the words. She felt his body harden, and he grasped her so tightly she couldn't move.

When they were finished, they lay in each other's arms, their bodies pressed against each other. And Nell thought she had never in her life felt so warm.

Nell awoke when the door opened and fresh air rushed into the room. There were no windows in the cabin, so she didn't know whether the blizzard was over. But when she looked out the door, she saw the sun glinting off snow.

"Storm's done with, and guess who's back?" Buddy said from the doorway. He held a blanket in his hands.

"Bean!"

"He was standing just outside when I went out." He paused and gave her a sly look. "I'm kind of glad he didn't come back last night."

Nell blushed as she went to the door, thinking of what had happened in the night. She felt shy and a little embarrassed.

Everything seemed different in the bright sunlight. She wondered if Buddy would talk about the night. "Are the cattle still there?" she asked, when Buddy didn't say anything.

"Right there in the trees."

"Are we going to herd them back to the ranch?"

"I reckon that's why we came."

"We ought to go. Lucy will be worried."

Buddy nodded, but he led Nell back into the room. The fire was blazing, and she thought he had built it up before she awoke. "I guess we've got some things to say."

Nell looked away. She wondered if they had done a terrible thing and Buddy was disappointed in her. He might think Charlie was right, that she was indeed a chippie, a loose woman. He might even say he didn't want to marry someone who was so easy, someone he didn't respect anymore.

Buddy put his arms around her, then tipped up her face so that he was looking into her eyes. "Maybe we ought to move up our wedding day. What say we get married in the fall instead of next winter?"

Nell grinned at him. "I'd like that just fine."

CHAPTER NINE

Lucy came into Nell's room one afternoon not long after Nell returned from the mountains and confided she and Buddy were going to marry. She had hoped to keep the engagement secret for a time. But Lucy informed Mr. Archer, who forgot it was a secret and congratulated Buddy at supper that night, and the word was out. The cowboys were happy, because Buddy was a favorite among them, and they liked Nell. No one was surprised, though; Nell wouldn't be the first hired girl to marry a Rockin' A hand.

No one but Alice and Owen, it seemed. "I hope you're happy you broke my brother's heart, Miss Hired Girl. You should be ashamed of yourself, leading Owen on like that," Alice told Nell when they ran into each other in Las Vegas. Then she added, "You certainly set your cap for my boyfriend. Well, he isn't married yet. I didn't come home all the way from New York to see him hitch himself to some cook's helper. There's still time for him to come to his senses."

Nell was too shocked to think of a response. Not until she was on her way home did it occur to her that she should have said that Buddy had indeed come to his senses. That was why he had proposed to her instead of Alice.

Now Lucy sat down on the edge of Nell's bed and handed her a flour sack. Nell reached inside and removed a length of fabric. "My aunt Mary, your grandmother's sister, cut out this dress long ago," Lucy explained. "She was going to wear it at her wedding, but her fiancé was killed in the War Between the States. Aunt Mary never married, and she never finished the dress. The style is old-fashioned, but I believe we could remake it as a wedding dress for you." Lucy spread out pieces of fragile white silk on the bed, some of them overlaid with lace. "The lace is hand-made. It might have been old even back then."

Nell ran her fingers over the thin silk.

"Aunt Mary probably intended to wear it with a hoop skirt. Look at how much material there is. But the bodice is a nice cut, and I believe it would fit you. Aunt Mary was tall like you." Lucy smoothed the top of the dress, its seams held together by pins that were rusty with age.

"It's beautiful," Nell said. "I would love to wear it."

Lucy smiled. "I thought *I* might wear it myself one day, but I won't." She paused. "Some might think it bad luck wearing a wedding dress made for a woman whose intended died, but I don't hold with that."

"Me either," Nell said. "In fact, I think it might honor Aunt Mary to wear her gown. I remember her. There was always something sad about her."

"And sour, after she got older. She told me once that without a husband, she felt incomplete. She thought of herself as a failure."

Nell stared at her aunt. "And you? Do you feel that way,

Aunt Lucy?" Nell turned away, embarrassed at her impertinence. "I'm sorry. I shouldn't have said—"

"Sad? Sour? Not at all," Lucy interrupted. "I have the benefits of marriage without the fuss." She gave Nell a look of defiance. "Marriage is fine for most women, but some of us can get along without it." Then she added, "I'm not sure you're one of 'us.'"

After Lucy left, Nell picked up each piece of the dress and studied it. She would change the sleeves a little and rework the skirt, making it less full. She reached into the bottom of the sack and pulled out a crumpled piece of lace. It was indeed very fine, and Nell thought she could wear it instead of a hat. She hadn't even thought about a wedding dress—instead, she had begun making a wedding quilt for Buddy—and here was one already cut out for her. Of course, the dress would take work, but there was plenty of time. She and Buddy wouldn't be married for months. Her grandparents would come to the wedding. Nell was sure of that. They and Lucy were the only family she had, and it meant everything to her that they would all be together. They would invite the Rockin' A cowboys and ranch families who had been nice to her, along with people in town. They would invite the Mackintoshes, too, even Alice. Especially Alice, Nell thought.

She wanted the wedding to be held at the ranch. They'd stand with the minister on the portico, decorated with golden aspen, and Nell would carry a bouquet of chamisa and purple asters and daisies. She'd wear her great-aunt's gown with the piece of old lace on her head. Lucy would stand up with her, and Mr. Archer or maybe Wendell would be the best man.

* * *

Nell was aware that war was coming. They all were. Everyone on the Rockin' A knew that the USS *Maine* had been blown up in the harbor in Cuba and that the newspapers blamed the Spanish. Everyone was calling for the government to drive them out of Cuba. But Cuba was so far away that the cowboys hadn't paid all that much attention to the war talk, and Nell had been too engrossed in Buddy and the ranch to give it a thought.

Then at supper one night, Mr. Archer announced he'd heard the army was recruiting cowboys from New Mexico Territory to join the 1st U.S. Volunteer Cavalry, which would invade Cuba.

"Cowboys?" Wendell asked. "How come cowboys?"

"I guess they don't want no eastern dudes that never slept anyplace but a feather bed. Cowboys can ride and shoot and roll up at night on the ground. If you had to choose between a cowpuncher and a greener, who'd you pick?" Mr. Archer replied.

"You're right about that," Wendell said.

"Now, I'd hate to see any of you boys go, but I got to do my patriotic duty and tell you if you want to join up, I'll hold your jobs open till you come back." He added, "I hear Willy Burden's already volunteered."

"Willy? He just got married," one of the hands said, which caused snickers around the table.

"I wonder if he don't like married life," Monty said.

"He's a red-blooded American with a wife to come home to," Buddy told him.

"Then maybe you ought to get hitched to Nell right now, if you're thinking of joining up," Wendell replied.

"Maybe I will."

Nell glanced at Buddy, but he wouldn't look at her. He'd never told her he was thinking of joining the army. They'd never talked about it. They hadn't even talked about the USS *Maine* being blown up or the possibility that America would go to war. She couldn't stand it if he left. He might get killed. She wouldn't let him go. Nell thought of the aunt whose wedding dress she would wear and how *her* fiancé had been killed in a war, and she wondered if the gown was some kind of omen. She would never let that happen to Buddy. Ever. When he asked her about joining the army, she would tell him no.

Buddy left the table as soon as supper was over. He had work to do in the barn. And in the morning he left just after he bolted breakfast. Mr. Archer was sending him into Las Vegas to pick up supplies. Nell had hoped to be invited to go with him, but neither Buddy nor Mr. Archer suggested she accompany him, and Nell, afraid she would be turned down, didn't request the time off.

Buddy returned late in the afternoon, and at supper, he announced that Owen Mackintosh was joining the army. People were calling the unit Roosevelt's Rough Riders. "It will be the most exciting adventure since the War Between the States," he said.

"Are you joining up, then?" one of the cowhands asked Buddy.

He glanced at Nell. "I just might."

Without talking to me? Nell wanted to ask, but with others at the table, she couldn't protest. "Well, let me know," she said, sure that everyone heard the displeasure in her voice.

She thought Buddy would seek her out after dinner, but he went off with Wendell to doctor a horse, and it was the next day before they talked. Nell was on the porch churning butter.

"They don't let just anybody join the Rough Riders, but Mr. Archer knows a man. He's sure I can get in. If they'll take Owen Mackintosh, they'll surely want me."

"How did you know about Owen?"

"Alice told me."

"Oh, you've seen Alice?" Nell tried to keep the anger out of her voice.

"Well, sure. I stopped at the Mackintosh house to say hello. You aren't jealous, are you?"

"No more than you are of Owen." Nell gave the churn a vicious whack, knowing she was indeed jealous. She didn't trust Alice, and she wondered now if she trusted Buddy. She and Buddy weren't married yet. He could still change his mind.

Buddy frowned. "You've seen Owen? Maybe you already knew about him going for a soldier."

"And Alice, did you tell her you were thinking of joining the army before you told me?"

Buddy didn't answer. Instead, he said, "Come on, Nell. I thought you'd be right proud if I joined up. It's a chance to do a little pirooting before I settle down."

"And me, do I get to do a little pirooting, too?"

Buddy looked startled. "You're a woman."

"I'd think you would have talked to me before you made a decision."

"You mean I got to ask your permission?" He reached for the churn, but Nell held on to it.

"You don't have to ask me for anything. You just suit yourself." The churning was done, and Nell poured the buttermilk into a pitcher so fast that it slopped over the side. Then she took the butter to the sink, where she washed and salted it. She wouldn't let Buddy help her.

"Give here," He yanked the butter from her and put it into the icebox. "You're one stubborn woman."

Nell glared at him.

"I take it we don't think alike on several points, but it sounds like you're telling me what to do. I wouldn't abide a wife who did that."

"But you tell me what to do." She removed the butter and put it into a wooden mold.

"I disremember telling you anything. Besides, so what if I did? A husband's got the right."

"Not my husband," Nell said.

"Well, good luck to him, then." Buddy stomped out of the kitchen, letting the screen slam, and Nell, angry herself, took off her apron, balled it up, and threw it at the door.

For a day or two, Buddy sulked. He didn't come around except for meals. Then he showed up one afternoon with a bouquet of roses he'd picked from Lucy's garden. Lucy would be furious, but Nell was pleased at the gesture. It was Buddy's way of apologizing, she thought. She held the flowers to her nose for a moment to take in their sweet smell, smiling a little as she remembered the bouquet of brown-eyed Susans with the bee inside. She put the flowers into a Mason jar of water and set it on the kitchen table.

"I hope you aren't still off your feed. I gave you time to cool down," Buddy said. He didn't apologize. Instead, he told her, "I got it all figured out. That ranch I told you I was buying, I signed the papers yesterday. The bank hurried it through when I telegraphed I was going off to be a Rough Rider. You can quit the Rockin' A and go on up there and get things ready. This war isn't going to last but a minute, and I'll be home before you know it. I won't buy the cattle till I'm back, so you don't have to worry about them. Or hiring hands." Buddy beamed at her. "I even arranged for us to get married on Friday. The judge is coming out here, and Mr. Archer said he'll give you away. It's all took care of."

Nell was stunned. She pushed aside the tin cans of geraniums and sat down on the window ledge, clasping her hands together because they were shaking. "You did this without asking me?"

"There's not a thing for you to worry about. I took care of everything."

Nell tried to think of some way to tell Buddy she wasn't pleased, but suddenly she was angry, very angry. How dare he order her life without even consulting her! And getting married that week, without her grandparents present? She'd never agree to that. "Didn't you remember I said you ought to consult me before you made those decisions? Didn't you?" She clenched her fists.

"You don't have anything to do with it. It's my ranch, and it's my decision to join up."

"And your decision to get married—to get married on Friday."

"You rather wait to Saturday?" He smiled at his joke.

Nell didn't. "I thought we were getting married in the fall."

"I changed my mind."

"Well, I did not."

"I'm going off to war, and I want a wife to come home to. I'm not going less'n I'm married. So you'll just have to go along with it."

"Then I guess you'll stay home." Nell glanced out the window and saw Lucy standing there with Mr. Archer. She wondered how much of the conversation they had heard, but she didn't care.

Buddy kicked at the table leg, nicking the wood with his spur and jarring the table, knocking over the roses. The water ran across the wood, but he only glanced at it and didn't soak it up. Neither did Nell.

Suddenly Buddy lowered his voice. "I said I'm getting married before I join up. If I go under, I want there to be somebody who'll remember me. If you don't want to marry me, then I know a girl who will."

Nell looked at him in astonishment. Did he mean it?

"Alice?" She threw the word at him.

"She's not so balky. She'd marry me in a minute. Just you wait and see."

"Then you'd better go find her. I wouldn't marry somebody as high-headed as you."

"You going to marry that Lane Philips fellow back in Kansas, then?"

How did Buddy know about him? Then Nell remembered she had mentioned him once—*once*! "Just maybe I will."

Buddy kicked at a chair with the toe of his boot, then stopped and stared at Nell. "I guess it's a good thing I found out how pig-headed you are. You go marry that Lane Philips or Owen or somebody else cultus. They'll be glad to let you be in charge. I just guess I can marry Alice if I want to. It's easy done, and it's for sure I won't marry you."

"And I wouldn't marry you."

Buddy stomped out of the kitchen, stopping to use his arm to brush the roses and the jar from the table.

Nell watched through the doorway as he mounted his horse and rode off in the direction of Las Vegas. Then she used a cloth to wipe the water from the table and knelt and picked up the roses and broken glass from the floor. After she'd thrown them into the trash, she went into her room and closed the door. She took out the flour sack and began shoving her clothes into it.

In a moment, Lucy came in. She didn't knock but shoved open the door and stood by the bed, watching Nell. "I know it ain't my business, but I got to ask. What do you think you're doing?"

"He got hot at me, and I'm leaving. Now." Nell shoved a skirt into the bulging flour sack, then reached for another.

"He's just on the prod. He'll calm down."

"No he won't. He's stubborn. He means what he says. I wouldn't be surprised if he's already halfway to town to propose to Alice Mackintosh. I mean what I say, too. I see him now with a clear eye, Aunt Lucy. It's over." She glared at her aunt, too angry to cry.

"Now, Nell. You'll work it out. That's the way marriage is."

"Not marriage with Buddy. He thinks he'll be in charge and I'm to do what he says."

"Well, men are that way. That's one reason I chose not to marry again."

"We said too much that we can't ever take back, Aunt Lucy. It's the meanest luck, but it's done with." Nell looked around for anything she might have forgotten. She picked up her Bible from the bedside table and shoved it in with her clothes. "You heard what he said. He's going off to marry Alice."

Lucy sat down on the bed and smoothed a shirt that had fallen out of one of the flour sacks, then folded it and put it back. "If you don't stop him, I expect he'll do just that."

"I don't care. I have too much pride to go after him." Nell stood and made a final sweep of the room. "Aunt Lucy, will you ask Wendell to take me to the depot?"

Lucy sighed. "Ask him yourself. I'm not aiding and abetting." She left the room, and Nell heard the screen door squeak.

A moment later, Nell hurried to the barn and found Wendell and said she had to go to town right away. While she waited for

Wendell to hitch up the carriage, she went back inside and wrote a note to Mr. Archer, but she did not write one to Buddy. He'd know why she was leaving. Then she slung the flour sacks over her shoulder and waited on the porch until Wendell drove up in the buggy, and she climbed in. No one waved to her, and no one said good-bye. Nell looked straight ahead as she left the ranch. She didn't see the cattle that had stopped grazing to stare at her as she passed or the flapping windmill that she had fixed with Buddy. She didn't look up as she rode by the broken wagon. And she didn't see Buddy, who was stopped just off the road, watching her ride away.

CHAPTER TEN

When Ellen was finished telling the story of Nell and Buddy, June leaned forward in her chair and asked, "She left just like that?"

"Stupid, wasn't it? She should have stayed and worked it out. But she was too stubborn."

"Did Buddy go after her?

"No, and that made her mad, too. She realized later that he didn't know where she was, because she'd asked her aunt not to tell him."

Nell had returned to her grandparents' farm in Kansas, Ellen explained. The farm was home. She might have gone to a city, but she needed to be where she felt loved. And safe. Besides, Nell wasn't so adventuresome anymore. She wanted to sleep in her own bed and wake up to the sounds of cows and chickens. She'd always loved chickens. Ellen paused and looked out at one of her own chickens that was pecking at the dirt. They wouldn't have chickens if she and Ben moved into Durango. They'd have to eat store-bought eggs from the Piggly Wiggly and chickens that had been killed and plucked in a factory. They'd taste like cardboard. Damn grocery stores, she thought.

Ellen moved her chair to get out of the sun. It was midday now, and the sky was cloudless, the sun very hot. An apartment wouldn't have a porch either. Where would she go to cool off from the summer heat? She'd probably have to depend on that wretched air-conditioning people were starting to put in. You couldn't even open the windows in some of those places. The veranda was one of the first things she and Ben had added to their honeymoon cabin. Except in the winter, they sat there almost every evening, looking out at the stars. Ben would talk about cattle prices, ask her opinion on improvements, because their marriage had always been a partnership. Sometimes they didn't agree, and they'd argue, argue loud enough that Maria would come outside and shush them. But sooner or later, one of them would give in, and there would be peace. Ellen almost missed those fights, the times she'd win Ben over to her way of thinking or Ben would convince her he was right. They would make up and know that they really did beat with one heart.

When the children were young, they played on the porch, galloping back and forth on stick horses, and when they were older, they honed their roping skills on chairs and tables. The veranda was their rumpus room. The children did their homework there, too. Ellen remembered how John had filled out his college application forms at a table on the porch. She had been sitting there when he came in from the mailbox one afternoon with a letter saying he'd been accepted at Harvard.

Although the nights were cold now, Ellen and Ben still sat on the veranda after dinner, watching the sunset streak the sky with violent swaths of purple and orange and pink. Ben would remember times long past, and they'd call each other by pet names they hadn't used in years. Sometimes they didn't need to talk. They just sat and held hands.

"Buddy and Nell might have worked things out, I suppose, but they were both too stubborn," Ellen continued, setting her sewing on the table. She had stitched while she told the story—intricate embroidery stitches that covered the seams between the patches of fabric.

"Like you?" June asked.

"Oh, no, she was much worse." Ellen smiled, as she ran her hand over a patch from a silk gown, a wedding dress that had been in the family. Maybe she shouldn't have cut it up, but some of the silk was split. The top was shredded, and only part of the skirt was any good. What was the point of keeping it?

A second chicken came along, and the women watched as the two chickens fought over a worm. They squawked. The first chicken triumphed, and the other walked away.

There was an afternoon train out of Las Vegas, and Nell barely made it, Ellen said, going back to her story. "You have to wonder what would have happened if she'd missed it. She might have changed her mind. Or Buddy might have come after her. Of course, neither of those things happened."

"Did she believe they'd make up somehow and she'd marry him after all?"

"No," Ellen said, shaking her head. "After Nell was home, she realized it was over. There had been too many hurtful words. Once she was back in Kansas, Nell knew she'd never marry Buddy after what they'd said to each other. She wouldn't be happy with someone who felt he had the right to tell her what to do," Ellen said.

"Like me?" June asked.

Ellen thought a moment. "That's for you and Dave to decide."

Nell had other complications, she explained. She'd pretty much convinced herself that Buddy didn't really love her, and that maybe, after what had happened in that cabin, he no longer respected her. She knew that ranching is lonely work, and that Buddy wanted a wife. Maybe Buddy chose her because she was strong and worked hard. Nell was aware there were other girls if she turned him down. "There are men who think one woman is pretty much like another. And then, of course, Alice was waiting in the wings," Ellen said, staring into the distance. "Nell convinced herself of a lot of things."

"What became of Buddy?" June asked. "Did he survive the war?"

"Yes," Ellen replied. "The Spanish-American War lasted only a few weeks, and there weren't all that many men in the fighting. Or that many casualties. In fact, some soldiers never even made it to Cuba before the war ended. All war is awful," she said, "but Buddy's war was short, so it wasn't as bad as the two world wars with all their carnage. Or Korea." Ellen glanced at her granddaughter when she mentioned Korea, but June didn't react. "You know, of course, that Theodore Roosevelt, who was second in command of the Rough Riders, became president."

"Maybe Buddy went to Washington with him. Was his picture ever in the paper?"

Ellen shook her head. "Not that I know of."

"Maybe he came looking for her after the war."

He hadn't, because he didn't know where she'd gone, Ellen said. Lucy might have told him, but she died not long after Nell left, kicked in the head by a horse. Nell might have gone back for the funeral, but it was a long time before she learned what had happened to her aunt, and by then, it was too late.

"Lucy never married Mr. Archer?"

"No. It's funny. *He* might have married *her*, but she held out. Maybe Lucy giving Nell the dress she'd once intended for her own wedding was like admitting that she'd never marry again. Lucy was awfully independent."

"Like Nell?"

"Do you think Nell was really independent? Oh, she moved out west to live on a ranch in New Mexico, but she was after a husband. That was the main reason she went there. And that was why she moved on later." Ellen twisted her embroidery thread to make a French knot.

"What happened to Buddy?"

"He married, all right."

Just then, the screen banged, and Maria came out and asked if they wanted their dinner on the porch.

Ellen pushed aside the quilt and stood, saying that would be nice. It wouldn't be long before it would be too cold to eat outside. "June and I can fetch it."

"I'll do it. You're supposed to take it easy. June, you make sure your grandma don't work too hard. The doctor says for her to rest."

"Oh, hell, I'm not an invalid," Ellen said. "Sometimes you treat Mr. Ben and me like we've got one foot in the grave."

"Well . . ." Maria crossed herself.

Ellen waved her hand. "Don't rub it in. We still have one foot *out* of the grave. If I'm going to die, I don't want to do it while I'm sitting in a chair."

Maria threw up her hands and went back inside. June asked her grandmother, "Is your heart that bad?"

"No, of course not. I just have to take my pills and be careful climbing stairs. The doctor won't let me on a horse anymore."

"So you don't ride?"

Ellen didn't answer.

"Granny?"

"Your grandfather doesn't understand when I tell him I'm supposed to stay off horses." Just the day before, Ben had saddled Ellen's mare and shown up at the kitchen door with the horse. When Ellen told him she wasn't supposed to ride, he looked as hurt as if she'd slapped him in the face. He said he wanted to ride out to the creek, and there wasn't anybody else to go with him. Lord, June had thought, she couldn't let him go alone. He'd have ridden into the next county, and she never would have found him.

"So you went with him?"

Ellen shrugged. "Somebody has to look after him." They'd had a nice time, too. Ellen had asked Maria to fix a picnic, and they'd spread an old quilt on the ground under a cottonwood and eaten the lunch. Then Ben had napped on the quilt, his hat over his face, while Ellen took off her boots and put her toes into the cold water. It was as nice an outing as they'd had in a long time. When Ben woke up, he thought for a moment it was fifty years earlier, not long after they moved to the ranch. They had made love in that very spot. He seemed to remember and reached for her hand, and they had sat holding hands until suppertime. Maria feared that Ellen had been bucked off her horse and Ben had wandered away to get help. She was ready to send Wesley to search for them when they finally showed up.

"Can't Maria take over some of your work?" June asked.

"She already has, but there's just so much she can do. She can barely read and write." There was no way the housekeeper could keep books and fill out government forms. After all the years she'd lived with them, Maria didn't know a thing about beef except how to cook it.

"What about Wesley?" June asked.

Ellen smiled. "He's as loyal and honest and hardworking as the day is long, and there's nothing he wouldn't do for us, but would you trust him to run a ranch?"

"At least he can read and write."

"Can he?"

"I see your point."

June held the door, and the two of them followed Maria into the big kitchen. It was Ellen's favorite room in the sprawling ranch house. The man from Sears, Roebuck who designed kitchens had drawn up a plan with metal cupboards and a linoleum floor. It looked like something from a women's magazine, not like a real ranch kitchen. Ellen had thrown away the drawing and hired a carpenter to make big wooden cupboards. She'd put in a countertop of bright Mexican tiles, some of them broken now, and a wood floor that had been worn down over the years by hundreds, maybe thousands of boots. There was a pantry with bins that held hundred-pound sacks of flour and sugar, a freezer big enough to accommodate an entire beef or maybe two, a stove with six burners—and a dishwasher. The heart of the kitchen was the scrub-top wooden table that could seat a dozen, and during roundup, there were often that many men gathered around it. Ellen had found the table at a ranch sale. Then she'd picked up old pressed-wood chairs that nobody wanted anymore. They were sturdy enough that a man could lean back in one until it rested on two legs and not fall over.

Maria went to the stove and stirred a big pot of chili with a long wooden spoon. She tasted it and nodded her satisfaction. "It's not too hot for you," she said.

"I'm not an invalid, Maria," Ellen told her. "I don't want chili that tastes like junket. You can't make a chili that's too hot for me."

Maria waved away the insult as she dished up bowls of meat and beans and sprinkled cheese on top. She wrapped hot tortillas in a towel, then set everything on a tray.

"Will Grandpa Ben be back in time to eat with us?" June asked.

"He won't be back till late afternoon. I imagine he'll have his dinner in Durango. He should be home by suppertime." Ellen hoped so, at any rate. Ben was liable to start jawing with the vet about horses and bulls that were long dead and lose track of the time. He could be stubborn when Wesley insisted he get back into the truck. "Who works for who?" he'd asked more than once. That was why Ellen generally took her husband into town on errands. She could argue him down.

"Well, good, because that gives you time to tell me about the two other weddings your friend ran away from."

Ellen started to pick up the tray, but Maria elbowed her aside and said, "My job. Too heavy for you, old woman."

"I'm no older than you," Ellen replied, although Maria was twenty-five years younger. Still, she let Maria carry the tray. The doctor had told her not to lift heavy things. She smiled at the housekeeper, who had been with her for more than twenty years.

Ben had found Maria hiding in the barn with a young boy. They were illegals and scared to death, he'd told Ellen. "She asked could they sleep in the hay, but it isn't right when we have a place inside where she can sleep."

No, Ellen agreed that it wouldn't be right. She remembered a neighbor who had found Mexicans hiding in one of his sheds and had driven them out with a pitchfork.

"I told her they could stay the night in the foreman's cabin, since it's empty."

"The night?" Ellen asked.

"Maybe a little longer."

Ellen was sure it would be a lot longer. Ben was softhearted. He'd never been able to shoot a horse with a broken leg, and one of the hands had had to do it for him. He was always bringing home stray puppies and kittens. Maria and her son were more than homeless animals. So Ellen and Ben made the two feel at home, and before long, Ellen knew they would be a part of the ranch as long as they wanted to. Two years ago, the boy had been drafted into the army, but he'd promised to come back when he was mustered out and work as a cowhand. At least he would if Ben and Ellen still owned the ranch. Ellen wondered what Maria would do if they sold the place. They wouldn't have room for a cook and housekeeper in an apartment. And what about Wesley and Durrell, the other cowboy, who'd been with them for decades? They were getting along in years, too, and with mechanization, there wasn't so much employment for ranch hands, not the way it used to be when cowboys drifted from ranch to ranch, always looking for better jobs. Where would Wesley and Durrell go?

June and her grandmother followed the cook outside. As Maria set the food on the table, June snatched away the quilt. "Just what we need, spilling chili on this." She brushed yellow cottonwood leaves off a chair and set Ellen's stitching on it.

"I wonder if Nell ever forgot Buddy," June said after Maria went inside.

Ellen shook her head. "I wouldn't think so. You never forget first love." She glanced at her granddaughter, who was looking off toward the barn, thinking.

"Maybe I've done a stupid thing," June mused. "I should have stayed and talked to Dave after we both calmed down. Running off like that was foolish, wasn't it? It seems like I was just as impulsive as your friend Nell. But Dave is always so sure of himself. He'd have tried to convince me I was wrong. I didn't want him making the decision for me, Granny. I couldn't go through with it. I just couldn't. Do you think I was wrong?"

"There's not a right or wrong to it."

"If I don't marry him, do you think I'll regret it later?"

"Sometimes. If you marry him, you'll always wonder what would have happened if you hadn't. And if you don't marry him, you'll still have what-ifs . . . Nell had a lot of what-ifs . . . Three of them. Remember, she ran away three times. The second man was James."

"And he tried to tell her what to do, too?"

"Not exactly. She left him for an entirely different reason. And it didn't have a thing to do with stubbornness."

"What happened with him?"

Ellen sat back on the bench and pushed away her bowl. Then she picked up a fork and took a bite of the Mexican chocolate cake that Maria had made. The icing was as thick as the cake. The doctor had told Ellen to watch her diet, but she didn't. Why deprive herself if she was going to die anyway? she'd asked him. He hadn't had an answer. "James Hamilton was the second man Nell was engaged to, and oh my, was he a looker."

"Was he like Buddy?"

"Not in the least. In fact, he looked just like that young actor we saw in the movie in Durango when you and Dave were here last summer, Van Johnson. He was blond and freckle-faced. He was the picture of the all-American boy. You could have put his face on a *Saturday Evening Post* cover." Ellen used the tines of her fork to catch the cake crumbs on her plate, thinking she'd like a second piece. "Maybe Nell was attracted to him because he didn't seem at all like Buddy. And he seemed like prime marriage material. Don't forget, she was still looking for a husband. She was a lot more serious about it this time."

CHAPTER ELEVEN

Nell cried all the way home on the train. She cried for weeks, months really. Her heart was broken. It was almost as if she were a Spanish-American War widow instead of a girl who had run away on the eve of her wedding. She grieved for Buddy, and at night, when she couldn't sleep, she sat by the window in the moonlight, the pieces of her wedding dress in her hands, weeping. The dress had been in one of the flour sacks she'd used to pack her clothes, and she had taken it with her when she fled. Some nights, she didn't sleep at all but lay in bed, shivering under the red-and-gray Indian rug. She didn't know why she had snatched it up when she left, but she was glad. It was the only thing that kept her warm. She tried to find solace in her Bible, but when she opened it, she discovered the chamisa flower Buddy had picked for her on the way to the Mackintosh house, and she cried again.

There were times when Nell was tempted to write to Buddy in care of the Rockin' A. But she knew that their marriage would have been a disaster. They were both too strong-willed to make it work. They had said too many cruel things to each other. Besides, he had married Alice and moved away to his ranch. Nell didn't even know where it was.

She missed New Mexico, the dry air of the High Plains, the long vistas, the clang of the dinner bell sounding across the prairie. And the people. She felt guilty about leaving so abruptly and wondered what the cowboys thought of her. They had been nice to her; Lucy and Mr. Archer had been grand. She had let them all down, hadn't even said good-bye. So she couldn't go back even if she'd wanted to. She didn't want to, however. Her New Mexico days were over.

The farm in Harveyville was comforting. Nell loved working in her grandmother's kitchen garden, picking beans and eating tomatoes still warm from the sun. The two of them worked together, putting up the blackberries that grew beside the barn, the brambles home to chiggers that caused them to scratch their arms and legs for days. They made apple jelly, putting the mash into a sugar sack and letting it run through into a kettle. In the afternoons, they snapped wax beans in an old yellow earthenware dish and wilted lettuce by salting it and dousing it with vinegar and bacon grease in the blue feather-edge bowl.

Nell took over the hen house, feeding the chickens and collecting eggs. She was fascinated with the chickens, their beady little eyes and their iridescent feathers. She loved the way the hens cocked their heads when they looked up at her, and she found their clucking soothing. Each hen had her own personality. Nell called them "the girls," and it saddened her when she had to stretch the neck of one on the chopping block. Each time she did that she remembered the old rooster at the Rockin' A, and she grieved over Buddy.

She quilted with her grandmother, the two of them sitting side by side in the shade of the trumpet vine on the porch, cutting out squares and rectangles and piecing them together. Nell even quilted with her grandmother's stitching group. They called themselves the Pickles, after a paisley fabric one of the members had acquired. Often, before the hot of a summer day came on, she walked barefooted down the country road to town for a spool of thread or a quarter of a yard of new fabric, pinching the stuff between her fingers to make sure the quality was good, wondering what had happened to the quilt top she had started for Buddy as a wedding gift. She had left it behind.

On winter mornings, when the frost etched patterns on the windowpanes and snow sifted through cracks in the walls onto the quilts on her bed, she crept into the kitchen, where her grandmother already had a fire going in the cookstove. She poured herself coffee, hopping from one foot to the other on the cold linoleum because she had forgotten her slippers.

One afternoon, she took out a handkerchief, and a dozen aspen leaves the color of gold coins spilled onto her dresser. They'd come from a branch of aspen that Buddy had given her. The leaves had dried and fallen, and Nell had scooped them up and saved them. Now she gathered the leaves, brittle as old paper, and held them in her hands remembering. She went to the window and crushed the leaves, then tossed them into the wind, watching as they were swept away. One leaf had escaped and fallen onto the floor. Nell picked it up and studied it for a moment, tracing the veins of the heart-shaped leaf with a fingertip. Then she laid the leaf in the palm of her hand and held her hand out of the window. The leaf swirled away in the wind, and Nell watched it until it was gone. She knew then, it was time to end the mourning, to stop feeling sorry for herself. She could not hide out on the farm forever. She had to take control of her life. The year after she had fled New Mexico, Nell knew it was time to move on.

Leaving Kansas wasn't as easy this time. There were encumbrances. It wouldn't be as simple to go away as it had been when she left for New Mexico Territory. Still, her grandparents agreed she should leave. "You need to be out on your own again. You're young yet, Nell, too young to be cooped up here with no chance to meet young men. And you need to find a husband," her grandmother said. "Leave everything here and go out in the world for six months, maybe a year. Find someone you can spend your life with. You don't want to end up by yourself like Lucy, bless her soul."

"Go to a big city this time," her grandfather advised. "Find yourself a go-getter, a young fellow who's coming up in the world."

Topeka was too close. So was Kansas City. So she boarded the train to Denver. It was spring, too early to find a teaching job. Besides, Nell wasn't sure she wanted to teach again. The pay was poor, and there were too many restrictions on a female teacher. She had to be docile and respectful and live a public life, and what if someone delved into her secrets? Nell didn't want to get turned down because somebody found out about New Mexico and decided she'd led an immoral life. Living on a ranch had made her too headstrong for all that.

Since she had been a ranch cook, Nell looked for a job in a restaurant. If she could make three meals a day for nearly a dozen people, she surely could find a job cooking for customers. Besides, she liked cooking—the smells of bread and cinnamon rolls fresh from the oven, the challenge of making chili that was rich and hearty but not too sharp, of frying steak so it was crusty on the outside but tender within. The cowboys had said she was the best cook the Rockin' A ever had. Cooking on a big restaurant stove would be easy after the balky wood-burning cookstove at the ranch.

But restaurants, she discovered, didn't want female cooks— even restaurants that served food so greasy and overcooked it was barely edible. So she applied for work at cafés and diners. She didn't find cooking jobs there either, but at Buck & Betty's Café, a woman said she could use a waitress who would fill in in the kitchen if needed.

Nell figured she could take the job until she found something better and agreed. The owner, Betty, who did the cooking, was a no-nonsense woman who reminded Nell a little of Lucy. There was no Buck. "I thought it sounded better to have a man's name on the sign. Buck's my last name," Betty explained.

The café was downtown near Union Station. It was a breakfast-and-lunch counter, with a few tables over on one side, that catered to business and traveling men. "I expect you to be friendly but not too friendly, if you get my meaning. And you'll have to watch out for some of the customers," Betty explained. "I have a repu-tation to maintain, and it wouldn't do if the customers thought they could have their way with my waitress." Nell wouldn't just have to deal with the flirting, but she'd have to learn how to turn down too-friendly men without insulting them. Betty wanted them to keep coming back, but she expected them to keep their hands to themselves.

The work suited Nell. She had to be at Buck & Betty's at five in the morning, but then, on the ranch, she'd gotten up early to start breakfast for the hands. A few customers usually were waiting when Nell opened the door at six, and after that came a rush of diners. There was no chance to flirt even if Nell had wanted to. In fact, she barely had a chance to say hello and take orders before she was called into the kitchen to deliver plates of food. The customers were steady until Buck & Betty's closed at two thirty, although there was a lull between the breakfast and lunch crowds. The few customers who came in then ordered just coffee and doughnuts, and often the place was deserted for a half hour or so, and the two women could sit down with coffee themselves.

The café was closed on Sundays, and that first Sunday, Betty helped Nell find a place to live. Nell had been staying in a hotel, but it was expensive. Besides, she wanted a place she could call her own. Betty knew of a rooming house near downtown that was clean and owned by a woman who insisted her roomers be respectable but was not a snoop. "Some landladies will go through your things when you're away," Betty warned.

Nell liked the house and the room that was available. The sun streaming through the window made her think of the bright days in New Mexico. There was a chicken coop out back, too. The woman offered two meals a day, but Betty negotiated a rate that included only supper, since Nell ate breakfast at the café.

At first, the landlady, Mrs. Bonner, was skeptical because Nell was young. Her three other boarders were maiden ladies in their forties and fifties, all of them schoolteachers. But when Nell mentioned she loved to quilt and asked where the best place was to purchase needles and thread, Mrs. Bonner became almost motherly. She even offered to let Nell use her treadle sewing machine.

"I expect you won't be here long, a pretty young thing like you. Some young man will snatch you up."

"I'm not interested in getting married," Nell protested, thinking the woman would not rent to her if she knew there might be young men coming around to court her. She *was* interested in getting married, however. That was why she'd come to Denver. She'd have to be discreet.

She wouldn't find a husband among the customers at Buck & Betty's, Nell decided after a week or two. Most of them were male, but they weren't the marrying type. Betty had been right about their trying to flirt with her. A good many of them, Nell figured, were already married. Betty had warned her that as traveling men, they likely had wives at home but were looking for a little fun on the side. She warned Nell to watch out for them. The worst ones, Nell decided, were older, old enough to be her father.

"If I had a girl as pretty as you, I wouldn't let her sling hash," one man told her.

"What would your granddaughter do, then?" she shot back.

The man was startled and blushed, but then he laughed.

Another man whispered that he was an artist and would like her to pose for him. He said he'd pay. Nell took her pencil out of her hair, which she wore in a pompadour on top of her head, and handed it to him along with a page torn from her order pad. "Help yourself, and I won't charge you."

Nell didn't find her retorts especially clever, but Betty laughed at them and told Nell she'd do. "Where'd you learn to talk back like that?" Betty asked.

"From a bunch of cowboys," Nell told her, and it occurred to her that maybe the practical jokes on the Rockin' A had done her some good. She thought of Buddy's prank with the handkerchiefs. She had to admit that after she cooled off, she'd thought the joke was clever. She wondered if Buddy still had her handkerchief. No, Alice would have noticed Nell's initials and thrown it out.

Some of the customers tried to show off with their knowledge of café lingo, ordering "white wings," which were eggs over easy, or "draw one in the dark"—black coffee. But Nell quickly caught on to the jargon. A few of the men were more forward. One or two pinched her, and another put his hand on her bottom and squeezed. Nell was so offended that she dumped a cup of hot coffee on him. He jumped up, red-eyed angry, and Betty came out from the kitchen and tried to clean him off.

"Your girl just about killed me. I know the mayor. I ought to get you shut down," he sputtered.

Betty looked at Nell for an explanation, but it was another customer who spoke up. "Yeah, I seen what he did, and you ought to get the vice squad down here pretty quick, Betty. He's a masher. He's lucky your girl didn't take a whole pot of coffee and dump it on his head." Betty told the diner to get out and never come back. He was one customer she didn't mind losing.

The bulk of the customers actually were gentlemen, especially after the coffee incident, which someone brought up whenever a customer's attentions to the new waitress were too obvious. "Best watch yourself, bub," the regulars would say. "Unless you like your coffee in your lap."

After Nell had been there a few weeks, several customers asked her out on the town. She turned down the gasbags and the ones she suspected were married. She was lonely, however, and did go out to the flickers with two of them. They were traveling men who, as it turned out, invited her back to their hotel rooms. She knew what that meant and made it clear she was not interested.

It would be better if she found men outside the café, she decided. But so far, she hadn't met any, and she spent a good many evenings with her quilting. She hadn't moved to Denver to sew, though, and she pondered how she could meet someone. Maybe she should start attending church or ask one of the schoolteachers at the boardinghouse to go with her to a dance. When she mentioned it to one of them, the teacher shook her head. Her principal wouldn't approve, she said. In fact, the landlady looked at Nell crosswise at the suggestion of the two women going to a dance without escorts, so Nell said quickly, "Of course you're right. I'm from New Mexico. The customs are different there."

In those first months in Denver, Nell enjoyed herself most when she was with Betty. They window-shopped at the downtown stores, rode the trolley to City Park to look at the flowers and feed the ducks, and dined out on Saturday nights, comparing the food and the service to Buck & Betty's.

Nell's boss was twenty years older and skeptical when it came to men. She had arrived in Colorado during the gold rush and lived in Swandyke, a mining town in the mountains. Her husband, Foster, Betty confided one morning as the two sat drinking coffee between the breakfast and lunch rushes, had been a hard man. He'd come west to get rich. Nobody ever came west to get poor, she said with a laugh. But he failed to find pay dirt and had had to work as a common miner. He took out his frustration on Betty, but that was what a wife was for, she had believed.

They had two children, a boy and a girl, and the father preferred the boy. He treated the girl the way he did Betty. When the little girl was two, she skinned her arm and wouldn't stop crying. Foster yelled at her, which only made her cry harder. He became enraged and slapped her back and forth, hitting her so hard that she passed out. The child was never the same after that.

She had fits and often fell to the ground, her eyes rolling back in her head. Foster blamed Betty for the girl's condition, told her she was a poor mother and said the child was an idiot. He took to ridiculing both of them.

The boy was better treated, and he learned that his father liked it when he, too, bullied his mother and sister. So he disobeyed his mother and tormented his sister.

Betty began holding out money from the little her husband gave her to purchase necessities. When Foster was passed out drunk, Betty stole money from his pockets, and since when he sobered up he couldn't remember how much he'd spent, he never suspected her. Betty wasn't sure why she did it—it never occurred to her that she would actually leave her husband—but she thought she might need the money one day.

The girl was five, and she spoke only gibberish. The family had gone into the mercantile, where the father bought a peppermint stick for his son. The girl pointed to the jar of candy and then to her mouth, muttering excitedly. "Shut up," Foster told her. When the girl didn't, Foster turned to Betty. "Shut that dummy's mouth."

A man laughed, and Foster exploded—not at the man but at his daughter. He struck her with his fists, telling her to be quiet. He yelled that she was worthless and he was ashamed of her. Betty tried to stop him, but he flung her aside. He didn't stop hitting his daughter until she was lying on the floor unconscious. She never came to her senses, and a day later, she was dead.

If Foster had struck the girl at home, no one would have known. But a crowd had gathered around him when he began beating her, men grabbing his arms to stop the abuse. So word of the incident reached the sheriff, who came to the house to make an arrest the day of the funeral.

"Let me bury my daughter first," the father said, and the sheriff, who was a decent man, agreed. No matter how foul a father Foster had been, he was still a man who had lost a child to death. He seemed shaken and mortified at what he had done. Foster sent Betty on ahead to the burying, but he never showed up. Instead, he took their son and got on the train to Denver. Betty never saw either one of them again.

Except for the money she had hidden from her husband, Betty was destitute. A mining town was no place for a woman alone. The miners took up a collection for Betty, but times were hard, and the collection wasn't much, only enough to pay for the funeral. Betty set herself up as a laundress, but washing clothes in mountain water made her hands crack and bleed. So with the little she had saved, she bought supplies, rented a shack, and set up a lunchroom for the miners. She cooked breakfast and packed lunch pails. She made enough to leave the mountains, and she moved to Denver, where she opened Buck & Betty's.

As she finished the story, Betty had tears in her eyes, and Nell took her hand. She was moved by her friend's plight. She had been caught up in her own troubles, but now she realized others had had things worse, and one of them was her friend. "You don't know what happened to your son?" she asked.

Betty shook her head. "My guess is Foster took him back east, where we came from. I hope he didn't turn out like his father, but most likely, he did. He was a nice little boy, but toward the end . . . It worries me." She smiled, although tears were running down her cheeks. "I don't talk about this very often," she said. "It tears me up. My daughter wasn't right in the head, but she was the sweetest thing you ever saw. She was my sunshine. I'd have taken care of her for the rest of my life and been glad for it."

Nell, moved, reached over and squeezed Betty's hand. "What were their names?" she asked.

"Tom. That was my boy's name. He'd be twenty-eight now." Betty stared down at the table a moment before she looked up and whispered. "The girl . . . her name was Nellie. My daughter's name was Nellie."

CHAPTER TWELVE

Before long, Betty trusted Nell as if the two had worked together for years. When business slacked off in the late mornings, Betty often ran errands, leaving Nell in charge.

One summer morning when Betty was gone and the café was empty, Nell sat at the counter writing a letter to her grandparents. She liked Denver, and she loved her work, she wrote, but she was lonely, and she hadn't found a man she cared about.

The screen door banged, startling Nell, and for an instant she thought she was in the kitchen of the Rockin' A and the slam meant some cowboy had come in. She half expected to look up and see Wendell or Monty, until she came to her senses and realized where she was. She pushed the letter aside and stood up.

"Looks like I'm your only customer," a man said. Nell had seen him walk by the café window earlier when the place was filled with people and remembered his sallow face and mustache. Nell had never cared for mustaches. She wished Betty or another customer were there, because she didn't want to be alone with this man. She didn't like his looks or the way he clenched and unclenched his hands.

"Looks like. What can I get you? We've still got doughnuts, fresh made this morning. Shall I bring you a couple?" She tried to sound cheerful and hoped he didn't catch the edge in her voice.

"Yeah, do that. Coffee, too." Nell went into the kitchen for the doughnuts and heard the man cross the room to sit down on a stool.

"You alone?" he asked when Nell set down the doughnuts in front of him. She reached for the coffeepot and held it in front of her for a moment before she poured the coffee into his cup. He glanced up and down the counter but saw no one. "Looks like you're alone. I guess you don't get many customers this time of day."

Nell frowned a little. She didn't remember the man coming into the café before. Most likely, he was just being friendly. Nonetheless, she said, "Betty went out. She'll be back in a minute. And we've got customers coming in all the time. It's hardly ever this quiet. I can fix you ham and eggs or pancakes if you like. I'm a good cook." The man stared at the coffeepot until she put it down.

"I just bet you are," he said.

"I learned to cook on a ranch," she said, and then she added, "I learned to shoot there, too." She wasn't sure why she'd said that.

"I don't see no gun."

"Oh, I don't need one. We have so many customers that I always feel safe."

"I don't see none of them, neither."

Nell glanced at the door, as if a customer were about to enter, and saw that the man had shut both the screen and the heavy inner door when he came in. The OPEN sign that hung there had been turned to read CLOSED. He must have done that when she went into the kitchen.

"I seen Betty go on down the street. I guess she won't be back for a time. It's just you and me. Ain't that nice?"

Nell felt uneasy and reached for the coffeepot, but the man grabbed it away from her. "Now, don't go thinking you can pour that on me." He threw the pot on the floor and took Nell's wrist.

"What do you want?" she asked, her voice high-pitched with fear. She'd never been afraid of a man before, even of Charlie. The cowboys might have teased her, but they had always treated her like a lady. So had the customers.

"What do you think I want, girlie?" He leaned over and kissed her hard, his teeth black and his mouth reeking of chewing tobacco. When Nell tried to slap him, he grabbed her hand and twisted it. "So, you want it rough," he said, shoving Nell down onto the counter and pushing at her long skirt. "We can do it that way, or you can be real quiet, and I'll be nice." His eyes, which were hard and bleached blue, roamed over her body.

"Don't!" she said. Nell's hands were strong from carrying heavy plates, and she grabbed at the man, but he caught both of her wrists in one hand and held her arms above her head. With his other hand, he reached into her blouse and fondled her breast. His fingernails were ragged and dirty, and he scratched her skin.

"Stop it!" Nell yelled, hoping someone would hear her. And then, "Help me! Somebody help me!" But with the door closed, nobody on the street heard her. And with the CLOSED sign, no one was likely to come into the café. She knew Betty would be away for a long time. Nell looked around frantically, but there was no one to rescue her. "Let me go. Please," she begged.

The man slapped her and told her to shut up or she'd be sorry.

Nell twisted one hand loose and reached behind her on the counter for something to use as a weapon, but the man had shoved the plates and cutlery onto the floor. She struggled, and he slapped her again and ordered, "Lie still, or I'll hurt you bad." Nell was quiet for a moment, and he said, "That's a good girl. This won't hurt." He stared at her with his awful eyes, clawing at her clothes with his gray hands.

Nell couldn't let him force himself on her like that, and she struggled. She kicked at him and cried out, until he put his hand over her mouth, and she gasped for breath. She had almost passed out when she heard the door slam open and another man enter the restaurant. For an awful moment, Nell wondered if the two men were partners, if the second man would take her when the first was finished. She struggled, kicking her legs, but it did no good. She was only kicking into the air.

The man who held her turned his head in surprise, and at that moment, Nell reached over her head and grasped a heavy china coffee cup. She brought it down on his head, shattering the cup. The man made an "oof" sound and slid to the floor, where he lay still.

Nell sat up, pushing down her skirt, gasping and grasping the broken cup handle like a weapon.

The second man held up his hands. "I was trying to stop him. Miss, are you all right? I'll call a copper."

Nell went limp and dropped her hand. "He tried . . . he tried . . . if you hadn't come in . . ." She began to cry.

"Hey, hey," the man said. "It's all right." Slowly, so as not to startle Nell, he reached out and took the broken coffee cup from her hand. "You'll be all right. I'll go to the police box and come right back, so you won't be alone for more than a minute. I doubt he'll come to by then. You hit him awful hard."

"No! Don't leave me alone with him," Nell begged.

The man nodded. "You use the call box, then. I'll stay here with him, and if he wakes up, I'll clobber him over the head again." He grinned at her, his face so open and friendly that Nell felt better. "My name's James—James Hamilton," he said as he helped her to her feet, then opened the door for her, and Nell, wobbling a little, rushed across the street to the police box.

When Nell returned to the café, her attacker was still passed out on the floor. "You have a mighty strong arm, young lady. You used him up pretty good. I sure wouldn't like to get on your bad side," James said, smiling at her until Nell smiled back. He looked around and asked, "How'd you like some of your coffee? You sit right here on the stool and I'll get you a cup. You got to promise not to smash the cup on my head."

Nell nodded and smiled again. The joke wasn't very funny, but at least the fellow was trying to make light of the incident. Then she glanced down at the man on the floor, who had started to moan and move around a little. She drew back.

"Don't you worry about him, miss. The police will be here any minute, and you and I can take care of him till they show up."

"He tried to . . . he . . ." Nell couldn't say the word "rape."

"But he didn't, did he?" James said. "You can't worry about what didn't happen." He patted her shoulder, and Nell drew back. But he smiled again, then poured coffee into two cups and handed her one. He stood over the man on the floor for a minute. "I guess I'll pour this on him when he wakes up."

The CLOSED sign still hung on the door, and no one came into the café until a police officer yanked open the door and stepped inside. He looked at Nell, then at James, and finally at the man on the floor. "What's going on?" he asked.

Nell started to reply, but instead, she began crying, shaking her head back and forth. James held the coffee cup to her lips and told her to drink. Nell grasped it with both hands but then shook so hard that she spilled the coffee on her uniform. James took the cup. "It's all right, miss. You're safe." Then he turned to the officer. "It looks like this man tried to have his way with her. I saw it through the window. The sign on the door said the café was closed, and I thought that was odd, because it's always open in the morning. So I went to the window to see if somebody'd forgotten to turn around the sign. I saw this man here"—he kicked at the man on the floor with the toe of his shoe—"forcing himself on her. He'd have raped her if he could."

Nell bowed her head at the word. "If you hadn't come in—" she said, but James hushed her.

"Any man would have helped you. I was just here. All I did was open the door. You're the one who hit him over the head. You saved yourself." He grinned at the officer. "He sure did pick the wrong woman to fool with."

By then, the man on the floor was awake, and he sat up, rubbing his head.

"You got anything to say?" the officer asked.

"Yeah, you arrest her. She tried to murder me."

"Too bad she didn't," the policeman said. He yanked the man to his feet and reached into his pocket for handcuffs. Then the officer told Nell, "We had reports about a fellow that looks like this. Goes into stores where a woman's alone. I hadn't heard he tried it in a café."

By that time, several men were standing outside the door, wondering if the café was open, and then suddenly Betty was inside. She looked around and grasped what had happened. "Go home," she told Nell. "Just go home and take a warm bath and go to bed, and we'll talk about this later."

"I don't know, Betty. I don't want to be alone," Nell said. Her voice was like that of a little girl.

"You let her stay if she wants to," James said. "She should keep on working, doing what's normal. That's the best way to deal with something unpleasant."

"You a doctor?" Betty asked.

"Just a customer," he said.

Betty studied him for a moment.

"He helped me. The CLOSED sign was on the door, but he came in anyway. He saw what was going on. I was almost passed out," Nell said. "I want to stay here. I want to pretend it's just a regular day and that this didn't happen. Besides, I feel safer now that you're back." That wasn't entirely true. What Nell really wanted was to be in the kitchen on the farm in Kansas, with her grandmother fixing her tea. Then she'd truly be safe.

Betty studied Nell a moment. Finally she said. "If that's what you want. Go brush your hair. We got customers." She turned to James and said, "So you saved her? You like steak, do you? I got a porterhouse back there."

"Just coffee," he said. "Give me a broom, and I'll sweep up this mess first. You take care of your customers."

Nell went to the sink in the kitchen and splashed water on her face. She combed her hair, which had come loose in the scuffle, and twisted it back on top of her head. For a long time, she stared into the mirror over the sink, but she didn't look any different, just tired. She buttoned her blouse where the man had forced it open and found a fresh apron, tied it around herself, and went into the dining area.

The half-dozen men in the café had been chatting among themselves, gossiping about what they thought had happened, but when Nell appeared, they were silent, and they sent her sympathetic looks. She felt better when she realized that the diners liked her, that they were glad she was all right. They were curious, but they were gentlemen. And they didn't know what to say.

Then James put aside the broom and said, "I sure would like a cup of coffee and maybe a doughnut. You got any?"

"You bet," Nell said, her voice high. She swallowed and said, "Yes."

James grinned at her, as if to encourage her. "How about two, then?"

"Yes, sir," Nell told him, her voice better now.

The men in the café exchanged glances. Then one spoke up. "I'd like coffee, too. Cream." The others gave their orders, and before long, things did indeed seem like normal. They weren't, of course, and for a time Nell acted in a daze. But then the lunch crowd came in, and she was able to shove the happenings of the morning to the edge of her mind. When there was a lull, she looked for James, thinking he might like more coffee, but he was gone. She cleared his dishes and found a silver-dollar tip under his saucer. She hadn't even thanked him.

She and Betty were about to close the café when James came back. "I went to the police station. That man's locked up. He won't bother you again. In fact, the cops were razzing him about being knocked out by a woman." He grinned, and then he handed Nell a bouquet of violets that he had held behind his back. "I didn't want the entire day to be a bad memory."

Nell took the flowers and said formally, "I am in your debt."

"No, ma'am, I'm in yours. You see, I always wondered what

THE PATCHWORK BRIDE 141

I'd do if someone needed me. I worried that I wouldn't be man enough. But now I know I am, even though it was you who knocked out that fellow." He grinned at her, a smile that lit up his face and made his eyes shine.

Nell smiled back, but Betty didn't. In fact, she watched him, as if wondering what he wanted. Nell knew Betty didn't trust men, even the good ones. She believed they were always after something. "You want that porterhouse now?" Betty asked.

James shook his head. "I imagine it's time for you ladies to go home." Later, Betty said she'd thought James would ask to escort Nell home, and then who knew what he might try. But instead, he said, "I hope you're all right, Miss . . . Miss . . ."

"Nell," Nell said.

"Nell. I always did favor that name." Then he turned and said over his shoulder, "I'll see you around, Miss Nell."

Two weeks passed before Nell saw James again, and by then she was disappointed, thinking he wouldn't be back. She wanted to thank him, but more than that, she wanted to see him again. He was the nicest man she had met in Denver, and she hoped he wasn't married. Then one midmorning, when the café had only two or three other customers, James sat down on a stool and ordered coffee and doughnuts. "I just thought I'd stop by and see if you're all right," he said.

"I'm pretty well, I guess," Nell told him, but of course, she wasn't. She had gone home the night of the attack and taken a bath and climbed into bed, but she couldn't sleep. Every time she dozed off, she saw the bleached-out eyes of the man who had attacked her. She felt his hands clawing her, scratching her breast, pulling at her skirt. After a time, she got up and went downstairs, where she had left her quilting, and sat in a rocker, her sewing in her lap. But she couldn't take a stitch. She picked up the needle, but instead of inserting it into the fabric, she pricked her finger and watched a tiny drop of blood seep out. She put her finger into her mouth.

"Can't sleep, can you?"

Nell jumped when she heard the voice, and she clutched the rocker, her elbows poking into her sides as if she could make herself smaller.

"I can't either." Ignoring Nell's startled state, her landlady, Mrs. Bonner, sat down on a hard chair. "I came downstairs to make myself a cup of tea. It's chamomile. I dried the flowers myself last summer. You want a cup?"

"Yes, please," Nell said. She wasn't sure she wanted the company, but she didn't care to be alone either.

"Any reason you can't sleep?" Mrs. Bonner asked when she returned with the tea.

Nell shook her head. She was too ashamed to confess what had happened. "A bad dream, I guess." She sipped the tea, which almost scalded her mouth.

"Bad things happen sometimes," Mrs. Bonner said, and Nell wondered if Betty had told her about the incident in the café. "Like the fellow says, you got to remember the good things, not the bad ones."

"Oh, nothing like that," Nell said, determined no one should know what had happened. "It was just a dream."

"A man came by today," Mrs. Bonner said, and Nell turned to look at her, startled. Had James Hamilton followed her home? Or worse, had the police let her attacker go and somehow he'd found out where she lived?

Mrs. Bonner studied her a moment. "He asked if I took male

boarders. I said no. I wouldn't have taken him even if I did. He was older than I am, all bent over. He couldn't have climbed the stairs."

Nell gave a slight smile, glad Mrs. Bonner had diverted her attention to such a small thing, and glanced down at her quilting, although she didn't seem to have the energy to stitch on it.

"What are you making?" Mrs. Bonner asked.

"A Lone Star," Nell replied, holding up the patchwork.

"A Texas quilt. Didn't you say you'd been living in Texas?"

"New Mexico Territory."

"Well, same thing. Looks like a cowboy quilt."

Did it? Nell wondered. Had she chosen a cowboy pattern? "I picked it because I like stars."

"I do, too. Last quilt I made was an Evening Star." Mrs. Bonner chatted as she picked up her own quilting, Nell only half listening. In fact, the drone of the landlady's voice made her sleepy. After a few minutes, she finished her tea and said good night.

She went right to sleep, and in the morning, she wondered if Mrs. Bonner had known the conversation would make her drowsy. Women, she thought, could be wonderful friends. She'd hoped to find a husband in Denver, but it wasn't such a bad thing that she had found two good friends.

Nell was thinking about James at the very moment he came into the café. He had been like a medieval knight rushing in to rescue her, then disappearing into the sunlight. What reason was there for him to come back? There really was no reason he should come around, and Nell had given up seeing him again.

Then he was there, grinning at her and sitting at the counter, removing his hat. He was smartly dressed in a fashionable suit, with a tie and a high starched collar, but the fine clothes didn't hide the boyish look.

Nell's eyes lit up when she saw him. She poured him a cup of coffee. "Cream?" she asked.

James shook his head. "Don't need it. Your coffee's too good." Then he inquired how she was.

After Nell told him she was fine, he said, "Well, I'm glad for it. With a day like this"—with a wave of his hand, he indicated the sun outside—"who wouldn't be fine? I love Denver. I surely do. Can't stand to be away from it."

"You're a traveling man, then?" Nell asked. Apart from his name, she didn't know a thing about him.

"Colorado, Wyoming, Utah, Nebraska."

"New Mexico?"

"No, not there."

"What do you sell?"

"Fabrics, mostly, and notions. I work for a big company. We manufacture anything you need to stitch a dress or make a tablecloth. I have clients all over." He opened a case and took out some fabric samples. "Pretty, aren't they, and high quality. Just the thing to appeal to a housewife."

"Or a quilter," Nell said.

"You quilt?" he asked. "I thought you just might be too elegant for something as simple as quilting."

Nell laughed. It felt good to laugh with a man again. "I'm pretty simple."

"Well, these are for you, then." He laid the samples on the counter.

Nell touched one of the swatches, and James put his hand over hers. She savored the warmth of his touch before she took her hand away. "Oh, I would like to buy them someday," she said. The fabric looked expensive, and she was close with her money.

"They're not for sale. I'm done with them. I was going to throw them out. I'd like to know they will end up in a quilt. I'll give them to you if you promise you'll use them for something pretty."

Nell was flustered and not sure it was proper to accept such a gift. Then Betty came into the room from the kitchen and said, "Take them. You can make them into a quilt for me." She added, "That porterhouse is getting awfully old."

James shook his head. "Coffee. If you'll give me a cup of coffee, I'll call it square."

Nell thought James might ask her out then, and she was disappointed when he finished his coffee and rose, putting another cartwheel under his saucer. "See you next trip," he said.

Betty watched him go. "Here I thought he was ready to ask you to go to the pictures with him. Maybe next time. He'll be back."

"Do you think so?"

"Oh, yes."

"I hope so," Nell said, remembering how the touch of his hand had warmed her.

CHAPTER THIRTEEN

Nell began to look forward to James's visits. Each time the door opened, she looked up, hoping to see him. She never knew when he would show up. Sometimes he came by two or three times a week, and then he'd skip a week or two because he was calling on stores in another state, he said. He told her little about himself other than that he'd grown up in Idaho.

"On a ranch?" Nell asked.

"Oh, my, no, in a town. My father had a dry goods store. I could have taken it over, but I get restless staying in one place. That's why I became a purveyor of yard goods and such." He removed a spool of thread and set it on the counter. Each time he came into the restaurant now, he gave her samples of notions he sold—snaps, buttons, thread. "Try this, it has a new twist," he said, taking a skein of embroidery floss from his sample case.

Nell thanked him, and as she did, she removed a quilt square from under the counter. "I kept this here to show you how I used the fabric scraps you gave me." The square was wrinkled, and she smoothed it with her hand. She had brought the best of the squares, the one in which the corners matched perfectly.

James touched Nell's arm as he leaned over to study it. "What's the pattern?"

"Lady of the Lake." The quilt was for Betty. Nell had chosen a pattern she thought her friend would like, but she wondered if she had really picked it because she thought it would please James. That was foolish, because, as Nell reminded herself again, James really had never been more than a customer, although he was a friendly customer. Betty thought perhaps he was married—or maybe he had a girl at home, wherever that was. That would explain why he'd never asked Nell out.

After he inspected the quilt square, James admired Nell's workmanship, and she wondered what other man ever paid attention to the stitching on a quilt.

"I like the way you use the blue against the purple. You have a way with colors," James said.

Nell glanced at Betty, who was listening in the kitchen and rolling her eyes.

"I'd say you're an artist—an artist with fabric." He smiled at her, his eyes lighting up. "Say, there's a painting show at an artist studio uptown. I passed it yesterday and wanted to go back to see it. Would you like to go with me? I could come for you when you get off work."

"Yes. Oh yes, I would," Nell stammered, glancing over her shoulder at Betty for approval. Betty shrugged. Nell didn't know a thing about art. She remembered the print of the lone wolf in her grandparents' living room and the one of dogs playing cards that she'd seen in the bunkhouse. She was pretty sure *they* wouldn't be in the art show. "I love pictures," she said.

"I enjoy them, too. I do a bit of painting myself."

"You're an artist?"

"I wouldn't say that. I just like to paint."

"There was an artist wanted to draw Nell, wanted her to pose for him. Are you like him?" Betty called from the kitchen.

James blushed, which made his freckles stand out. "I wouldn't do that. I mean, if I painted people, Nell would be a fine subject. But I only paint landscapes and still lifes."

Nell was pleased he no longer called her *Miss* Nell.

Betty came out from the kitchen then and looked James up and down. "I thought maybe you was married."

James laughed. "That's a good one. Do you think I'd be asking Nell to go out if I was?"

"When's that ever stopped a man?"

"You don't think much of me, do you, Miss Betty?"

"Sure I do. You saved Nell from that scapegrace, didn't you? It's just that I don't think much of men in general."

"I'm sorry about that, but maybe I can show you we're not all bad—show Nell, anyway."

After James left, saying he'd come back when the café closed, Nell said, "I like him fine. More than fine, in fact. Why don't you?"

Betty was staring at James's back through the window. She shook her head. "I don't know. There's something . . . Maybe it's what I said, that I just don't like men. I'm suspicious of all of them. It doesn't matter who they are." She paused. "Don't pay any attention to me." Betty picked up James's empty cup and saucer and slid the silver-dollar tip along the counter to Nell.

"He's nice, and I think he's a gentleman. And after the way he came in that day . . . I sort of feel I owe him."

Betty swirled around. "You don't owe him. You don't owe anybody. That's what gets girls into trouble."

Nell studied Betty. "I'm not as naïve as you think. I can take care of myself."

"Can you?"

James returned just after the café closed, with a corsage of violets for Nell. She started to pin them to her throat, then realized she was wearing her uniform. "I ought to have brought another dress," she said, embarrassed.

"You look fine. Take off your apron and put on your coat and hat, and nobody will know you're wearing a uniform. They'll just see the violets," Betty said.

Nell did as she was told and looked at her reflection in the mirror over the sink and decided she didn't look so bad. The New Mexico tan had long since worn off, and her skin was fair. She'd changed her hair when she moved to Denver, thought the new style emphasized her blue eyes.

"Why, you look grand," James said when Nell returned from the kitchen. "After we view the pictures, I'll take you to tea at the Brown Palace Hotel."

"Hotel," Betty muttered.

Nell didn't acknowledge the remark. Although she barely knew James, she trusted him.

"We could ride the trolley, but I'd rather walk," James said, taking her arm. She liked that, liked the warmth of his hand on her. His touch made her feel safe.

The street was crowded. Because the café was near the depot, most of the passersby were men, hurrying to catch the trains or walking from one appointment to another. They were dressed in suits and high collars, like James, and walked quickly, occasionally giving Nell a glance. She and James passed a beggar girl dressed in rags, her face dark from dirt or maybe bruises. She held out a tin cup and repeated, "Help me. Help me," over and over in a kind of rhythm. The girl couldn't be more than five or six. James reached into his pocket and took out a silver dollar, dropping it into the cup. The girl looked into the container, then stared at James, her eyes wide in disbelief. She was too surprised to thank him.

"That was generous," Nell said, pleased at his kindness.

"Oh, not so generous. She has one silver dollar, and I have a pocketful of them. Poor tyke." They watched as the girl ran over to a man and handed him the money. "Her father will drink it up, but maybe he won't beat her tonight."

"How do you know that?"

James shrugged. "That's the way it is with those poor kids. Their fathers send them out to beg money for liquor and punish them if they don't get it. I can't stand that. I love kids. I hate to see them treated that way."

Nell liked that about James, liked that he loved children, and smiled at him, noticing then how tall he was. In the bright sunlight, she saw that he was older than she'd thought. There were wrinkles—laugh lines—around his mouth and touches of gray in his hair. They made him look distinguished. She stared at a scar on his chin and wondered how he'd gotten it.

James saw her looking at him, and he tightened his hand on Nell's arm. "The violets look nice on you. I was hoping they were your favorite flower."

They weren't, but Nell said, "They are now." She glanced down at the violets but was distracted by the music coming out of a saloon. Someone was playing "There'll Be a Hot Time in the Old Town Tonight" on the piano.

James hummed a few bars. "That was the favorite song of the Rough Riders," he said.

Nell knew that perfectly well. "Was it?" she muttered.

"The Rough Riders," he said, as if she didn't understand. "They fought in Cuba under Theodore Roosevelt. They were the most famous fighters in the war. Do you know about them?"

Nell nodded.

"Some of them went to fancy schools in the East, like the one Roosevelt went to. But there were westerners, too. They came from Arizona and New Mexico Territories—" He stopped. "You said you lived in New Mexico once. I bet you knew some of them."

"Probably."

"Probably." James studied her a moment but didn't say more. They had reached a tiny brick building with an ART SHOW TODAY sign in front, and he led her inside.

Nell had never been to an art show, and she stared at each picture as she stood in front of it, frowning a little and not commenting. In fact, she found most of the pictures boring and didn't know what to say. James told her they were the latest trend in art, but they didn't make sense to Nell. "Is this what you paint?" she asked.

"No, but I like them. Look at the way the paint is applied, thick as butter. And the lines on that one. I like the way they intersect."

"But what is it? All that doesn't mean anything to me. Look at this one. The woman's foot is bigger than her head. It doesn't make sense. And that one over there; the man looks like he's starving."

"I see that I'm going to have to take you in hand and teach

you about painting. You don't want to make statements like that around people who really know art."

For a moment, Nell bristled. Who was he to tell her what she had to know? "What if I don't care?"

James turned to look at her. "You're a funny one. You say violets are your favorite flowers because I like them, and now you say you don't care about art after I tell you I want to teach you. I don't know if you're trying to please me or not."

"I please myself," Nell said. If James was going to try to control her, she wanted to know it right off.

"Of course you do," he said, throwing up his hands. "I misspoke. How about if I make it up over tea?"

Nell was a little ashamed of herself then. She'd been too outspoken, and she had offended James. She wanted so much for him to like her. "You don't have to," she said. "I was perfectly awful, wasn't I?"

"Not at all. I like a girl who thinks for herself." He tucked Nell's hand under his arm, and they left the gallery. Then he whispered to her, "I thought some of them were pretty awful myself."

"Really?"

"Someday I'd like to show you what I paint."

"I'd like that," Nell said, then stiffened the slightest bit, wondering if James might find her too bold. Would he think she was saying she would accompany him to his hotel room to see his paintings?

If he did, James didn't pursue the idea. Instead, he asked, "Would it be all right if I brought one or two to the café? I don't have them displayed anywhere. In fact, I don't sell them. I just give them to friends." He squeezed her hand, which was still on his arm. "I'd like to think you are my friend."

Nell nodded. "I am."

"I'm glad you don't hate men like Miss Betty does. You have the right to, of course, after what happened to you. It was an awful thing. I hope you don't think about it all the time."

"No," Nell said. "When I do, I remember the man who saved me. It makes me know that while there are bad people in the world, there are good ones, too."

"I'm glad," he said, stroking her arm.

James didn't ask Nell what she wanted but instead ordered tea and crumpets for both of them. Nell didn't mind. She'd never been to tea in a hotel dining room and wouldn't have known what to ask for anyway. She was awed by the Brown Palace's eight-story rotunda with the stained-glass ceiling and the thousands of feet of onyx on the walls; she called it marble, but James corrected her. "More onyx than any other building in America," he said.

The dining room with its starched white tablecloths and heavy silver was a far cry from Buck & Betty's. The walls were painted with designs in gold and green, and there were heavy draperies at the windows. As James seated her, she looked around at the elegant women in their tea gowns and smart suits, their hats as big as washbasins and decorated with feathers and artificial flowers. She felt dowdy in her waitress uniform, and at first she thought she shouldn't have come. Then she looked down at her hands, strong from carrying heavy dishes, and she smiled to herself. How many of those women could gallop a horse across the plains, survive a mountain blizzard, even fight off a masher?

James saw the smile, and he grinned at her. "Are you thinking you're the prettiest girl in the room?" he asked.

"I'm wondering how many of these women worked all day in a restaurant."

"Good girl. You're a woman who doesn't mind hard work."

"And who doesn't care about art?"

"Next time I'll find a show with pictures of babies and puppy dogs. Girls like those."

He was teasing her, and Nell didn't like that, but she wanted to be agreeable and said only, "Maybe."

The tea arrived, and Nell took a sip. She preferred coffee—coffee with canned milk. The tea wasn't bad, however, and she loved the crumpets, especially since she had skipped dinner. She and Betty usually ate after the café closed, and James had arrived just at closing time.

"Do you want more crumpets?" James asked. She did, but she had gobbled them up like a ranch hand and thought she should say no.

James poured more tea, then looked at her from across the little table. "I would like to know all about you," he said.

"There isn't much to tell," she replied. But there was, and she told him more than she had intended, not about Buddy and what had happened in New Mexico, but about growing up in Iowa and spending summers on her grandparents' farm in Kansas, then moving there after her parents died. "It's the best place I know," she said. "Whenever I'm unhappy, I think about quilting under the trumpet vine on the porch with Grandma. That always makes me feel better."

"Is that what you thought about when . . . you know?"

Nell nodded. "Yes, afterward. I still do when I can't sleep."

James reached across the table and took her hand, and Nell felt a thrill when his fingers wrapped around hers. "You can't blame yourself. It wasn't your fault, you know. It was his." He glanced around the room. "I wonder how many of these fine ladies could have fought off that man with a coffee cup. Why, I'd say you were pretty remarkable."

James smiled at Nell, who smiled back at him. He slowly withdrew his hand and stood up. "Shall I walk you home?" he asked.

Nell wanted him to, but she thought things were already moving fast. So she told him no.

"I hope you'll let me take you out again," he said.

Nell placed her napkin on the table and looked down at it for a moment so that James wouldn't see how excited she was at his words. She had wanted to see him again outside the café. She'd hoped to find a husband in Denver, and James was the nicest man she'd met. She had already begun to care about him. "I'd like that," she said. "I'd like that very much."

CHAPTER FOURTEEN

One Sunday, James took Nell for an outing at Elitch Gardens. Located at the northwest edge of Denver, Elitch was a large park with flower beds and fountains and a zoo. Old couples sat on benches while children ran in and out of hidden places. Families brought picnics and ate at tables scattered throughout the park.

As they walked along a path, James held Nell's hand. He often did that now, and Nell liked it. James's hand was warm and firm. Holding hands seemed genteel, something appropriate for a gentleman like James. She'd become very fond of James in the weeks they had known each other. He was sophisticated, with lovely manners, and he was polite to everyone. In fact, despite Betty's skepticism that something about him seemed off, Nell couldn't find anything wrong with him. She'd asked Betty again why she didn't like James, but Betty had chalked it up to her suspicious nature. "He just seems too good to be true," she'd said. "There has to be something wrong."

Nell thought there wasn't a single thing wrong.

Now the two stopped beside a display of roses to watch a woman in an ostrich-drawn cart talk to a group of boys and girls. The children gathered around the ostrich, hands reaching out to pet the bird, all except one little boy who was squatting in the dirt, a blade of grass in his hand, teasing a grasshopper. The grasshopper jumped, and the boy, surprised, fell over, laughing.

"This is a good place for children," James said, watching as the ostrich bit off the boy's shoe button. "There's fresh air and animals and places for them to run about and play. It's so much better than the streets. I'm glad children are welcome here."

Without thinking, Nell squeezed James's hand. She was glad he cared about children. That was more important to her than he could know. She watched as a robin redbreast pecked at a crumb, then flew off with it in his beak. Perhaps he was taking it to a nest of babies.

James squeezed back and smiled at Nell. His face was red in the sun, and his freckles stood out. "You must like children, too. I can't imagine a woman who doesn't. I certainly wouldn't care to know such a woman." They walked on, past a pond with water lilies, the green pads as big as stepping-stones. After a time they stopped beside a plot of pansies set out in a formal display, a lovers' knot of yellow and purple.

"My grandmother called them heart's ease," Nell said.

"They have faces like little old men." He screwed up his face, and Nell laughed, feeling carefree.

"You look grand," he said.

Nell was pleased. She had dressed with care. She wanted to show James she was stylish, because although they had gone out several times now, he generally saw her wearing a uniform. She'd chosen a black skirt that came above her ankles in the new style, with a white blouse with puffed sleeves. She had made the blouse on Mrs. Bonner's sewing machine. There was a black tie around her neck, and her hat was a small black straw with a white egret feather. She'd slipped a smart black drawstring bag over her arm. No one would have guessed she was a waitress or had once been a hired girl.

"It they had violets, I would pick a bouquet for you," James continued. "But violets grow only in flower shops this late in the season. What other flowers do you like?"

"Daisies. They're such happy flowers. They're my favorite."

"You like them more than violets?" he teased.

"They go together," Nell said.

"Like a wedding bouquet."

The remark flustered Nell, and she dropped James's hand. She thought how she had changed since the first time she'd left the farm in Kansas, looking for both adventure and a husband. She was no longer headstrong or as sure of herself. She'd lost some of her confidence and become more deferential. Maybe it was because of the man who had attacked her. Or it could be that she was older now, more mature. Besides, more was at stake. She was a little more desperate for a husband. She wondered what kind of husband James would be. Kind and thoughtful, a good father. She was sure of that. But thinking of the way he handed out silver dollars, she wondered if he was a spendthrift. She wished James was more forthcoming about himself, but then, Nell hadn't told James everything about herself either.

They arrived at a refreshment stand near where a band played in a gazebo-like shell, and James bought her a glass of lemonade—bought lemonade, too, for half a dozen urchins who were standing nearby. "Sometimes I think you *can* buy happiness, at least for a minute," he said as he and Nell watched the children gulp down their drinks. He led Nell to a small iron table next to a planter of petunias, and they sat down in dainty iron chairs whose backs were a profusion of scrollwork. "If I painted portraits, I would paint you there, sitting in that white chair, your head turned to the sun, the purple flowers behind you," he said.

"But you don't paint people," Nell reminded him.

"Perhaps I should start. You make an awful nice picture sitting there."

Nell looked away, not sure how to respond. She wasn't used to compliments, although she had to admit she liked them, especially when they came from James. "Why not just paint the flowers?" she asked.

"Without the girl, they're only flowers."

Had she pushed for the compliment? Flirting didn't come naturally to Nell, although it seemed natural enough for James to flirt with her.

"You are very pretty, you know." He grinned at her. "But maybe you don't know. You are so modest, so lacking in artifice. I like you awfully well. Do you know that?" He picked up her hand and kissed it.

Nell blushed and looked out over the gardens, at the wild grasses and a pond, at the bright displays of blooms. She turned back to James. "What I don't know is about you. You never tell me much. About yourself, that is."

"That's because there's not so much to tell. I grew up in Idaho. My father was a businessman. I think I told you that. Mother died when I was a boy, and Father a few years back. I'm alone, an orphan, you might say. I once had two younger sisters, but they died when they were very small, both from pneumonia. They were in the same little bed." He looked off into the distance, then ran his hand across his eyes as if he were wiping away tears.

"I was alone with them when they died. My parents were worn-out, and I said I would sit with Beatrice and Anna— those were their names—while they rested. Beatrice was seven; Anna was six. I remember watching Beatrice's chest rise and fall as she tried so hard to breathe. Then she stopped. She just didn't take another breath. I looked at Anna, and she wasn't breathing either. I got up to call Mother, but I didn't. She needed her sleep. There was nothing she could do. So I sat there for hours, holding their little hands and waiting for Mother to wake up."

"But what if they weren't really dead? They might have just been sleeping."

"No, they weren't. I can't say why I was so sure, but I was. Beatrice's hairbrush was on the dresser. I brushed her hair and then tied it with a ribbon. Pink. It was her favorite color."

"And Anna's hair? You brushed it, too?" Nell whispered.

James shook his head. "No. Beatrice's hair was straight. Anna's was curly. She had ringlets all over her head." He looked down at his hands. "I miss them still."

"I'm so sorry." The story brought tears to Nell's eyes. She brushed at them with her gloved hand. She smiled at James, and he reached over and held her to him.

"I suppose that's why I care so much about children. They seem so fragile."

"That must have been awfully hard on you. On your parents, too." She felt very close to James at that moment. She was glad he had confided in her, and she laid her head against his chest.

"I think that's what killed Mother. For a long time, it was just Father and me." He was silent, remembering. "I never tell this story. I'm sorry to sadden you. But you are so easy to talk to. I guess I forgot myself."

"I'm glad you told me." Nell straightened up but put her hand over his. For a moment, they sat without talking.

The band had begun another tune, a waltz, and Nell hummed it, thinking she should change to a happier subject. She smiled at James and said, "Tell me something else about you. Do you go to church? Who did you vote for? Do you ever go by Jim or Jimmy? What's your favorite color?" She wanted to ask if he had ever been married—or if he was married now—but Nell couldn't bring herself to really quiz him, not after the story he had told her about his family.

"No. McKinley, and I'll vote for Teddy Roosevelt next time. I don't care for Jim, and only Mother called me Jimmy. Orange."

"Orange?" Nell laughed. "Not violet?"

"Maybe there are orange violets."

Nell made a face. James's story about his sisters had drawn her to him, and she felt they were connected. She felt very close to him now. She could not remember when she had had such a wonderful time. "You could paint a picture of orange violets."

"You wouldn't like it because the violets would be a lie. You said you like only art that's realistic."

"I think I should like them if *you* painted them." Nell wondered if she had been too forward.

"Then I shall indeed do it. I will bring you a painting of orange violets if you promise to hang it in your room."

"Will you? Oh, yes, I promise I will." She would hang the picture over her bed, where she would see it in the morning light. She liked the idea of waking up thinking of James.

They walked on and stopped at a formal garden where roses

bloomed in pink and red, yellow and peach. James leaned over to smell a white rose, then glanced around, and when he saw no one was looking, he plucked it and gave it to Nell.

Nell frowned at him. "You shouldn't have, James. Didn't you see the sign saying not to pick the flowers? They'll ask us to leave," she told him, although she was pleased. She put the rose to her nose to take in its scent.

"Tuck it into your purse, and they'll never know. It's so pretty I thought you should have it." He paused, then added, "As pretty as you are." Suddenly he reached over and pulled Nell to him and kissed her.

Startled, Nell nonetheless leaned into the embrace and kissed him back.

When Nell pulled away, James apologized. "I couldn't help myself. I hope you won't think I'm fresh."

"No. I . . . I liked it."

"I did, too." He took her hand, and they walked on. As they stopped to watch the animals in the zoo, Nell realized how different her life had become in just a few years. She was no longer a headstrong girl but a woman whose beau had just kissed her. She was happy now—perhaps for the first time since she'd left New Mexico. *He* made her happy. Nell glanced over at James, who was watching the deer, and thought how lucky she was that he had come into the café that morning. When she thought of the attack now, she remembered it had brought James into her life.

Late in the afternoon James took Nell's arm, and they left the park for the trolley stop. They hadn't been watching the sky, hadn't seen the dark clouds gathering, and suddenly it began to rain. They had not brought an umbrella, and James hustled Nell across the street to a gloomy little café to wait out the storm. "It's not as classy as Buck & Betty's, but at least we'll be dry," he said, and Nell laughed, because Buck & Betty's was nice enough, but it was hardly classy.

They had not missed the rain, and Nell's neck was wet with drops of water. She brushed them away with her hand until James took out a white linen handkerchief, starched and embroidered with his initials, and gave it to her to wipe away the damp.

They sat down in a wooden booth near the window where they could watch the rain, the drops heavy now, falling onto the dark street, and they ordered coffee and doughnuts. The doughnuts were pale and hard. James tasted one and muttered, "Not as good as what I'm used to." The coffee was fine, however, and it warmed them after the cold rain.

"I must look a mess," Nell said, opening her purse to take out a little mirror. The rose had fallen apart in the little bag, and it fell onto the floor.

"I'll buy you another—a whole bouquet of them," James said.

"No, I like this one. I'll save the petals and press them in my Bible." Nell plucked the petals from the floor.

James gestured to the handkerchief, saying, "Keep it."

So she wrapped the petals in the white linen. "They'll remind me of a wonderful day." She ran her hand over the initials.

"I'm glad you think it was wonderful, because I think you are wonderful, too," James said.

He had been saying such things all afternoon, and Nell thought over the words. A shadow of doubt came into her mind. Was he serious, or was he after something else? Perhaps it was all a play to get her to go with him to his hotel room. She knew Betty believed that. But Nell dismissed the idea. James was a decent man. He was . . . well, he was wonderful, too.

"I hope you like me just a little," he said, after Nell did not reply.

"Oh, but I do," Nell said quickly. "I mean, I'm awfully glad I met you."

"I hope so."

The waitress poured them more coffee, and Nell stirred cream into hers, watching the white swirl through the dark liquid, turning it into a velvety light brown.

"But your friend doesn't?"

"My friend?"

"Betty."

"Oh, she likes you fine."

"I don't think so. She doesn't trust me, does she?"

Had Betty been that obvious? Nell answered, "She doesn't trust men, and I don't blame her."

"Why? Did something happen to her?"

"Oh, not what you think, not like that man in the café," she answered quickly. "Betty was married, and her husband was a terrible man. He beat her. Their daughter died, and he took off with their son. She hasn't seen either one of them since then." Nell blurted it all out without thinking.

"I guess I wouldn't like men much if that had happened to me. Buck, was that her husband's name?"

"His last name. She's Betty Buck." Nell wondered if she had said too much. Betty's story wasn't hers to tell. She looked out the window at an iron fence. Rain had accumulated on it, and the drops made long trails as they slid down the iron spikes. "I think the rain is letting up. I suppose we should go."

James glanced at the window but didn't make a move to get up. "What was her son's name?"

"I don't know. She told me, but I can't remember." Nell thought a minute. "It might be Tom. Betty said she thought her husband took him back east. Why do you ask?" The trolley rumbled along the tracks in the distance, and Nell stood. "If we hurry we can catch the car."

"There'll be another," James said. He pushed the plate of doughnuts aside. He'd eaten only half of his, and Nell hadn't eaten hers at all. "I suppose that son would be, what, twenty-five or thirty by now?"

Nell shrugged. "Betty told me, but I don't remember. Why?"

"Oh, the name Tom Buck is familiar, that's all." He stood. "Maybe it's familiar because of Buck & Betty's. Well, let's see if we can spot another trolley." He set down enough money for the coffee and doughnuts and left a dime tip under his saucer. He didn't tip all waitresses a silver dollar, Nell observed.

They walked across the street, avoiding puddles of water that had collected in the dirt. Nell was glad that she had put on boots instead of the kid slippers she had intended to wear. They had missed the streetcar and had to wait for another. A delivery wagon went by, splashing water, which soaked the bottom of Nell's skirt. Rainwater dripped off trees onto their clothes, and Nell thought her hat must be ruined. She took it off and looked at the egret feather, which was spoiled. She pulled it out of the hatband and dropped it onto the ground. "Wet feathers look better on birds," she said, which made James laugh.

The wind came up, and Nell shivered a little. James took off his jacket and put it around her; then he put his arm around her shoulder and drew her to him. "You need to warm up," he said, rubbing her shoulder. Nell wasn't *that* cold, but she liked the feel of his arm holding her tight, protecting her. In a few minutes, they heard the clang of another trolley in the distance, and the screech of metal wheel on rail, and looked up to see the car coming toward them. James paid the fare, and they sat down on one of the rattan seats. The trolley was fragrant with dampness and cigarette smoke.

"Do you mind if I smoke?" James asked. When Nell shook her head, he took out a tin case of cigarettes, selected one, and lighted it. "I suppose I should offer you a cigarette, but I really don't approve of women smoking, especially in public."

Nell nodded as if she agreed. She'd tried smoking at the Rockin' A, had rolled her own like the cowboys did, but she didn't like the taste of tobacco and had given it up. Still, she didn't care for the idea of James telling her what to do. Were all men like that? The air in the car was stuffy, and Nell tried to open the window next to her, but it was stuck. James stood and forced it open. Then he tossed out the remainder of his cigarette and apologized, saying he'd been rude to light it.

As they got closer to town, more and more people climbed into the streetcar, perhaps to get out of the rain, which had started up again. James stood up and gave his seat to a woman, and when the car got very crowded, Nell offered her seat to an old man with a cane.

"You didn't have to do that," James said.

"I can stand better than he can."

James put his hand on her arm and leaned forward and whispered, "You're very thoughtful, Nell. That's one of the things I love about you."

Nell felt a thrill go through her at the word "love." Of course, that could have been just a manner of speaking, but she hoped James meant it.

Did she love him, actually love him? Nell pondered that as she held on to the back of a seat, wedged against it by the crush of people around her. Did she love him as she had Buddy? For a moment she pictured Buddy, but then his face faded and disappeared. She didn't love Buddy anymore, Nell thought, at least not as much. She would never forget him, never stop wondering what could have been between then, but she had met James.

She smiled up at James, and he reached for her free hand and held it against his lips, kissing it in front of all those people.

CHAPTER FIFTEEN

One afternoon not long after that, James came into Buck & Betty's and whispered, "Will you meet me for tea at the Windsor Hotel at four? I need to talk to you about something. It could be awfully important." He glanced around as if afraid Betty would hear, and Nell frowned. What in the world was so mysterious? She couldn't imagine what he had to tell her, what was so important that he had to whisper. And why the Windsor Hotel? Then she smiled to herself. Perhaps he had chosen the fine old hotel as the place where he would declare his intentions. Nell thought about that for a moment before she decided no, it was too early for that.

As soon as Betty closed the café, Nell hurried to her rooming house. The Windsor was near the café, but she didn't care to wear her uniform, especially not if this was to be a special occasion. She wanted to change into something presentable, something that would please James. Although the Windsor Hotel, once Denver's finest hostelry, had seen better days, it still was a decent address. Gold and silver kings who were down on their luck lived there, and drummers often preferred its rooms to the better hotels because it was cheaper and close to Union Station. Many of them ate at Buck & Betty's. Nell had passed the hotel many times, but she had gone inside only once—out of curiosity. She wanted to see the rotunda and the infamous devil's-head staircase, which cast such a sinister shadow on the wall that some guests refused to use those steps. She had been overwhelmed by the hotel's old elegance, but the Windsor's time had passed, and the hotel was worn.

As she dressed, she wondered if the Windsor was a place for trysts, and she was not so quick to dismiss the idea that James might try to entice her to his room. If he did, how would she respond? She could hardly pretend—to herself, at least—that she was above such a thing. Should she tell him about her past? Not just yet. If things went further—if James declared his intentions—she would have to tell him. Besides, James was too much of a gentleman to try to seduce her.

She glanced at herself in the mirror. She had put on a white linen suit that she had made, with Mrs. Bonner's help, and embroidered with white flowers. The skirt came above her ankles, and the jacket was long and fitted. With white gloves and the black straw hat—now decorated with artificial flowers instead of a feather—she thought she looked as chic as any guest at the Windsor. Or the Brown Palace, for that matter.

"I hope you are going someplace fine," Mrs. Bonner said when she caught Nell coming down the stairs.

Nell started to say she was having tea with a gentleman, but she remembered that Mrs. Bonner and Betty were good friends, and James had been secretive about their meeting. She didn't want Betty to know. "Oh, I'm just going out," Nell said, wishing she had been quick enough to invent some story that would satisfy the old woman.

"Betty tells me you have a young man."

"He's not my 'young man.' He's just a fellow who comes into the café sometimes. He took me to Elitch Gardens once."

"Well, bring him 'round. I'd like to meet him."

And I would like you not to meet him, Nell thought. She didn't want Betty and Mrs. Bonner gossiping about James. Betty with her dislike of men was bad enough. No wonder James didn't want Betty to know he had invited Nell for tea at the Windsor.

Nell could have walked to the hotel, but she didn't want to be late. Nor did she care to soil her white shoes by walking through the dirt and horse droppings on the streets. She took a trolley instead, standing up so that she didn't wrinkle her linen outfit.

James was waiting in the lobby for her. He had changed clothes, too, and was dressed in a soft gray summer suit. Gray made him look distinguished. He was studying a pocket watch that was attached to a chain across his vest, although Nell was not late. In fact, the lobby clock showed she was a few minutes early. James did not comment on her outfit but said only that he was glad she had come. Nell started for the dining room, but James took her arm. "We're not going in there."

Nell wondered then if James stayed at the Windsor, not the Brown Palace, when he was in Denver. He'd never said. She glanced at the massive walnut staircase, wondering again how she would respond if he asked her to go upstairs with him. She would say no, she decided, although she would be tempted. She loved the thrill of James's touch, and she longed for him to hold her. Still, she would be firm, although not indignant. She had no reason to be self-righteous.

James did not start upstairs, however. Instead, he took Nell's arm and led her to the bar. "I thought you might like a glass of sherry instead of tea. I hope I don't offend you. You do take stimulants on occasion, don't you?"

"No, you don't offend me," Nell replied and almost laughed. She had worried for nothing. James had been anxious only because he'd thought she might take offense at being invited into a barroom instead of a dining room. He did not know she had had more than one shot of whiskey in her life, and frankly, she liked it. They really knew so little about each other.

Nell allowed James to lead her into the room, which was decorated with old-fashioned elegance. It was heavy and dark, and electric lights illuminated the silver dollars that studded the bar, remnants of the days when Colorado had been famous for its silver mines. Nell glanced around and saw that most of the customers were men, a few of them elegantly dressed with diamond stickpins and gold-headed canes. The other women in the room looked respectable, too. This was certainly not a place where prostitutes hung out. Nell was aware of hookers. They came into the café sometimes, and Betty treated them like any other customers. "They have to eat," she'd explained to Nell. "Poor things. Maybe if I hadn't known how to cook and run a café, I'd have been one of them."

At Nell's look of surprise, Betty had said, "What choice do most of them have? Hooking is better than doing laundry or cleaning rooms or working in a factory, which are about the only things a woman alone can do, unless she's got some learning. The reformers want to rescue them and send them to farms, but most of those girls come off farms and will never go back. They think being a fallen woman, as they're called, is a better life, although most of them don't make it for more than five or six years." She added, "Some of them have kids. Imagine how hard it would be if you had a little one and no father."

Nell could imagine, and after that, she had been especially nice to the women. Besides, they tipped better than most of the male customers.

James indicated a table near the bar and pulled out a chair for Nell. "Sweet sherry or dry?" he asked, and Nell told him dry. In fact, the only time she had had sherry was at the Mackintosh home, and she wasn't sure what it was. But she thought dry sounded better than sweet. James ordered a whiskey for himself. Nell hoped she looked as if she belonged in a barroom with a man who appeared so distinguished. James seemed at home there, and she basked in the idea that people might think them a couple—even a married couple.

When their drinks arrived, James downed his shot, then smiled at Nell as if seeing her for the first time. "You look awfully nice," he said. "I should have brought you flowers to wear."

"They would wilt in the heat," Nell said. The weather was hot, and the room was close, and Nell herself felt warm. The sherry was heavy and sticky, but she didn't mind. She felt elegant sitting where Colorado's gold and silver kings had once bought and sold mines. She loved being there with James among the faded opulence.

"I like this place. It's solid and fine. Did you see the marble floor in the lobby? And the woodwork? It must have taken an entire forest of black walnut trees to build this place. There's a ballroom upstairs." James leaned forward. "The state legislature used to meet across the street, and I've been told there's a tunnel from that building to this so that the legislators could come to the bar here without being seen from the street."

"I didn't know you were interested in history," Nell said. "Is that why you wanted to meet me here?"

James shook his head. He took out his cigarette case and removed a cigarette, and impulsively, Nell asked if she could have one.

"You smoke?" James asked, frowning a little.

"If I can sit in a hotel barroom drinking liquor, a cigarette won't harm my reputation," she said. She felt a little like the old Nell then, more sure of herself and not caring if she shocked anyone. She threw her head back in what she hoped was a sign of confidence.

Nell glanced around the room and noticed another woman smoking a cigarette. She turned and saw James looking at her. "I guess times are changing," he said and offered her the case. He lighted her cigarette and then his own. "I suppose you'll tell me next you can roll your own." He laughed at the idea.

"I can. You forget, I used to live on a ranch."

"You are full of surprises."

Nell nodded, thinking she had other surprises he didn't know about, some more shocking. "I'm so glad you invited me to come here. It's a wonderful adventure."

"It's more than that." James inhaled, then turned away to blow smoke out of his mouth. "I stay here sometimes. I prefer the Brown Palace, but this place is convenient, and my customers like to come here for a drink. I've gotten to know the bartender."

The cigarette was harsh, and Nell placed it in an ashtray. She turned to study the young man behind the bar. He was of average height with sandy hair and a mustache, nice-looking but ordinary. She would not have noticed him on the street. "He seems pleasant enough."

"Look at him again."

Nell stared. "What am I looking for?"

"Does he appear familiar?" James asked.

Nell narrowed her eyes. Was he someone she had met in New Mexico? A cowboy perhaps, a man who knew about Buddy, someone who was aware they had been caught in a blizzard and spent the night in a cabin together? Well, so what? He wouldn't know for sure what had happened in that cabin. Not even Lucy knew. There was nothing wrong with James finding out she'd once been engaged. And then she thought the man might be from Kansas, a boy who lived near her grandparents' farm. Perhaps he knew about her there. Then she remembered the man who had attacked her in the café, and she shivered. She'd recognize *his* face. She'd never forget it. She looked at the bartender again, but he wasn't the one. In fact, he wasn't the least bit familiar. She was certain she'd never seen him before. "Should he?"

"I don't know."

Nell was confused. Surely he had not brought her there to meet a bartender. James sat forward in his chair and stared at her. Then she followed his gaze as he turned again to the bartender. "Have I met him?" Nell asked.

"No, of course not. I just thought he might look familiar." James picked up his glass, but it was empty. "His name is Tom Buck."

"Tom Buck? You mean . . . ?" Nell turned to stare at the man again, harder this time. She tried to see Betty in his features. "Is he . . . Oh, James, is he Betty's son? Have you found him?" She grasped James's hand. "That would be such an exciting thing. How good of you."

James shrugged. "I don't know, Nell. Maybe. How would

Betty feel if we introduced her to her son? That is, if he is her son."

"She'd be thrilled." Then Nell stopped and thought. "I suppose she would be, but I don't really know. She'd be shocked, of course. She thinks he went east with his father. She hasn't seen him since he was a little boy and doesn't know what happened to him. In fact, she hasn't heard a word about him since his father took him away. That was years ago." Nell sat back and sipped her sherry, thinking. "Betty said he wasn't a very nice boy. He took after his father. Maybe he hates her. What if he's a terrible person? Have you asked him if he's Betty's son?"

"Not yet, but I did talk to him yesterday. You see, after you mentioned his name, I remembered the bartender here was Tom Buck. I didn't want to tell you for fear he was somebody else. It's not such an unusual name, I suppose. So I got to talking to him last night. He said his mother was dead and he'd run off from his father. Do you think he looks like Betty?"

Nell turned to stare again at the bartender. "Maybe. He has her coloring."

"I didn't want to pry too much until I talked to you. What if Betty wouldn't want to see him?"

"Of course she would, even if he turns out to be a disappointment. Wouldn't you?"

"I can't imagine not wanting to know your own child." He reached over and squeezed Nell's hand. "Let's give it a try." James got up and went to the bar, leaning over and saying something in a low voice, while Nell watched, barely able to contain her excitement.

"Sure," Tom Buck replied.

"I asked him if he could join us for a minute," James said after he returned.

They waited, not talking, watching Tom pour whiskey into a glass and hand it to a customer. He took a dirty glass off the bar and washed it. Then, after looking around to make sure no one wanted anything, he came to the table. "Everything all right here, Mr. Hamilton? Ma'am?"

"Everything's fine, Tom. Can you sit down?"

The bartender glanced around the room. Most of the patrons had left. "Sure thing. You want another?" He gestured at the glasses.

Nell shook her head, and James said no. She was nervous and ran her handkerchief through her fingers. She picked up her glass and sipped the sherry. It was sticky, and she decided she didn't care for it.

Tom wiped his hands on his apron and leaned forward in his chair. He waited for James to speak.

"I was telling my companion here that you and I had an interesting conversation yesterday. She thought you might know someone in common."

"Me?" Nell mouthed, wondering why James had suddenly made her responsible for telling him about Betty. She clasped her hands in her lap because with the warm air and the excitement, they were damp with perspiration.

"Who's that?" Tom asked.

Nell didn't know what to answer. After all, she didn't want to blurt out Betty's name. So she picked up her drink again, buying a little time. She finished the sherry and set down the glass. "First, I want to ask you a question. Did you live in a mountain town when you were a boy?"

"Yep. Swandyke. It was a nice place back then, but cold in the winter. My God, it was cold. And the wind!" He shook his head. "I've heard Swandyke's played out." He started to say more, then stopped and narrowed his eyes at Nell. "Why?"

"Did you have a sister?"

Tom's mouth formed a straight line, and he clenched his fists in his lap. "Who are you? What's this about?"

Nell didn't answer, and she was silent for a moment, waiting for her heart to settle down. This was Betty's son! Finally she said, "Your sister was . . . well . . . not quite right in the head. She died. You were mean to her. And your father's name, was it Foster?"

"My father . . . What's that to you?" Tom started to rise, but James put out his hand and told him to take it easy, that everything was all right.

"We don't mean to pry, but you see, I believe we know your mother," Nell said. She let out a deep breath. Now she had said it!

"My mother?"

Nell nodded.

"Not likely. My mother's dead." He rose and said, "I'll thank you not to mind my business, Mr. Hamilton."

"Please," Nell pleaded. It hadn't occurred to her that Tom wouldn't believe them. "How do you know she's dead?"

"My father told me so." He paused, thinking over his answer. "But maybe he made it up because he was such a liar. Maybe she just ran out on us. I always wondered about that. It doesn't matter. She's dead to me."

"Or you ran out on her," Nell said in a low voice. She looked down at her handkerchief, which was wadded up and damp now. She glimpsed the initials embroidered in it and realized it was the one James had given her at their Elitch Gardens outing.

She had washed it and meant to return it to him, but she must have slipped it in with her own handkerchiefs by mistake.

Tom stared at Nell for a long time, then slowly sat down again. "Why are you here?"

"My friend is a waitress. She believes she works for your mother, who runs a café near here," James said.

"What café?"

"Buck & Betty's," Nell said.

Tom nodded. "I've seen it. I thought it was funny that it was just like my mother's name. Her name was Betty." He absent-mindedly picked up the empty glasses. "I'll get you another drink."

"No," James said.

"On the house." Tom rose despite their protests, then was gone for several minutes. Two men had sat down at the bar and involved him in a lengthy discussion about the merits of the various whiskeys before they ordered. Then a man called from the other side of the room, asking for another glass of beer. When Tom returned, he set two fresh drinks on the table. "Is she really my mother?" he asked.

"I don't know for sure, but she must be. She told me about your sister. She said you used to torment her," Nell said.

Tom bit his lip, then nodded. "It wasn't right, but my father told me to do it. He hated her. She embarrassed him. Me, too." He looked away, ashamed. "After Nellie died, Papa took me away. He told me that my mother was going to die, that the sheriff had arrested her, and she was going to be hanged, that she'd killed Nellie. He said I'd be arrested, too, if we stayed, because I'd been mean to Nellie, that she was a dummy because I'd hit her when I was little. I didn't remember that, but I believed him."

"That's not true. None of it."

"How do you know?"

"Betty told me."

Tom closed his eyes and took a deep breath. "She could have lied."

"I don't think so."

"Then what did happen?"

"It's not my place to say. You'll have to ask Betty."

"I doubt she'd want to see me."

"Of course she would. She's your mother," James told him. He picked up the shot glass but only sipped. "This is your best whiskey, isn't it?"

Tom shrugged. "Maybe you deserve it." He nodded at Nell's glass. "You'll like that sherry better than the other."

She tasted it and decided he was right.

"You really think she'll see me?" Tom asked.

"She'll *see* you if you walk into the café. It's up to you if you want to tell her who you are," James said.

Tom thought that over. A customer called to him to order a drink, but Tom waved him off. "I don't think I can do that, tell her who I am with a bunch of people sitting there. What if she asks me to leave?"

"I'll be there," James said. "You can walk in just before closing. She shuts down at two thirty. Why don't you come by tomorrow."

Tom stood up and started for the bar. "I don't know. It's been a long time. I'll have to think about it. If I decide to do it, I'll meet you there a few minutes before closing." He paused. "But maybe I won't go."

"Please," Nell begged. "Please give her a chance. Give yourself one, too."

Tom went back to the bar, and Nell asked James, "Do you think he'll show up?" She sipped the sherry, thinking she still liked whiskey better.

"Of course he will. You know, he's like those waifs we saw at Elitch's. What they want more than anything in the world is a mother. I think we've done a good deed, Nell. We've brought together a mother and her little boy."

Yes, they had, Nell thought, or at least James had. What a kind, decent man he was. She shivered as she wondered what it would be like to lose your son, then meet him again after twenty years. What would she do if that happened to her?

CHAPTER SIXTEEN

James sat at the café counter, a cup of coffee half full in front of him.
The coffee was cold with a shimmer of oil on top, and when Betty
wasn't looking, Nell threw it out and gave James a fresh cup. He
let that grow cold, too. He was the only customer, and from the
looks Betty sent him, it was obvious she wanted him to leave so
that she could close up.

"That clock right?" he asked. He seemed to have forgotten
the pocket watch he carried in his vest.

"Just as right as the last time you asked," Betty called from the
kitchen. She had long since cleaned the top of the stove and
washed and dried the dirty plates and cups and cooking pots and
put them away, and she had taken off her apron.

"No sign of him. I guess he's not coming," James said in a low
voice to Nell.

She was disappointed. James had done such a kindness in telling Tom about his mother. If Tom didn't show up, Betty would

never know what a good man James was. "Maybe he doesn't have a watch, or he doesn't know where this place is."

"Maybe." James poured sugar into his coffee and stirred it—the third time he had added sugar, and Nell thought the coffee must taste like syrup by now. It was a good thing James wasn't drinking it. He leaned forward and whispered, "If I was going to meet my mother for the first time in fifteen or twenty years, I'd sure know the address. Besides, he told us he'd been by here—that he knows where this place is."

"I guess he doesn't want to come, then." Nell felt sad for Betty as well as Tom. After all those years, how could he stay away? If nothing else, he must be curious. But perhaps he believed the stories his father had told him. It was a good thing they hadn't said anything to Betty about her son. She would have been in turmoil all day and then might have been devastated when he didn't show up.

They heard a clock chime in a tower far away.

"Café's closed," Betty called out. She turned off the light in the kitchen. James gave Nell a look of resignation and shrugged. "Maybe another time," he whispered.

But just then the door opened, and Tom came in. He wore a clean shirt, and it looked as if he'd just been to a barber. His hair was neatly trimmed, and his face was smooth and pink from a shave.

"Café's closed," Betty repeated, not bothering to look at him.

Tom stared at Betty, but her back was turned. He sent a questioning glance at James, who nodded. "I been walking up and down outside, not knowing if I should come in," he whispered. He straightened his tie, then ran his hand across his hair, patting it into place.

"You're too late," Betty said.

"I'm glad you did," Nell whispered back, then spoke up. "You want coffee?"

"Coffee's gone. We're closed," Betty said for the third time.

Tom looked confused. "You didn't tell her?"

"We didn't know if you'd come."

"I guess I didn't either."

Betty came out from the kitchen, her purse over her arm. She stopped when she saw them whispering. "What's going on?"

The three of them exchanged glances, not sure who should speak.

"Nell?" Betty asked. Her voice was sharp. "What are you up to?"

"This is your . . . I mean, we want you to meet someone," Nell said.

"Who's that?"

"Me," Tom said.

"Yeah, who are you?"

Tom started to reply. He opened his mouth, but the words wouldn't come. Sweat was beaded on his lip, and he wiped his hands on his pants. He looked ready to bolt.

"Well?" Betty said, and when the three were silent, she added, "I haven't got all day. What's going on?"

Tom seemed to panic. He took a step backward and said, "Maybe I better go."

He edged toward the door, but Nell grabbed his arm and stopped him. She was perspiring, too, and thought this wasn't going well. "Betty, he's somebody you ought to meet," she said again. "He's a bartender at the Windsor Hotel."

"That's nice," Betty said. "He looking for a job as a waiter?

Tell him we don't hire men, only women, and I got a good one right now. Is she planning on quitting? Unless she is, she'd better tell me what she's up to."

Nell took a deep breath and rubbed her palms on her apron. Then she gripped the material in her damp hands. "The bartender . . . he's . . . his name is Tom Buck."

"What?" For a long time, Betty stared at Tom. Then she grabbed the counter and slid onto a stool. Her purse fell to the floor. "Tom Buck?" she repeated, her voice hoarse, shaky. "You're Tom?"

"I . . . I . . ." His voice gave out, and he nodded.

"You're . . . ?" Betty couldn't finish.

Then Tom said in a soft voice, "Mama?"

Betty stared without saying anything.

"I'm your son. At least I think I am. They say I am." Tom looked wretched, as if he still might flee.

"He must be," Nell added. "He's the same age, and he looks like—"

Betty held up her hand to stop Nell. She began to shake. "I know who he is. I should have recognized him, but I never thought I'd ever see him again."

Tom opened and closed his mouth a few times, before saying, "Me either. I thought you were dead. Papa told me you were dead."

"He would have. Does he know you're here? Did Foster send you?" Suddenly Betty looked wary.

"I don't know where he is," Tom said quickly. "I ran off as soon as I was old enough. I'd have looked for you, but like I said, he told me you were dead."

"I thought he'd taken you a long way away, back east somewhere."

"Not so far. Just to Pueblo."

"If I'd known . . . I would have looked for you, but I didn't know where. And I didn't know if you'd want me." Betty began to cry.

Tom rushed to her and got down on his knees. "Mama, is it you? Mama?"

"Tommy," Betty said. "My little boy."

"I cried for you. I didn't want to go away. Papa said you didn't want me anymore, not after Nellie died. He said it was my fault and you didn't love me. You only loved Nellie."

"That's not true. I always loved you. But you didn't like me. And you were cruel to Nellie." She reached out her hand, holding it over Tom's head before she touched his hair with the tip of one finger. Tom's hair was ginger-colored and curly, like her own, and she ran her hand through it.

"I didn't want to be. Papa said Nellie was a dummy and I had to treat her like one. I tried to be nice. Once I gave her half an apple, and Papa saw me do it, and he knocked the apple out of my hand and slapped me down, said I wasn't to waste food on such as her. He hit her, too, for taking it. Papa said you spoiled her because you didn't care about him or me."

"And you believed him?" James asked.

"He was only a little boy," Nell said. She had watched the scene with more emotion than she'd expected, wondering what she'd do in Betty's place.

Tom stood then and stepped behind his mother, his hand on her shoulder. Nell thought the scene was too intimate, and she went into the kitchen and lighted the stove to make coffee. She filled a teakettle with water and ground the beans. When the water was hot enough, she poured it over the grounds in a pot and let it steep. James came into the kitchen and took out cups. They felt like intruders. "Maybe we should leave," James whispered.

"Not yet." Nell put her hand on James's arm. "Betty might need me." Nell wasn't sure that was true, but she didn't feel right leaving her friend.

"You didn't say good-bye," Betty told Tom.

"I didn't know we were leaving," Tom replied. "Papa took me to the depot, and we got on the train. We didn't take our clothes with us. I had to leave my jackknife behind and even my sack of marbles." He swallowed. "And the bear. Remember you cut up an old coat and made a bear out of it for me? That hurt me the most, not taking it. I loved that bear."

"I have it," Betty said softly. "I kept it all this time."

Tom took a deep breath, then blurted out, "Papa said the sheriff arrested you for killing Nellie and that they'd punish me, too, because I'd been mean to her. He said they were going to hang you. He said he didn't want me to see you hang."

"Hang me?" Betty looked at her son in surprise. "I never hurt Nellie. I protected her. Your father was the one who beat her that day. People saw it. There were witnesses. He beat her until she was senseless. She never woke up. Someone went for the sheriff. He arrested your father. The only reason he got away with you was because the sheriff said he could go to the funeral."

"Papa killed Nellie?" Tom was astounded. "I thought you did it."

"It was your father."

"Did you ever try to find me?"

"I would have, but how could I? I didn't know where you'd gone."

Tom sat down on a stool next to Betty, his head in his hands. Nell busied herself pouring coffee into the cups. She started to carry them into the café, but James stopped her and nodded his head at Tom, who was shaking with silent sobs. "Wait," James mouthed.

Nell set down the cups and leaned against the drainboard. She started to cry, too, and she placed her fingers over her eyes to stop the tears. James put his arms around her, and Nell leaned her head against his shoulder. Nell loved Betty, and she was shaky with emotion. When her tears stopped, Nell looked up at James and whispered, "This is all because of you. I don't know how to thank you."

James shut his eyes for a moment, as if he, too, were taken up with feelings. "*We* did it. If you hadn't told me about Betty, if you hadn't cared so much about her, I never would have connected her with Tom Buck. I didn't even know Betty's last name until you told me."

"It was you who did it. You are an extraordinary man," Nell said, and she thought how true that was. She had never known anyone so thoughtful. In that moment she loved him. She wanted a life with James. He was her future. Nell leaned her head against his shoulder, thinking how comfortable she felt touching him.

Tom had stopped crying. With a final look at James, Nell picked up the coffee and a pitcher of cream and carried them out of the kitchen, setting them down on the counter. The four were silent as they drank the coffee. When they were finished, Nell took the cups back into the kitchen and said she would wash them in the morning. Betty should be alone with her son now, and Nell hung up her apron and picked up her pocketbook. "I'll see you in the morning, Betty," she said as she walked to the door, James behind her.

Just as she did, a man came into the café and asked, "You still open?"

"We closed a few minutes ago," Betty told him.

"Sign says open. All's I need is a bowl of chili and some crackers."

"It's shut, bub," Tom said, pushing the man outside. "Mama says it's shut."

Nell smiled and turned around the sign so that it read CLOSED. Then she switched off the light and shut the door, leaving Betty with her son in the shuttered café.

As they walked down Seventeenth Street, James grasped Nell's arm and held it tight, and he did not let go. "Betty should be pleased with you."

"And with you, too."

"Oh, she doesn't like me."

"She does now."

"And you?" James asked. "Do you like me?"

"Of course I do."

"Really, really like me?"

That was an odd thing to ask, and Nell was cautious. She didn't intend to make her feelings known until James did. *If* he did. "What do you mean?"

"Oh, nothing. I was just hoping you would think I'm a grand fellow."

"Anyone who brings together a mother and son has got to be swell."

James grinned at her. "You are being careful. I intend you should like me a great deal. More than like."

Nell shivered. She and James hadn't known each other very long, not even three months, but sometimes it didn't take long. She'd been attracted to James that very first day, and in just a short time, she had fallen in love with him. But of course, she couldn't tell him so. He had to declare himself first. Was he asking *her* to?

He squeezed her arm and said, "We have done a good deed today. Are you as pleased as I am?"

"I am."

"Then I believe we should celebrate. What say I take you to dinner at the Brown Palace Hotel? It is the finest place I know. And you are the finest girl that ever was."

Her uniform was wrinkled and soiled, and she would have to change clothes first, Nell told him. She would meet him at the hotel later on.

"I won't allow you to be away from me that long. I shall walk you home, and when you are ready, I'll take you to the Brown."

There was no reason he shouldn't come with her, Nell decided. It was perfectly proper for a gentleman to wait in the sitting room of the boardinghouse while she changed her clothes. Nell had been reluctant to introduce James to Mrs. Bonner for fear she would gossip about him with Betty, but after what had happened that afternoon, Nell no longer feared Betty's disapproval.

They walked along arm in arm, not in any hurry, stopping to smell honeysuckle that hung over a fence and then to admire the hollyhock dolls a ragged little girl was making. A sign in front of a cup read DOLL 1 CENT. It was empty.

James grinned and reached into his pocket. Just as he did, a well-dressed boy came up and handed the girl a nickel. Then he ran off before the girl could give him a doll.

"I should like to have a son as compassionate as that," James remarked, after he dropped a coin into the cup.

Without knowing it, Nell tightened her hand on his arm. He would someday, she hoped.

CHAPTER SEVENTEEN

Despite whatever Betty might have told her, Mrs. Bonner was charmed by James and sat with him while Nell slipped out of her uniform and donned a clean white dress.

"White is so becoming to you, so pure and fine," James said when they were out on the street again. He had stepped behind her so that he walked next to the street in case a wagon splashed mud onto the sidewalk.

Nell shuddered at the word "pure," wondering what James would think of her if she told him about Buddy. *When* she told him, she thought, for if he were interested in marriage, he would have to know. As much as she wanted to wed, needed to wed, Nell would not deceive a man who wanted her as his wife. James would be shocked, of course. He had called her pure. But she put such dark thoughts out of her mind. She was being presumptuous. She did not know that James would propose. If he did, she would worry then about the consequences.

When they reached the Brown Palace, James led her to one

of the leather-covered chairs in the lobby while he headed to his room, saying he would change his collar and cuffs before he escorted her in to dinner. "You are staying here, then?" Nell asked, a little apprehensive.

"I prefer this hotel to all others, although I don't always choose it. The customers I am seeing this trip like to come here," he said, ignoring any hint of impropriety.

When she was alone, Nell studied her gloves for a minute, taking one off and straightening the fingers, then putting it back on. She had worn them to the Windsor and realized one was not quite clean. She rubbed at a speck of dirt on the back of it. She should have washed the gloves the night before. Mrs. Bonner had taught her the trick of washing her hands with her gloves on. It was far more effective than dipping the gloves into a basin of water.

After a time, Nell lifted her head and stared at the stained-glass lobby ceiling high above her. Then she studied the people, women in afternoon dresses, men in summer suits and soft collars. A man in a Stetson and boots stood at the cigar stand, his back to her, and for a moment, she imagined he was Buddy. But the man turned around, and Nell saw he was an old rancher whose face was etched from the sun. What if he had been Buddy? Would she have ignored him? Or maybe James would have come down just then, and she would have sent Buddy a triumphant look as she rose to meet her handsome friend. She smiled to think she had left Buddy in the past. He didn't matter anymore. He was only a small ache, like a scratch on her heart, that didn't hurt so much now that she cared about James.

"You're smiling," James said. Nell had not noticed his approach.

"I was just watching that rancher over there. Look at the

way he walks. I think every cowboy must be a little bit bow-legged."

"It's good you rode sidesaddle, then."

"Oh, but I didn't," Nell told him, thinking she liked being truthful about herself now. James ought to know who she really was.

He took her arm, and they rode the elevator to the dining room, with its stucco columns and onyx wainscoting, so different from the heaviness of the old Windsor Hotel. "Would you like a sherry—dry sherry, as I recall?"

Nell started to nod, then stopped. She might as well be honest. "I would rather have whiskey."

"A shot?" James asked, surprised.

"No, a cocktail with whiskey in it."

"Another habit from your cowboy days."

Nell wasn't sure that he approved.

"There aren't a lot of ladies' drinks on a ranch. It was whiskey or water."

"And next you'll want another cigarette?" James frowned.

"No, I'm really not so fond of tobacco. Just sometimes."

"To show me you are independent, I think. I will have to get used to a lady who thinks for herself."

"Do you not like it?" She hoped James didn't think she'd gone too far. "Do you think I'm terribly fast?"

"No, I quite like it. You are just the right speed. I believe that . . . that incident in the café when I met you must have made you timid, and now you are yourself again. I think highly of a lady who can be unconventional."

Nell glanced down at her hands. Sometimes James overwhelmed her. She couldn't imagine with all the beautiful, stylish women he met—she'd seen the way women looked at him—that he cared for her. She stole a glance at him, thinking again how handsome he was, how lucky she was to be with him.

The waiter brought their drinks, giving Nell's whiskey cocktail to James and his beer to Nell. She switched them around and saw the waiter glance at James out of the corner of his eye. "Madam," he said, giving her a lady's menu with no prices on it.

James raised his glass. "To mothers and sons," he said after the waiter left.

"And to bringing them together," Nell added.

"It was a fortunate coincidence, just like my meeting you." They smiled at each other until James picked up his menu. "The quail is awfully good. I recommend it."

"Then I shall have it."

"You will let me make the decision? Good. I prefer a little independence in a woman, but not so much that a wife believes she should be in charge."

Wife? Was James testing her? Nell shivered and didn't answer.

"I would not want a wife who tried to instruct me," he added.

Nor would she want a husband who would instruct *her,* Nell thought. James was not like that, however. She still said nothing.

"You didn't reply," James said.

"Are you testing me?" Nell asked. They were flirting, and she wanted to stop because it made her uncomfortable.

"Perhaps I am. You are full of contradictions, and I do not always understand them," he said and turned to the menu.

Their suppers arrived, and they ate without talking. After the plates were cleared, James ordered a dessert. The waiter brought it on a cart and made a great to-do of pouring brandy over a cake and lighting it. Then the waiter set down tiny glasses of a golden liqueur. James raised his glass and caught Nell's eye. She thought he would toast Betty and her son again, but instead, he said, "To us. To a long life for both of us. Together."

Nell held her glass in the air, watching the reflection of the candles on the cut crystal. The liquid was the color of James's eyes.

"You won't drink to that?" James asked.

"I'm not sure what it means."

"It means I just proposed. I just asked you to marry me."

Nell's hand shook, shook so hard that she had to set down the glass. "You're asking me to marry you?"

"I know we haven't known each other very long, but how long does it take to know you are in love?"

"With me?"

James laughed as he glanced around the room. "Who else?"

Nell was flustered. Of course she was thrilled. She had hoped James had fallen in love with her as she had with him. Still, she had supposed that even if he proposed, James would not do so this quickly.

"It has been such a good day that I thought we should top it off with a little excitement of our own. I want it to be a day you will remember for more than one reason." He reached across the table for Nell's hand. "I love you very much," he said. "I want you for a wife, and I want us to have a family with very many children."

Suddenly Nell's eyes were wet, and James said, "I hope those are tears of happiness, that they mean you will say yes."

"You don't know me. There is so much I need to tell you before you will want me as a wife. Perhaps you will change your mind when you know."

"You know I love you, and I believe you love me back. Does anything else matter?"

"I think it does." Nell took a sip from the small glass. She had spilled a little of the liquid, and the stem of the glass was sticky.

"Then tell me," he said. "I do not think anything could make me change my mind. But I do not want there to be secrets between us. If you think you must, then tell me about yourself." He paused. "It does not matter if I am not the first man you have loved." He grinned. "If that is the case, I will think only how lucky I am that I won you instead of the other fellow."

James reached across the table and took the glass from Nell's hand. "Tell me, dearest."

He had never before used that term of endearment, and Nell closed her eyes for a moment. When she opened them, she said, "There was a man, a cowboy in New Mexico." Across the room, someone dropped a glass that shattered on the floor, but Nell didn't flinch. She didn't even turn away but instead kept on staring at James. "I am not an innocent girl," she said, and then she told James about Buddy, told him everything, about the night in the blizzard, how they had fought, and she had fled, and he had married another girl. And the aftermath of it all.

Sometime during the telling, James let go of Nell's hand. He picked up his glass and drained it, and when the waiter appeared to ask if he wanted more, James waved him away without looking up. When Nell was finished speaking, finished telling her story, James stared at her for a long time. "Do you still love him?" he asked at last.

"No," and Nell was sure then that she did not.

"You have forgotten him?"

"I will never forget him. But he is past. I no longer care about him." She paused and added, "I haven't since I met you."

James smiled. His smile was warm, and it went into his eyes, which sparkled like the crystal glass in front of him. "I do not think you have told me anything that makes me change my mind about you. You are still very dear to me. I want to care for you and our children. So I ask you again, Nell, will you marry me?"

Nell felt a great surge of happiness. She had wanted a husband, and now she had found not only a man who wanted to marry her but one she could love wholeheartedly, a man who accepted her with all her faults and mistakes. Her heart was so full that she could barely murmur, "If you still want me, then I would be proud to marry you."

James reached across the table for her hand and brought it to his lips. "My dearest love," he said. "I want us to marry very soon." Then he stood, and still holding Nell's hand, he said, "Come."

Nell thought he would take her home then. It had been a wonderful evening, a wonderful day, one she would remember all her life. They went into the hotel lobby, James holding Nell's arm now. She turned toward the door, but he held her and nodded at the elevator. "Please," he said. His dark eyes glistened, and Nell thought they were filled with tears. "I want to hold you in my arms. I don't think your landlady would approve, and the café is not the place. Come with me."

Nell knew what he was asking. He wanted more than just to hold her, and she demurred. "Not yet," she said.

"I would have waited, but after what you told me . . . Is there any reason we should not express our love to each other now? You are so precious to me."

Nell looked into his face. It was open, loving. He was right. What reason was there to wait? For a moment, she thought about the consequences. What if she conceived? But they would be married in weeks, days maybe. It didn't matter. And she desired him, too. Suddenly she wanted to be in his arms. More than anything, she wanted him to hold her, to caress her, to whisper he loved her. She ached to have him touch her. She looked at him wistfully and then nodded.

James smiled and, gripping her arm, led her to the elevator and his room upstairs. "We will think of this as our wedding night," he said.

She did not stay the night with James. Mrs. Bonner would be worried—and shocked—if she did not return to her room. So, late in the evening, they dressed, and they walked hand in hand through the dark streets to her boardinghouse. As they lingered under a gaslight near Nell's front door, James held her close and whispered, "Oh, my dear. It was so much better than I'd imagined. Let us be married at once."

Nell nodded and kissed him. She went inside and turned out the lamp that Mrs. Bonner had left burning. As she quietly climbed the stairs to her room, she thought how lucky she was to have found James. She shivered as she thought of what had happened between them. She undressed and lay in her own bed, unable to sleep. She remembered the warmth of James beside her on the cool, starched hotel sheets, the way his body fit hers, the joy that they brought each other. She knew James was a man she could love forever.

CHAPER EIGHTEEN

When James stopped at the café the next morning, he told Nell he would be gone for two weeks. He didn't want to stay away that long, he said, but something had come up. He would be thinking of her every minute he was away, he promised. And although he wouldn't be with her, he would send her an expression of his love.

Nell wondered if that meant she could expect flowers, or perhaps a piece of jewelry. But the package that arrived was large, and heavy. When she opened it, Nell found a length of China silk brocade, printed with violets. The fabric was very fine, and James intended it for Nell's wedding dress. They would be married soon after he returned. They would not have a formal wedding, of course. Neither of them cared for that. They would be married by a judge with only Betty and Tom as attendants. And her grandparents, Nell said. She insisted they be there. James would be part of her family.

Nell ran her hand over the silk, which she knew was expensive, then crumpled it. When she released it, the silk was not wrinkled but held its shape. She had never stitched material so elegant and was reluctant to cut it. James had included a paper pattern for a gown. There were pinpricks in the pattern, and Nell thought it must have come from a buyer at one of the stores that stocked James's fabrics. The pattern might even have been for a dress used in a display. "If you don't care for it, you must choose your own style," he wrote in the note that accompanied the package. James had such wonderful taste, Nell thought. Nell loved the pattern and was pleased that James knew what style would flatter her.

Nell confided in Betty that James had proposed. Betty said she was happy for Nell, but she did not seem excited. She was distracted by Tom, Nell thought. Although mother and son were happy that they had been reunited, their relationship was shaky, and they were sometimes at odds. Betty remembered things that Tom had done, meannesses to both her and her daughter, and she told Nell she was sure that Tom, too, was dealing with conflicts from his boyhood. His father had told him so often that his mother didn't love him that he found it difficult to accept her affection.

He often came into the café at closing, and he and Betty sat there talking until it was time for Tom to go to work. Sometimes as she cleaned up the kitchen, Nell heard their voices rise. Once Tom stomped out, but he came back a day or two later. Nell wondered what it would be like to meet a parent you thought was dead. After the initial joy, there would be disappointment, recriminations, most likely guilt. How did you connect with a mother or father you had not seen in years—or maybe ever? What excuses did you make, or truths reveal? Nell brooded over Betty's situation, wishing she could say something to cheer her friend. But what? Betty and Tom had to work things out for themselves.

Nell wrote to her grandparents to tell them she would be married and wanted them to come to Denver for the ceremony, but they replied that they did not dare leave the farm that time of year. They suggested Nell visit them on her wedding trip, and she thought that was a grand idea.

She told Mrs. Bonner she was engaged, and the woman busied herself making nightgowns and underwear for the bride and helped Nell cut out the pieces for her wedding gown. The sewing machine needle was too harsh for the brocade James had sent. So in the evenings, she and Nell sat in the parlor, stitching the seams by hand, Nell thinking this would be the most beautiful wedding dress ever created.

James did indeed return in two weeks. Nell heard the door open, but the café was crowded, and she did not look up. It was hot in the kitchen. Her hair had come undone, and the steam made it curl around her face, spilling into her eyes. Someone had slopped coffee onto her apron, and it had soaked through to her skin. The customers had been hot and sweaty and hard to please. One had berated her because his toast was too dark, and another complained that it was too light. She would be glad when the day was done and she could go home and take a cool bath, then work on her wedding dress. She was setting down platters of ham and eggs when she spotted James. He was stylish in a white linen summer suit with his gold watch chain draped across the vest, and he smiled at her.

Suddenly Nell forgot about the hard day. She felt cool and clean, the way she had that time in Elitch Gardens when James had said he would like to paint her among the flowers. He smiled at her, and Nell felt a warmth that didn't come from the hot kitchen.

A customer waved frantically because Nell had forgotten to bring him syrup, and another made an elaborate gesture and pointed to his cup. Nell ignored them. Instead, she smiled back at James and said, "Good morning, sir, would you like coffee?" When James nodded, she asked, "Do you want cream for your coffee?" James took his coffee black. He had said that first day that he did not want cream, but Nell had not remembered and had asked him about cream the second time he came into the café. Now it was a joke between them, and Nell thought she would ask James that on the morning after their wedding—and every morning after that.

"I have found a place for us to rent," he whispered. "It needs only your approval. I am anxious to show it to you."

"I can't leave now. It will have to wait until we close." Nell leaned close and confided, "Poor Betty. I don't know where she will find a waitress to replace me."

"Why would you quit? You know how much I will be away. You would be bored by yourself."

"I thought . . ."

"We will talk about it later. First I want you to see the house. It is small, but just right for us and a little one."

Despite herself, Nell blushed.

As soon as the café closed, James took Nell to see the house. It was indeed small and a little shabby. Nell hid her disappointment. Perhaps it was all James could afford. She realized she did not know how much he made. Of course, he was a salesman and had to travel, and she supposed he had heavy expenses. Did his employer pay for his train fare and for his hotel rooms and meals, or did James have to cover those costs from his pay-check? There was so much to learn about her future husband.

"If you don't like it, we shall find a more suitable place," James said.

"Oh, but I do," Nell insisted. She was not helpless. She could paper the walls and put up pictures, plant a flower garden, raise vegetables, and even install a chicken coop. Mrs. Bonner would give her the chicks. "It is a honeymoon cottage."

She glanced at the tiny fireplace. It was ugly and dirty, but she would scrub it and hang James's painting of the orange vio-lets over it. She would surprise him, just as he had surprised her by bringing the painting into the café one day. He had placed it in a paper sack, and she thought at first that the sack contained some of his samples. "For you," he said, a little embarrassed.

Nell pulled out the painting and gasped. "It's perfect. God didn't make orange violets, but you did!"

"Do you like it?"

"Of course I like it. I love it!"

James shrugged. "It's rather amateurish."

"Hardly! It's finer than the paintings we saw at the art show."

Now, she thought, the painting would be just the right touch in their living room.

"I wanted our home to be private—and not too expensive. I know you are not a spendthrift. And if you are working, we can save up money for our little family," James said.

"Of course." Nell would do what James asked, although she would have preferred staying at home.

"I have given much thought to this," he told her, and took a small box from his pocket and opened it. Inside was a thin gold wedding band that was very plain. "I have noticed you do not wear much jewelry, so I thought you would want something simple." He paused. "This was my mother's."

"Oh," Nell gasped, taking the ring from the box. It was a little worn, but she didn't mind, since it was a family heirloom. "It is just right." He slipped the ring onto her finger.

"Leave it there," James told her. "There is no need to wait until the ceremony to wear it." Then he took money from his pocket and handed it to Nell, telling her to buy what she needed for the kitchen. She wanted to ask about the furniture, because the pieces in the house were worn and ugly. But she would not let James think she was careless with his money. She would spend the money she had saved from her waitress job to replace the furnishings. And she would buy nice things. They were to last a lifetime.

James took Nell's hand and kissed the finger that wore his ring. Then he kissed the palm of her hand. He put his arms around her and led her to the bed and threw aside the cover. The mattress was tattered and dirty, and he spread his coat over it, then gently pushed Nell onto the bed. "We'll be married in just a week or two," James said as he fumbled with her skirt and petticoat. "I do not think I can wait."

She should tell him no, Nell thought, but she wanted him too much. Besides, they had already had their wedding night. Nell put her arms around his neck and pulled him to her.

Late one afternoon a few days later, Nell sat under the lilacs in Mrs. Bonner's garden stitching on the wedding dress. The blooms were Persian lilacs, very dark purple, and fragrant in the breeze that scattered tiny flowers across the pale silk. Nell blew them off, afraid if she scattered them with her hand, they would stain the material. Because the fabric was fragile, she stitched slowly, careful that the needle did not pull the threads. With the wedding only days away, when James returned from a business trip, Nell would have to hurry to finish the dress, would need to stop dreaming and concentrate on her sewing.

The house was ready. Nell had bought new bedding and a mattress, because the old one was so stained. Bright throws covered the sofa and armchair and would have to do until they bought new furniture. She had scrubbed the grime off the table and chairs, had cleaned the house from top to bottom so that it smelled fresh. She had hung the picture, too. James had yet to see it.

Nell had even planted rose cuttings and seeds that Mrs. Bonner gave her. With children playing next door and neighbors who were friendly, the house seemed more like a home now, and Nell was beginning to like it. Later, of course, when they had children of their own, they would move into something better, but the cottage would do for a time.

Since he was away, James had left the decorating to her. He had made other decisions, however. They would be married on the following Sunday in a judge's quarters. Then, after a wedding supper with Tom and Betty, they would spend their wedding night in the Brown Palace. James had arranged to get a week off from work so that they could take a wedding trip to Kansas, where he would meet Nell's family. Then he would settle her in the little house. He would spend as much time as he could with Nell, but his job required him to travel. Perhaps when he moved up in the company—and he was being considered for a promotion even then, he confided—he would live in Denver permanently. She would have to understand that she would be alone a good bit of the time. That was another reason she should stay on at Buck & Betty's. Nell understood. In fact, she agreed with the arrangement, because after she thought about it, she knew she would be lonely all day in the little house without James.

As she sat in the yard, Nell closed her eyes for a moment, feeling content and happy, perhaps happier than she had ever been. The sound of bees in the lilacs made Nell think of the Kansas farm, the wheat, amber-gold in the sun, the wheat field against the irregular fields of oats and alfalfa, like the patches in a crazy quilt; the red hummingbirds with their bills deep in the orange flowers of the trumpet vine, the cats, proud and arrogant as sultans, hissing at Old Bill as the dog lazed in the grass.

She pictured her grandfather pumping water over his head to cool off, drenching his shirt and overalls, drops of water clinging to his beard; her grandmother in the leafy shade of the bench beneath the cottonwood tree, shelling bright green peas into a white enamel bowl. Nell missed her family and wished they could come to her wedding. But she would see them soon. She would take James to meet them, and they would love him as she did.

A shadow passed over her face, and Nell looked up, expecting to see Mrs. Bonner. Instead, a woman holding a box stood in front of her. "Hello," Nell said, thinking the woman was someone inquiring about a room. Nell would be leaving the boardinghouse in a few days, and her landlady had already put out a ROOMS TO LET sign. "Mrs. Bonner has gone out."

"I came to see you," the woman said.

Nell put aside the brocade dress. The gown was almost completed. The seams were finished, but there was still fine sewing to be done on it. "Do I know you?" Nell asked, standing.

"No."

A little girl of about two peeped out from behind her mother, and Nell said, "Hello, what's your name?"

The girl stared at her and didn't answer.

"You're a very pretty little girl. You must have a pretty name."

The girl still didn't reply, and the woman moved as if hiding the child behind her skirts.

"I do not know that Mrs. Bonner will allow a child, but yours is so sweet. Perhaps she'll reconsider."

The woman shrugged. She was younger than Nell, but her face was worn and a little hard, her eyes black, almost beady. "I don't need a room. Like I said, I come because of you."

Nell was confused. She'd never seen the woman before and couldn't imagine what she wanted. Was she looking for a job at Buck & Betty's? Nell didn't think so. "Why are you here?"

"Are you the one marrying James Hamilton?"

Nell smiled. "Why, yes." She indicated her sewing. "This is my wedding dress. Beautiful, is it not?"

"So he give that material to you, too. He tell you he likes violets, did he?" the woman replied, her voice heavy with sarcasm.

"Who are you?" Nell demanded. She reached for a handkerchief—James's handkerchief—and touched it to her brow.

"My name is Emily Hamilton."

Nell frowned. "You're James's sister, then? I know two of his sisters died, Beatrice and Anna. He never mentioned a third one."

"Oh, is that what he said? He loves to tell that story. Got you all dewy-eyed, didn't it? Made you want to give him comfort. He told it to me, too, the scamp. That's why her name is Beatrice." She indicated the little girl. "Fact is, he never had no sisters that died, because he never had no sisters. Only brothers, and they're no better than he is." She paused, and her face grew hard. "I'm his wife."

"His what?" Nell gripped the arm of the chair. Her knees were shaky, and she needed to sit, but she did not want the woman looking down at her.

"His wife. Me and James was married three years ago. He promised I'd be the last one. I made that hanky for him, red cross-stitch with his initials—if they are his initials. His brothers got a different last name. Maybe he made his up."

Nell dropped the handkerchief. "James is divorced?"

"He tell you that?"

"No." James had never mentioned being married, and Nell had never asked. She'd just assumed . . .

"Oh, we're married, all right, even if maybe it's not legal. There was never no divorce."

"I don't understand."

The woman set down the box and arched her back. She was pregnant. "I guess you don't, do you? Well, the truth of it is that's because James already had him a wife when we got married, two of them, maybe more for all I know."

The idea was monstrous, and Nell said, "I don't believe you."

"Ask him, why don't you. Ask him why he travels around so much. He has to visit Agnes in Wyoming and Mary Beth in Idaho. I think there's another in Utah, but I don't know for sure. He has plenty of money, but with all us wives, there won't be much for you. I bet he wants you to keep on working. He's a big spender until after the wedding. Then it's root, hog, or die." She looked down at Nell's hand clutching the dress. "That silk's the same he gave me for my wedding dress. Didn't you ever wonder about the pin marks in the pattern? I put them there. And that old ring you've got on. Did he say it was his mother's? It's mine. I knew when it disappeared he was strutting around again." She took the little girl's hand. "This is his, and this one, too." She pointed to her stomach. The woman stretched again, then sank onto a chair. Nell sat down, too.

"If what you say is true—and I'm not saying I believe you— why would he marry me?"

"Oh, he can't help himself. He keeps falling in love with women. And children," the woman continued. "He'd have a hundred of them if he could. The last wife before me was a widow with two kiddies. He thought she was the gold mine." Emily gave a laugh that was more of a bark. "I bet he rescued you from something. He likes to do that. Me, he found me when my ma died. I was an orphan. It makes him feel good, helping women like that, makes them beholden. Me and Agnes talked about it. She got knocked down by a wagon, got her arm broke. He was standing on the street and took her to a doctor. I bet he was real nice and didn't rush you, didn't try to take advantage of you, didn't move too fast, but then . . . Well, you ain't a virgin no more is my guess."

Nell studied the woman a long time. She might have been attractive once, but she was too worn now to be pretty. "Did you know about the other wives when you married him, I mean if what you're saying is true?"

"Oh, it's true, all right. I'm thinking you know now it's true. I knew about them, and I didn't care, because, like I say, he promised I'd be the last. He's a yellow dog, but I love him. Then you come along. I knowed it when he painted that picture with the orange flowers, and then it was gone."

Nell cringed to think how she had already hung the picture in the little house.

"Truth be told, I despise you. You got no right to take him away from me. The others, they don't care about you, but I do."

"How did you find me? How did you know?"

"I seen a letter you wrote him. It come in the mail, and I had a feeling, so I opened it. I shouldn't have. James don't let nobody mess with his mail. He'd strike me down if he knew."

Nell remembered there had been a return address on the package of silk James had sent, and she had written to thank him.

"That letter was wrote real pretty, with all them big words. I burned it. He never seen it." She stood. "I come to tell you so's you'll know, so's you'll quit him. But if you don't, well, I brung you a cake to welcome you to the family. Us wives has got to stick together. You'll be needing us." She smirked at Nell then. "Don't you dare tell James I was here." She set the box on the chair next to Nell, then took the little girl's hand and was gone.

Nell sat for a long time, staring at the wedding dress. Was the woman some crazy person, or was what she had said true? Nell pondered the question. Then, slowly, she realized the woman had indeed spoken the truth. Although they were engaged, Nell knew nothing about James, not who his employer was or how much he made or even where he lived. He had explained his absences as sales trips, but he'd never said where he had gone. The night he proposed he'd told her he wanted there to be no secrets between them, but James's life, she realized now, was all about secrets.

Nell began to shake, and she put her arms around herself. She had been too anxious to marry, too easily taken in. Why hadn't she asked him to explain his long absences? She had simply accepted that they were sales trips. Why had he refused to tell her about himself or his family? Perhaps all this explained why he didn't care about what she had confessed, about what had happened with Buddy. Nell put her hands to her face and began to cry. She had thought they would have a wonderful life together. He was so kind and would have made a good husband and father. For a second, she wondered if she might go ahead and marry him. She had met no one else. If the other wives could accept each other, could she? She loved James. Despite what she had just discovered, she still loved him. But the idea of marrying him now sickened her.

She looked down at the box Emily had left, and opened it. Inside was a chocolate cake, a pretty cake with thick, dark frosting. She could give it to Mrs. Bonner to serve for dinner, but the idea repulsed her. She would never eat that cake, and neither would anyone else. She picked up the cardboard box with the cake inside and threw it into the chicken yard. The chickens would eat the cake as well as the box. There would be nothing left of either one.

Then she wadded up the wedding dress and went to her room. She would have to face James, ask him why he would do such a thing, and listen to his pretty words as he tried to talk her into marrying him. She knew he would do that. Even with the other wives, he loved her, she believed. Then she would have to tell Betty, who had been right all along about James. And she would let Mrs. Bonner know that the wedding was off, give back the delicate clothing the landlady had made for her.

Nell did not go down for supper that evening, and later Mrs. Bonner brought her a tray. The old lady's face was wet with tears, and Nell wondered if somehow she had discovered the truth about James, knew there would be no wedding and had come to offer comfort.

Nell was so immersed in her own sorrow that at first she didn't respond to Mrs. Bonner's sadness, but when the old woman said nothing about James, Nell asked what the trouble was.

"I am sorry to tell you, but you loved them."

Nell frowned, not understanding.

"I went to gather the eggs, and I found them."

"Found what?"

"The chickens. They're dead. All of them. The chickens are all dead."

CHAPTER NINETEEN

"How dreadful!" June shuddered. "That woman was going to poison Nell!"

Her grandmother shrugged. "That's what it looked like. Of course, maybe it was something else that killed the chickens, a virus perhaps. But the coincidence was just too great."

"What did James say? Oh, don't you wish you'd been hiding behind the door when Nell confronted him."

"She never saw him again. Why would she? She felt stupid, so damn stupid!" Ellen paused as she ran her fingers over a creamy white square in the quilt. Everything the woman said made sense to Nell, she told June. It explained James's absences and why he never really told her about himself. She'd been a fool not to press him, of course, but he'd protected her from that masher, so she wasn't very objective about him. She just believed he was wonderful. And she loved him. Ellen looked off toward the mountains and shook her head. "He was so handsome, so charming, so understanding. She cared as much for him as she had for Buddy. So Nell was devastated. Again."

"Do you think if that woman hadn't shown up, James eventually would have told Nell about his wives?"

"Who knows? I think he would have had to." Or else Nell might have found out on her own, Ellen added. Perhaps he thought that by then, she'd be pregnant and wouldn't leave him—or couldn't leave him. Indeed, how could a pregnant woman support herself? It wasn't as if she could have gone back to her grandparents. What would people in Harveyville have said? Ellen picked up a brittle cottonwood leaf and crushed it in her hand. "After all those years, I still shiver at the thought of what might have happened to her. Nell took the wedding dress and her clothes and the Indian blanket, the one Buddy had given her. She couldn't leave it behind. And she went back home to Kansas."

"Did she leave James a letter then?"

"Nell thought about that, but what could she say? Maybe 'Give my love to your wife—or wives.' She wrote a note to Betty, however, telling her everything and apologizing for running away like that. She knew that Betty would confront James— she'd relish it, in fact. Betty would get revenge, if that was what Nell was after.

"That wasn't the only reason she left so abruptly. Nell was afraid that wife would come back. Or maybe one of the other ones would. So she knew she had to leave fast. When she found out the poison didn't work, Emily might have shot Nell or run her down with a wagon. The woman was demented. And frankly, Nell was a little afraid of James. He certainly wasn't the man she'd fallen in love with. Who knows what he might have done.

He could have been cruel or vindictive. So Nell took her things and was gone by morning. She put her Buck & Betty's key in an envelope, with the note to Betty, and slid it under the door of the café on her way to the station. Then she took the first train back to Kansas. Nell felt awful about leaving Betty like that, but she knew Betty would understand. While Betty didn't know James was already married, she had always suspected there was something off about him."

June asked if James tried to contact Nell after she left.

"I don't think so." Nell had asked Betty not to tell him where she'd gone, and she'd never mentioned Harveyville to him, had only said her grandparents lived in Kansas. "Besides, why would he try to get in touch with her? How could he explain what a yellow dog he was?"

"And she never saw him again."

"No, but she did see Betty." Ellen smiled to think of what had happened. Nell had returned a long time later. She was in Denver and went by the café, which was still operating. Betty remembered her. It had been years since they'd seen each other, but Betty recognized her right off and asked, "Come for your wages? I didn't know where to send them." She told Nell that James had come into the restaurant the morning she left. He asked where she was, and Betty teased him along. Betty had read the letter, so she knew what a bum he was. He asked if she was going to close the café for the wedding. Betty said she hadn't closed it for his other weddings, so why would she close it for this one? "Number three, is it? Number four? Number seventeen? How many other wives do you have, James?" The blood drained out of his face until it was as white as a dish towel. He left, and he never came back.

The telephone rang inside the ranch house, and Ellen said,

"Maybe that's your grandfather." She rose quickly, thinking something might be wrong. Ben had grown careless. Perhaps he had fallen or walked in front of a car and been hit. "Is it Wesley?" she called when she heard Maria answer the phone.

"It's for Miss June. Somebody wants Miss June," Maria yelled back.

June and her grandmother exchanged glances. "You didn't tell anyone I was here, did you?" June asked. "I don't want to talk to Dave."

Ellen shook her head, then turned to Maria. "Do you know who it is?"

"Some woman."

"Probably Mother," June said.

"Most likely," Ellen said. "I don't suppose it was too hard for her to figure out that if you disappeared, you might have come here." She thought of offering to tell Evelyn that June wasn't up to talking but decided against it. June should fight her own battles.

"I'd better get it over with. She'll probably chew me out. I guess I deserve it since it was pretty rotten of me to take off like that without talking it over with her. I guess I owe her an explanation, more than what I told the maid, anyway." June rose and slowly started for the door.

Before June opened the screen, Ellen said, "June."

The girl stopped.

"Don't tell them about your grandfather. They know he's slipping, but they don't know how bad he's gotten. There's no reason for them to worry. I'll talk it over with them later, after I've made some decisions. You concentrate on yourself right now."

June went inside, and Ellen picked up the quilt and began to stitch. If John knew how things stood, he'd show up and make those decisions for them, and Ellen wouldn't have that. She'd make them herself, although not just yet, by God. She put aside thoughts of Ben and wondered instead where James was now, whether he had found another wife and how she got along with Emily. Had Emily tried to poison her, too? Maybe she'd been successful and the police had arrested her. Ellen shuddered. Or maybe Emily had poisoned James. It would serve him right. Was he even still alive?

After a few minutes, June came back and sat down quietly, chewing her thumb.

"Your mother?" Ellen asked.

June nodded.

"Was she angry?"

June looked up. "That's the thing. She wasn't. She didn't even sound disappointed. She said I was young and had plenty of time to get married. She didn't want me to make a mistake that would ruin my life."

"Evelyn's a remarkable woman. I've always liked your mother. John was lucky to marry her." Of course, they had wished that John would marry a western woman who would want to live on a ranch. She and Ben had hoped to pass on the spread to John or to his brother or sister one day. All three had married easterners, however, and moved away. You had to want to be a rancher—the work was too hard if you didn't love it. None of the three children seemed to have ranching blood in them, or maybe they had learned growing up that ranching was just too difficult. Ellen would have to face the reality that one day the spread she and Ben had worked for half a century would go on the market.

"Mom says that Dave's called half a dozen times. She thinks I ought to talk to him."

"Will you?"

"I asked her not to tell him where I am. I said I'd call him when I'm ready."

"If your mother knew you'd come here, perhaps Dave knows, too."

"Maybe. I hope I'm doing the right thing. It's such a muddle." June went to the edge of the porch and looked far off, at the patches of gold aspen among the green pines. Then she turned and sat down next to her grandmother. "Was Nell ever sorry she didn't change her mind and marry Buddy?"

"I suspect she was sometimes."

June laughed. "But I bet she wasn't sorry she didn't marry James."

"No, but still, it took her time to get over him. As I said, she loved him. And being deceived like that, it hurt."

The two sat there for a long time, until Maria came outside and picked up the dinner tray. It was midafternoon now, and clouds had moved across the sun, and the sky was gray against the purple mountains. Dead leaves blew across the porch as if escaping from a brewing storm. "You want hot chocolate?" Maria asked.

Ellen started to say no, but she changed her mind. What harm would a little more chocolate do? "How nice." She turned to June. "Maria makes it with Mexican chocolate and a little cinnamon. It's like liquid velvet, good for a day with fall in the air."

"That sounds perfectly lovely."

"Your grandfather and I used to drink it on winter afternoons."

June studied her grandmother a moment. "I'm sorry he's gotten worse. I can see it."

Ellen nodded, not looking at June.

"He was forgetful when Dave and I were here last summer. When did you first notice it?"

Ellen stuck her needle into the quilt. She didn't know how to answer. Ben's memory loss could have begun two years before, but she couldn't be sure. Little Texas had thrown him in the pasture. That had surprised her, because Little Texas was a good horse and Ben was still quite a cowboy. Maybe the horse had been spooked by a snake. Ben couldn't remember.

"You wrote that Grandpa Ben broke his leg a couple of years ago. You didn't say anything about a head injury."

"We didn't know if there was a head injury at the time. We still don't." Ben might have been developing dementia all along, and she hadn't noticed it. The leg wasn't badly broken, and it wasn't the first time Ben had been bucked off a horse and broken a bone. The real problem was that Ben was alone when the accident happened, and nobody thought to search until Wesley came into the house looking for him. Ben was supposed to help the cowhand doctor one of the calves. Ben wasn't there, so Ellen and Wesley went to the barn and found Little Texas gone.

Even then, Ellen didn't worry too much, because Ben might have stopped to talk to a neighbor or found a fence that needed to be mended, and he'd let the time get away from him. Still, the two of them saddled up and went looking for Ben. When Ellen saw Little Texas just standing there in the field, she knew something was wrong. Ben was lying on the ground, unconscious. They didn't know how long he'd been there. Wesley went back to get a wagon, and Ellen sat beside Ben, who finally came around. Maria called an ambulance. Still, it was a long time before they got him to the doctor. Maybe too long.

"So you think maybe he did hit his head?"

Ellen shrugged. "Who knows? When he got out of the hospital, he seemed to be okay. It wasn't until later that he started to forget. So maybe it wasn't a head wound at all."

"He doesn't forget who you are, does he? That would be terrible."

"No, he's not that far gone. Not yet, anyway. I first realized something was wrong the day he called me from town and said he couldn't remember where he'd parked the truck. So I drove in to get him, and passed him in the truck as he was coming home. He'd found it on his own and didn't remember calling me. What bothered me was not that he'd forgotten where he'd parked the truck. I mean, it was sort of strange, but anybody could do that. It's that he forgot he'd forgotten. Does that make sense?"

June laughed a little, then grew sober. "He was fine last night at the airport."

"Yes." Ellen nodded.

"But, Granny, when I was in the living room alone with him—you'd gone into the kitchen for something, I think—he asked me who I was. I thought he was joking at first. When I realized he wasn't, I said, 'I'm June.' Then he said, 'Oh, you're John's girl. I forgot.'" She turned away, anguish on her face.

"Oh, honey, I'm sorry. I hoped you being here would perk him up. He was so excited when I told you you were coming. He wanted to show you the newfangled watering system we've put in and how the colts have grown since last summer. He said the two of you could ride up to the old line shack and have a picnic. Then this morning, he forgot you were here. You don't need this when you've got your own life to worry about."

"You don't need this in your life either, Granny."

"He is my life." Ellen was silent then, listening to the sound of cattle bawling a long way away. In time, Maria returned with a tin tray holding Mexican cups with bright green designs on them. She set the tray on the table and waited until the two women sipped the hot beverage. "Good?" she asked, and they nodded. "When does Mr. Ben come back? Does he want supper?"

"He should be here by suppertime, unless he runs into somebody in town," Ellen said. "You know how he loves to talk. Wesley will call if they're going to be too late." She turned to June. "He can still carry on a pretty good conversation about cattle prices and land sales. A lot of people don't even realize he's failing. And you know, he's not always confused. Half the time he's perfectly normal."

Maria reached out and touched Ellen's arm but said nothing.

After Maria left, June sipped the chocolate, which was thick and rich. Then she changed the subject. "Why was Nell so anxious to get married, Granny?"

Ellen sighed, her mind returning to the story she had told. "Things were different back then. A woman had to have a husband. We were raised to think if we weren't married by the time we were twenty, we were destined to be old maids, and that was a terrible thing. A spinster, well, what could she do? Women didn't have many opportunities for jobs, not like today with you getting offered one with a bank. In my day, women weren't offered much of anything. A single woman couldn't earn enough to be independent. Most of them ended up living in somebody's upstairs. If they were lucky, they had a room in a relative's house, but they didn't want to be there, and the relatives didn't want them there either. Life didn't offer much for a single woman. Nell was already twenty-two when she went to New Mexico. The girls she'd gone to school with, they'd all married and had two or three babies."

"Were you that way, too, Granny?"

"Oh, yes. I didn't get married until I was even older than that. I thought all the good men were taken."

"And then you met Grandpa Ben?"

Ellen smiled. "That's another story. Maybe I'll tell you that one, too, sometime. There are an awful lot of stories I'd love to pass on if you'd care to listen to them. Most people don't, you know—want to hear them, that is. When I bring up the past to Maria, she throws up her hands and tells me I'm getting old." She stopped. "But we're not talking about me. We were talking about Nell."

"Couldn't she have married if she'd been willing to settle for just anybody?"

"Oh, probably. But she didn't want just anybody, not when she went to Denver. That changed a little after James. She wasn't quite so particular. She didn't believe in a knight on a white horse anymore—or even a cowboy on Old Paint." Ellen smiled at that, looking out at the poplars along the fence line. "After James, I think she lowered her standards," Ellen continued. "She really wasn't looking for true love again, just for a decent man. Then she met Wade. She would have married him. But at the last minute, she ran away from him, too—the third time she did that, as I said. He was a good man, and she hurt him. Nell was sorry for that, but in the end, she just couldn't settle down with him. She always knew she'd made the right decision."

"Was he another cowboy like Buddy or a salesman like James?" June stirred the thick chocolate in her cup, then drank it down and placed the cup on a weathered wooden table beside her. She straightened the Indian blanket in her chair and settled back, ready for the last of the story.

"Hardly. He was a banker, and he was a lot older. Like I say, he was a decent man. Wade Moran his name was. I think Nell would have died of boredom if she'd married him."

June grinned. "Tell me."

"This one isn't a very long story," Ellen said.

CHAPTER TWENTY

Nell returned to Harveyville, helping on the farm during the day and lying in her bed at night, shivering, wondering what would have happened if Emily hadn't showed up. For a time, she feared she might be pregnant. She and James had wanted children, and what did it matter if she conceived two or three weeks before they married? But now, how could she possibly stay with her grandparents if she was expecting a baby? Fortunately for Nell, she discovered, she did not have that concern.

She had loved James, but there were two Jameses—the gentle man who had rescued her and showered her with kindness and the devious one who had proved false. Although Emily had frightened her, Nell was glad, at least, that the woman had kept her from marrying. She could only imagine what would have happened if she'd discovered after the wedding that he had other wives.

Now Nell hated James, hated herself even more for being so

naïve. "Two men, I almost married them," she told her grandmother. "How stupid can I be?"

"Not stupid. Trusting, maybe," her grandmother replied. "There are good men out there. Truly, Nell. Your grandfather is one."

"He's already taken," Nell replied. She'd turned moody, and it wasn't fair to take her anger out on her grandmother, who had been so kind. Nell didn't know what she would have done without her.

"You'll find a man. I know it," her grandmother said.

Nell wasn't so sure. How could she trust a man again? The thought worried her. Would she ever find a husband? Certainly not in Harveyville, where Lane, the boyfriend she had left behind when she went to New Mexico, had married and started a family. None of the single men in town interested her. In fact, they seemed to avoid her as if she were soiled. Did people know she had gone to Denver in search of a husband and failed? Although no one, including her grandparents, knew that she called off the wedding to James because he had other wives— Nell had told her grandmother only that James was not the man she thought he was and had kept silent about Emily—Nell still felt that local folks were staring at her, whispering.

The farm was comforting, just as it always had been, a place of refuge. Through the fall and early winter, she resumed her old routine of working in the garden, and cooking and sewing with her grandmother. Still, she knew, she couldn't get too comfortable. The longer she stayed, the harder it would be to leave.

Then Claire, a college friend who was a teacher in Kansas City, wrote that a colleague had taken sick, and the school was desperate for someone to replace her. The school year was more than half over, and there were no teachers available. The position was Nell's if she wanted it.

Nell sat in her grandmother's rocker next to the cookstove, the letter in her hand, as she considered the opening. She had soured on waitress work, and she had left Harveyville for New Mexico partly because she hadn't much liked teaching. But she couldn't be choosey anymore. The position would get her away from the farm. Besides, a school sounded safe, and after Emily, as well as the man who had accosted her when she first arrived in Denver, she needed to feel safe. If she didn't like the job, she could leave after school ended in the spring.

Besides, Kansas City must have plenty of unmarried young men. The idea of finding another man scared her, but she needed a husband, and the longer she waited, the harder it would be to force herself to meet men. For a moment, she considered remaining on the farm, giving up altogether, but her grandmother encouraged her, even insisted that she leave, saying life wasn't meant to be lived alone. "You'll be so much happier married, and it's not likely you'll meet anyone here," she said. "You must try again."

Nell knew her grandmother was right. What if she ended up with no one? Could she live the rest of her life alone? She felt a pain in her heart at the idea. So Nell applied for the teaching job and was accepted. Her grandparents drove her into Topeka in the farm wagon, where she caught the train to Kansas City, to teach and to live with Claire.

"It's best you're going. If this doesn't work out, then you come back to the farm for good," Nell's grandmother said. "You need to try one more time—for your sake, for everyone's sake."

As they waited for the train, Nell's grandfather took her arm.

"There's a young fellow you ought to meet. He used to work as a hired man for us. Saved up his money and went off to Kansas City."

"That was more than twenty years ago. He's not such a young fellow anymore," her grandmother put in. "But he's a good man, trustworthy."

"Last I heard he was married and had a girl," the grandfather said. "But might be he could introduce you to somebody. He's a fine fellow."

"You must have forgot," Nell's grandmother said. "His wife and daughter died. I remember there was a typhoid epidemic. Poor fellow. He didn't deserve that. You be sure and give him a holler, Nell. Wade Moran his name is."

Nell wondered if her grandparents had rehearsed the conversation and were trying to set her up with the man. Her grandmother pressed Wade Moran's address into her hand as she climbed onto the train. She might meet him to please her grandparents, but she didn't hold out much hope for someone that much older. She put the paper into her pocketbook and never gave it another thought.

As it turned out, Wade Moran looked up Nell, but not until she had lived in Kansas City for months and had agreed to stay on and teach the following year. To her surprise, Nell found that she liked teaching again. Both she and Claire taught in an elementary school, and each morning, they packed lunches and rode the streetcar to work. They spent their evenings grading papers and planning lessons.

On the weekends, they explored Kansas City. The city was filled with lawns and gardens, and when the weather was good, they took picnics to Roanoke Park or Hyde Park and roamed along the lanes, then spread a cloth under a tree and ate their lunch.

Sometimes they took the streetcar to Armour Boulevard or to Millionaire's Row and walked along the shady streets, staring at the mansions' towers and turrets and porte cocheres. "They say they are built to last a century," Claire said as she stopped, awe-struck, in front of a massive stone castle on Troost Street.

"I'm afraid we won't be around to find out," Nell said.

They prowled around Westport, looking for traces of the pioneers who had crossed the Missouri River there on their way to the goldfields. Once they visited the stockyards, where Nell watched the cattle mill around the pens, but Claire complained of the smell, and they did not go back. When summer came, they attended an outdoor concert of ragtime music, then talked about buying a phonograph so they could play records. They took the trolley to Electric Park and rode the Mystic Chute. The amuse-ment park was connected to a brewery, and they finished up in the beer garden, laughing at the thought that they could be fired if a member of the school board caught them drinking beer.

On occasion, Nell went on dates. She went to the pictures with a male teacher from school. He had been silly and told too many jokes, and when Nell didn't appreciate them, he told her she ought to lighten up, that she was too serious. Claire intro-duced her to a former beau. She hadn't cared for him, but Nell might like him. He turned out to be too fresh and put his arm around Nell and tried to kiss her. When Nell resisted, he told her she was as cold as Claire, which, he added, was very cold indeed.

"My fault, I should have warned you," Claire said. "I thought he'd be better behaved with you." Claire, too, wanted to get married.

Neither man had invited Nell out on a second date, which was fine with her, because neither was suitable for a husband.

One evening in late summer, not long before the fall school term began, Nell came home from grocery shopping to find a man waiting in front of the screened-in porch of the little house that she and Claire rented. Claire had mentioned she'd met a new fellow, and Nell assumed the man on the steps was the one.

"Hi, I'm Nell," she said. "You can wait inside if you want to. Claire's still at the market. She'll be along any minute."

The man frowned. "Who's Claire?"

"Oh," Nell said, thinking how foolish she'd been to assume the man was Claire's new beau. She had just invited a perfect stranger to go into the house with her, and for all she knew, he was a masher, maybe just like the one who'd attacked her in Buck & Betty's. After Denver, she should have known better. Nell chided herself for being careless, as she looked the man up and down. He was medium height with dark brown hair slicked back, and he wore a fine black suit. He had a kind expression on his face, but what would that tell her? James had appeared nice, and look what he had turned out to be. "Who are you? Why did you want to come inside?"

"I didn't," he replied.

"Then what are you doing on our steps?"

The man had taken off his hat when Nell approached him, and now he placed it back on his head. "Perhaps I made a mistake coming here. I was looking for you, not Claire."

"What do you want?" Nell clutched her purse. Perhaps the man was a thief, although he didn't look like one. But then, what did a thief look like? And how would he know her name?

"Your grandmother wrote to me and asked me to call on you, but I can see she might have been mistaken. She said she had given you my name, but you hadn't looked me up, so she wrote to me. I'm Wade Moran. I was a hired hand on your grandfather's farm."

Nell had forgotten all about him and was embarrassed. "Oh, of course. I'm so sorry. She told me about you when I left Harveyville. I didn't mean to be rude. I'm just suspicious." She wondered if she would always be so. She'd changed because of both James and the man who had attacked her, just as she'd changed after she left Buddy. She smiled, as if to make up for her rudeness. "My grandparents told me to look you up, but I hadn't got around to it."

"Didn't want to, most likely," he said, smiling.

"How did you know?"

He tapped his forehead. "I might have had the same reaction if someone had asked me to meet up with a hired girl from twenty years back."

"I guess we're both snobs, then."

"You see, we have one thing in common."

"More than that. I really was a hired girl once."

"Then we've both come up in the world."

He'd taken off his hat again and held it in his hands, and Nell invited him inside. She thought to offer him whiskey—she and Claire kept a bottle in the broom closet—but decided against it. "I can make tea. Or coffee."

"I thought perhaps you'd like to have a soda. I saw a drugstore just down the block."

"I *would* like that," Nell said. Eating ice cream seemed like such an innocent thing to do. Besides, she was curious about the man. He was too finely dressed to be a farm worker—better dressed than she was. Nell thought of changing out of her wrinkled dress, but she didn't want to place too much importance on stepping out with this man. He'd worked for her grandparents probably before she was born, and while he didn't look it, he was nearly twice her age. She unlocked the door and once again invited Wade inside while she set down her groceries and combed her hair. But perhaps mindful of their conversation, he said he would wait on the porch.

Nell went into the bathroom and splashed water on her face, staring at herself in the mirror. Four years had passed since she'd gone to New Mexico, and she had changed. Her figure, she knew, was fuller, but then she had been too slender when she'd worked at the Rockin' A. There was a tiny scar on her cheek where one of the wild cats at the ranch had scraped its claw on her and a burn on her hand from where she'd touched the stove at Buck & Betty's. Fine wrinkles radiated out from her eyes and mouth, and her chin was not as taut as it once was. As she used a hairpin to sweep up strands of hair that had fallen from her pompadour, Nell spotted a white hair among the brown, but when she went to pluck it, she couldn't find it. Probably the light, she told herself. Nonetheless, she wasn't a girl anymore. In those last few years, she had become a woman.

As she patted her hair in place, she thought about the man waiting for her outside. Was she really ready to meet someone new? Of course she was. It had been a year since she had left Denver, although she had not forgotten James. She thought sometimes about what their life would have been if he hadn't had other wives. What if he had never been married? Would they have had a happy life in that little house? She remembered the painting of the orange violets. She hadn't thought about it since she left Denver and wondered if it was still there. Maybe James had given it to Emily or one of his other wives. Or perhaps he'd thrown it away. She hoped he was disappointed that Nell hadn't taken it with her. But she wouldn't have. It wasn't like the Indian rug Buddy had given her that brought back bittersweet memories. The painting would have been a reminder of falseness, of betrayal.

As they went along the sidewalk, Wade slipped behind Nell so that he walked on the street side—like a gentleman, she thought—and then she remembered that James had done just that, and he had turned out to be anything but a gentlemen. The thought of James intruding just then made her angry. They could have had a wonderful marriage if only . . . She shook away the idea. Time had passed, and the memory of him had begun to fade. She would have to force him out of her mind, just as she had Buddy. But when she thought of Buddy now, she remembered his smile, his good humor, the way he made her feel when he touched her. No matter how much time passed, she would never think of James that way.

Wade commented on the asters blooming in the yards, and the patches of corn, and Nell asked if he was still a farmer.

"Oh, no. Farming's too hard, sheer drudgery sometimes. That's why I went to college. I don't mind working, but with farming, no matter how hard you work, you never seem to get ahead. Look at your grandfather, up at dawn, work in the fields till dark, and then a hailstorm comes along and wipes out his crops. Where does that leave him?"

"But there are good times. I like farming."

"I do, too. I like being outside in the sun and watching things grow. They grow because of your hands." He held out hands that might have been hard and calloused at one time but now were soft, the nails neatly trimmed. "I miss the miracle of the harvest, the cycles of the earth, what the Bible says is a time to reap and a time to sow. I just don't want to depend on a farm to make my living."

"I'd miss the chickens if I didn't live on a farm," Nell said.

"You like chickens? So do I. In fact, I have a coop in my backyard. I'll bring you some eggs."

"We already have chickens."

"That's the second thing we have in common. We may become friends yet."

"I think we already are," Nell said. Friends, she thought. He was far too old to be a husband, but she liked the idea they would be friends. She needed them.

"Then you must call me Wade, and may I call you Nell—or is it Nellie?"

"Yes, Nell. No one calls me Nellie—anymore."

At the drugstore, Wade took her arm and steered her past the cigar counter and the various goods on display—perfumes and soaps, hairpins and straight razors, trusses and bedpans— to one of the small tables, where they ordered sodas. "So what do you do if you're not a farmer?" Nell asked.

"Your grandmother didn't tell you?"

Nell shook her head.

Wade grinned. "I'd rather not say, then."

"You mean you do something illegal?" Nell's heart sank. The one decent man she'd met in Kansas City, and already there was something wrong with him. She wondered if he was a confidence man or a second-story man or even a cattle rustler.

Wade waited while the soda jerk set down their drinks, then opened the glass container on the table to let Nell select a straw. "No, of course not. It's just that farm people don't always think well of my line of work."

Nell had put her spoon into her soda and was about to scoop out a bite of ice cream, but she stopped. "Maybe you better tell me what it is you do, then."

Wade stared at her a moment, then said, "I'm a banker."

"A banker." She laughed. "That's not so bad."

"I know your grandparents don't think highly of bankers."

"They have good reason for it. When I was living in New Mexico, Grandma wrote me that some cultus banker in Topeka tried to cheat them out of their farm."

"Cultus?"

"It means useless. It's a ranch word." Nell thought she should be more conscious of the way she spoke. Cowboy words were all right for a ranch cook—and for a waitress—but now that she was a schoolteacher again, she ought not to use slang.

"Cultus. I like that. Yes, that man was cultus."

"The banker said Grandpa hadn't paid his loan in six months, and he tried to foreclose on the farm. That wasn't true, of course. Grandpa never missed a payment. He went in the first of every month and paid in cash. It turned out the banker had applied the money to his own mortgage, but how would Grandpa know that? The man might have got away with it if my grandparents hadn't had a friend in Kansas City who went over the books—" Nell stopped. "That was you, wasn't it?"

Wade shrugged. "I took a look at the situation. It was pretty easy to discover what the fellow had done. He wasn't very bright."

"You saved the farm for them."

"Anybody would have found the deception. Your grand-parents just happened to ask me." He waved his hand to dismiss the idea that he had done anything out of the ordinary.

"That's not the way Grandma told it."

Wade didn't respond. He put a straw into his soda and sipped. "I always liked these things. I suppose I'm a little old to be drinking sodas. You won't tell anyone, will you?"

"Your secret's safe with me. Besides, I like them, too."

For a moment, Wade stared at his straw. Then he said, "You should know that I'm forty-four."

"I'm twenty-six."

"So I'm way too old for you."

"Not too old to take me to an ice cream parlor."

"No one's too old for that."

Nell liked his grin and smiled back. "I'm awfully glad you weren't Claire's beau," she said.

"Me, too." He stared at his straw for a moment, then looked up at Nell. "I ought to tell you about myself."

"This sounds serious." Nell hoped he would stop. She wanted to enjoy herself for a little while. Besides, she was conflicted. She knew why she had gone to Kansas City, but did she really want to get serious about a man so soon? It had been a year since she'd left Denver, but even so, her emotions were still raw, and she felt drained. Maybe she shouldn't have left the farm so quickly. She thought of the easy times she had spent with her grandmother making quilts. Then she thought of the quilt she had left behind half finished at the Rockin' A. She had begun it as a wedding present for Buddy, had pieced it and begun the quilting. What had become of it? Had Lucy finished it before she died? Perhaps it had gone into the dog's bed or had been cut in half and turned into a saddle blanket. Maybe one of the cowboys had taken it for a sugan. She hoped Wendell had, because she'd always liked him. She had thought to make a quilt for James, too, but he had wanted to be married right away, and with the wedding dress to complete, she hadn't had time to piece a top. Thank goodness, she thought. She wouldn't have wanted to keep a quilt made for James.

Wade stared at Nell until she looked up. "It is serious. I think before we go any further, you ought to know about me."

"Go any further?"

He blushed. "I suppose I'm making assumptions. It's just that I'm so much older. If we're to be friends . . ." His voice trailed off.

"Of course," Nell said. She tried to keep the mood light. "Are you going to tell me you're a criminal?" She smiled, but he was serious, and Nell felt foolish. "All right, if you think you must."

"I've been married."

Nell knew that, but she didn't tell him so.

"And I have a daughter—had, I mean. They were killed, both of them."

"Typhoid," Nell asked, remembering what her grandmother had said.

"No," he replied. "I wish it had been. They were murdered."

CHAPTER TWENTY-ONE

"Murdered?" Nell's voice was so loud that the soda jerk looked up and stared at them. Nell realized that she and Wade were the only customers at the fountain, but still, she lowered her voice. "How awful."

"Yes, it was. Terrifying. I'll never get over it."

"No, of course not." Nell thought of what had happened to her, of James's wife Emily, who had tried to poison her. No one was ever safe; she wasn't ever safe. Nell was holding her spoon, and her hand began to tremble, and then the spoon clattered onto the floor.

"I shouldn't have been so blunt. I'm sorry I startled you like that. I really don't know how to talk about it. That's why I hardly ever do." Wade picked up the spoon and set it on the table. He motioned to the soda jerk for another.

"It's just that . . ." Nell paused. Just that someone had tried to murder her, too? She couldn't say that, couldn't tell him that was another thing they had in common. "I guess I was just surprised. I've never known of anyone who was murdered."

"I call it murder. The police didn't. In fact, the young man didn't even go to jail." Wade reached for the discarded spoon and ran his finger along its handle. "Should I tell you about it? I don't have to. I don't want to shock you, but I just thought . . ." His voice trailed off, and he was silent as the boy put down a spoon next to Nell.

"Of course you should tell me, I mean, if you want to," Nell said, after the soda jerk moved back behind the counter. She did not really care to hear it. The incident with Emily in Denver was still too painful. "I should think it's very hard to talk about such a thing."

"It is. I almost never do, but you seem, well, as you said, we're already friends. I wanted you to know my life has been . . . different. I want you to know what you're getting into if we're to see each other."

Nell played with the straw in her drink, studying it for a moment before she looked up. Wade was searching her face, and she knew he needed to talk. She understood that, because she needed to talk, too. She had kept the story of Emily and the poisoned cake to herself. She had never revealed the details of why she'd run off, even to her grandparents. She'd never been able to share the pain in her heart. "Tell me," she said.

Wade nodded. He pushed aside his glass and leaned his arms on the table, clasping his hands together. He was a nice-looking man, not handsome, but solid. There was an air of trust about him.

"Abigail, my wife's name was. Abby. It was what you'd call love at first sight. We met when I was in college. She wanted to be a teacher, like you, but we got married instead, and nobody hired married women to teach. And of course, I didn't want her to work. I wanted her to stay home and raise our children. She wanted that, too.

"Abby was pretty, with violet eyes. I'd never known anybody with violet eyes. She loved children and animals—especially chickens. That's why I kept them after she died. She named them, and she couldn't watch when I slaughtered one. She cried when I chopped the head off of Topsy. That was her favorite chicken." He smiled at the memory. "I couldn't remember the names of the chickens after she died. That bothered me. I think Abby would have been disappointed." He smiled at the thought.

"I love chickens, too," Nell said. "And I name them."

Wade looked at her a moment, approval on his face. "We wanted a family, but we hadn't been lucky," he continued. "Abby didn't seem to be able to . . . you know. And then, almost when we'd given up, Margaret was born. She was a gift, as beautiful as her mother with those same eyes. I thought I was the luckiest man in the world. And I was. For five years."

He stopped talking and stared at his hands, and Nell had to prompt him. "And then?" She asked, touching his knuckle with her finger.

"I remember that day. I wish I didn't. I wish I could block it out. But it's as clear in my mind as if it had happened this morning, and I suppose it always will be." He looked up at Nell, who nodded for him to go on.

"There was a boy down the street. Boy! He was twenty-two! He was no more a boy than I was. His father worked for the mayor. The father was very powerful. He was one of those men who rise to power by knowing all the right people, flattering them, running errands for them. And then when they get to be in charge, they expect others to do the same for them. People in Kansas City kowtowed to him. The son was just like the father. The boy's name was—is—Alfred Sterling, and he'd always been—what's your word? Cultus. That described him. He drank too much. He'd sit out on his front stoop and swear at people when he was drunk. He got a girl in trouble. Everybody knew he was the father of her baby, but he denied it, and how do you prove it?" Wade looked up at Nell but didn't expect her to answer.

Indeed, Nell thought, you always knew who the mother was, but how could you be sure about the father?

"Whenever Abby walked past him, he'd whistle and make lewd remarks. When I found out, I confronted him, but it didn't do any good. In fact, his father said if I ever spoke to his son again, he'd get me fired. He knew the president of the bank where I worked, and he'd have done it. After that, Abby crossed the street to avoid Alfred." Wade shook his head. "I should have beat him up. I could have, too. He was such a weakling. And I'm, well, I was pretty strong from all that farm work. My job at the bank wasn't that important." Wade gripped his hands so tightly that the knuckles turned white.

Nell reached out and put her hand over his, and he looked up and smiled at her.

"I should have done something. Maybe if I had . . ."

"You can't worry about what didn't happen," she said, and then she remembered that James had used those very words after she beat off the masher.

Wade was silent a moment before he asked, "Are you sure you care to hear this?"

Nell wanted to say no, she didn't. She was afraid the man had raped Abby, and she didn't want to know about it, didn't want to relive her own horror. An attack by a rapist shouldn't be another thing she had in common with Wade. She knew he needed to talk about his wife's death, however, just as she had needed to confess to her grandmother all that had happened in Denver—but couldn't. She nodded, and turned away from Wade, because his face was drained of color and a little twisted. She sipped her soda, but the drink was gone, and her straw made noisy sounds as she sucked up air. She pushed the glass aside. "I do want to hear it," she said.

"All right." Wade sounded grateful. "Abby was on her way to meet me. On nice evenings, she and Margaret went to the trolley stop to wait for me, and the three of us walked home together. It was such a joy seeing them standing there. I always looked for them, even when I knew they couldn't come. I remember being on the streetcar that day and looking out the window at the lilacs. They were fragrant. The white ones and the very dark Persian ones smell the sweetest."

Nell nodded, remembering the Persian lilacs in Denver. She had been sitting under them stitching on her wedding dress when she'd looked up to see Emily.

"I thought that we should ask a neighbor for a start of one, and I would plant it beside our bedroom window so that we could wake up on spring mornings to that smell." He paused and added, "I can't stand the smell of lilacs now. I hate them. They bring back that day.

"I looked for them at the trolley stop, but they weren't there, and I was disappointed. Margaret always jumped up and down when she saw me, and no matter how hard my day was, she brightened it."

Wade leaned back in the chair. It was iron, and the arm was

attached to the underside of the table so that the chair could swing back and forth. "I thought Margaret might not have awakened yet from her nap, or perhaps Abby had taken her to the greengrocer or the butcher shop. I wasn't worried. I walked home by myself, not hurrying, because the day was nice. And then I saw a crowd of people gathered on our block. There was a police wagon and an ambulance. The minute I saw them, I knew something had happened to Abby or Margaret. I don't know why I thought they were the victims, but I did. There was a vicious dog in our neighborhood, and I worried that maybe he had attacked one of them. Then I saw Alfred's horseless carriage up on the curb. I knew it was his, because he was the only one in the neighborhood who had one. And I saw two white sheets on the ground."

Wade swallowed and shook his head, then took out a handkerchief and dabbed at his eyes. When he didn't go on, Nell whispered, "Your wife and your daughter?"

Wade nodded. "Both of them. I thought, why both? Why couldn't one have been saved? Why did I have to lose both of them?" He paused. "Perhaps I shouldn't tell you this."

"No, it's all right."

Wade gripped the handkerchief. "A police officer tried to stop me, said there'd been an accident and he didn't want any gawkers muddling things up. But one of the neighbors told him I was the husband and father, and the officer said, 'It's a terrible thing, sir. Don't look.'

"I waved him away. The crowd parted to let me get close to the bodies. I started to lift one of the sheets, but a woman took my hand and said, 'Don't.' I shook her off and said I had to see, that I owed it to them, and I lifted the sheets, first one, then the other. I don't know if I should have done it, because I'll never get the images out of my mind. But I had to look. I couldn't turn my back on them. They were my family, and I had to see them. I won't describe what they looked like, but they were tore up something awful." Wade groaned and touched his eyes with the handkerchief again.

"'It was the Sterling boy,' the woman told me. 'I saw it. They were walking down the street. He was drunk, and he cussed them out, and when your wife ignored him, he got mad. He jumped in his car and followed them.'

"The police officer stepped in then and said, 'Best we can tell, his foot slipped off the brake onto the gas pedal, and he hit them, slammed them into the ground and ran over them. Then he must have got confused, because he backed up over them, and they got caught on the underside, looks like, and they were dragged halfway down the block.' Then he told me, 'You can see the tire marks on them. Lookit there.'

"The neighbor woman told him to shut up, but the officer wouldn't. I guess he knew who Alfred's father was, because he said, 'You can't blame the boy, because he was drunk. It's an awful pity, but the boy was drunk, so he wasn't responsible.'"

"Not responsible?" Nell gasped.

A man sitting at the counter with a glass of soda water turned to stare at her. She hadn't seen him come in, and she hadn't been aware he was there.

"Did a jury agree?"

"It never got that far. He was charged with reckless driving. I think the judge was looking for a reason to dismiss the case. He was a friend of the Sterling family, had gotten his appointment because of old man Sterling. He said if Alfred was drunk, then it wasn't his fault."

"So he didn't go to jail."

Wade shook his head. "He was released and went out with his friends to celebrate. He was so drunk he ran into a tree."

"And was killed?"

"No, but he's blind. I see that as some sort of divine retribution. His father blamed me, of course, said if I hadn't pushed the police to file charges, there wouldn't have been a hearing and Alfred wouldn't have been celebrating. He tried to get me fired, but it turned out my boss was not so easy to push around."

"How despicable!" Then Nell asked, "Where is the boy now?"

"In an asylum. There was something twisted inside of him. He attacked his father and nearly killed him. That time he didn't get off because he was drunk."

She wanted to say it served him right, but instead, she asked, "How do you feel about that?"

Wade shook his head. "I don't care. I hated him at first, but now I don't care. Maybe the judge was right. Maybe it wasn't his fault, maybe being told all his life that he could do whatever he wanted spoiled him as a human being. I don't think about him much."

"But you do think about Abigail and Margaret."

"Yes, all the time. It's different now, however. For a long time, it was as if they were with me every day. Something amusing would happen at work, and I'd think I'd have to remember it to tell Abby. Or I'd see a toy in a shop window and start to go inside to buy it for Margaret. Each time, I would remember they were dead, and it was like seeing their bodies all over again. But now I accept that they're gone. I've put them in the past. A part of me is buried with them, but as for the rest of me, I'm still alive. I know it's time to move along. That's why, when I got the letter from your grandmother, I decided to call on you."

"I'm glad," Nell said, and she was. What had happened to

Wade was awful, and it made Nell put her own problems in perspective. She hadn't been raped or poisoned, and she hadn't married James. And she, too, had a reason—a good one—to go on with her life.

Wade cleared his throat and looked sheepish. "I'm so sorry. I hadn't intended to open up like that, but I'm glad I did. I feel better." He smiled at Nell. "You didn't know you were in for all this when you accepted my offer of ice cream." He glanced at the soda jerk, who was leaning against the counter, examining his nails. "I think we have outstayed our welcome." Wade rose and said to the boy, "We're just leaving." He slipped a silver dollar onto the table, and Nell was reminded of how James used to tip her with silver dollars. But James had done it to impress her. Wade was making it up to the boy for staying so long.

How long had they been there? Nell wondered. Outside, the sky had turned a deep blue, and she thought it must be late. She did not want to be obvious and look around the drugstore for a clock, but she figured they had been sitting at the fountain for two hours, maybe more. Claire would be worried. "I must be getting home," she said. "My roommate will wonder where I've got to. I left her at the butcher shop while I went on home, and now I've been gone for hours."

"I shouldn't have talked so much, but it just seemed I had to tell you. It's pretty heavy stuff for a first date."

So they had gone on a date, Nell thought. Well, why not. She hadn't met any other men in Kansas City who interested her, and already she liked Wade. Maybe the age difference didn't matter. Still, she wasn't sure he'd be anything more than a pleasant acquaintance.

"I hope there will be another, and I promise to let you talk next time. What would you say if I asked you to have supper Saturday night at the Savoy?"

"I would say yes," Nell replied, although she had no idea what the Savoy was. Later, as she thought about it, she realized that for the first time since she'd left Denver, she was looking forward to going out with a man.

CHAPTER TWENTY-TWO

"The Savoy!" Claire cried when Nell told her about her upcoming date with Wade. "Why, it's terribly nice. He must be in the chips."

Nell laughed. "He used to be the hired man on my grandparents' farm."

"Then he's certainly come up in the world."

"And he's almost twenty years older than I am."

"He doesn't look it." Claire had been sitting in the front room working on lesson plans for the fall term when Nell and Wade returned, and Nell had introduced them. "He looks like a pretty good catch to me."

"I'm not sure he'll be anything more than a friend. My grandmother approves of him. That's not especially promising, is it?" Nell had liked Wade well enough, but there hadn't been any sparks yet, at least not on her part.

"He didn't look at you like a friend."

"We'll see," Nell said.

Nell was awfully fond of Claire. The two had not been roommates in college, but they'd lived in the same dormitory and had often studied together. Claire was outgoing, and in the months Nell had lived with her, Claire had undertaken to heal Nell's wounds. At first, Nell hadn't wanted to go out. She was grieving over James and was content to sit on the porch in the warmth of the sun or curl up in bed under a pile of quilts. She spent weekends weeding the garden and cleaning the discarded chicken coop in the backyard. Then she'd bought four chickens.

Claire told Nell she was as broody as the chickens and took it upon herself to lighten her friend's mood, and in time, thanks to Claire, Nell's attitude had indeed improved. She'd begun to feel normal again, maybe not like the schoolgirl she had been when the two were young but comfortable, more sure of herself. She had not told Claire about what had happened to her in Denver, only that she had been engaged and that things had fallen apart. There had been someone in New Mexico Territory, too, she explained, but it hadn't worked either.

Wade had shown up at the right time. Still, as Nell told Claire, she hadn't felt a tug at her heart, at least not that first day. Did that really matter, however? Maybe she would grow to love him in time. After all, she'd spent only a few hours with him. If she didn't fall in love, well, Claire was right. He was a good catch. And then she laughed to think that she'd gotten ahead of herself. It wasn't as if Wade had proposed on the walk home.

"What should I wear to the Savoy?" Nell asked her roommate. Her best outfit was the white linen suit that she'd made in Denver, but it was too late in the year for linen. And the red dress she'd had in New Mexico was hopelessly out of fashion. She would have to buy something.

"You must wear my blue silk. It's the nicest dress either of us has, and it will look ever so much better on you than on me, especially with your blue eyes," Claire said. She added, "Your eyes really are an exceptional blue. I can't imagine a man who wouldn't notice."

Nell thought of Buddy calling her Miss Nellie Blue-Eyes, but she didn't tell Claire. She'd never told anybody about Buddy's nickname, not Aunt Lucy, not even her grandmother.

"Mr. Moran's not still a hired man, I take it," Claire said. The two had gone into the kitchen to prepare dinner. Claire had brought home two chops from the butcher shop, and she breaded and fried them as Nell snapped beans and brought a pan of water to boil on the stove.

"Hardly. He's a banker."

"Wade Moran," Claire mused. "It sounds like a banker's name. It seems familiar, too." She frowned, thinking, then turned away from the stove to where Nell was slicing tomatoes. "I think I read about him in the newspaper a couple of years ago. Is he . . . did he have a wife and child, a daughter maybe? Were they killed . . . ? I'm sorry. I shouldn't have said anything."

"Yes, he's the one. He told me all about it."

"I remember that it was awful. Some drunk hit them in his autocar. The story was in all the papers, because it was so unusual. Horseless carriages were awfully rare then, and I'd never realized they could kill. I mean, there are always runaway horses and wagons injuring people, but I'd never heard of an autocar running over anybody. It must have been terrible for him."

"It was."

"He got some sort of settlement. Did he tell you about that?"

Nell had finished slicing the tomatoes she had picked from the garden and was putting them on a plate. She shook her head.

"I don't remember the details. The man who killed them was someone important." Claire thought a moment. "No, he was somebody's son, some politician. I don't recall if Mr. Moran sued or what, but he ended up with a pile of money, several thousand dollars, I think. Anybody else would have kept it, but he bought up some land, and then he built a playground on it. I think he named it for his wife, or maybe it was his daughter."

"And he gave it to the city?"

"No, he was too smart for that. He gave the city a long lease, something like ninety-nine years. That way the city has to maintain the playground but can't tear it down or sell the land. Clever, isn't he?"

"He didn't say a word about it."

"I'd like him for that." Claire used a fork to remove the chops from the pan and place them on plates, which she set on the table.

"He helped my grandparents," Nell said as she drained the beans and dumped them into a dish. "Without him, they might have lost their farm."

"Like I said," Claire repeated, "he's quite a catch."

The blue silk dress fit Nell just fine, but Claire said her friend needed something to finish it off, so the two went to a millinery shop to buy a hat. The hats were gigantic, as big as turkey platters and covered with feathers, not just ostrich plumes and egret feathers but whole birds—pigeons and wrens and red-winged blackbirds, "anything that chirps," Nell observed. She selected a hat that looked like an upside-down serving bowl, with a chiffon crown and gigantic satin bow. She was self-conscious about the size, but when she walked into the dining room of the Savoy with Wade, she found herself looking at a sea of large hats decorated not only with birds but with flowers and bunches of fruit. Her hat was right at home.

Wade pointed to a couple seated at a table next to a palm tree in a huge pot. The woman's hat was even larger than Nell's. "I hope you don't mind. I've invited a colleague and his wife to join us," Wade said.

"No, of course not," Nell replied, although she was disappointed. She had decided she would tell Wade all about herself that night. She'd tell him about Buddy and what had happened and about James and how she had been taken in. Wade was a banker and very proper, and if her past offended him, he could drop her right now, before either of them wanted to go beyond friendship. But it was hardly a conversation she could bring up with a fellow banker and his wife.

Indeed, she would have shocked the couple if she had, Nell decided after she had talked to them for a few moments. Wilbur and Helen Harris were gracious but very proper. Helen was sipping sherry, and without asking Nell what she wanted, Wade ordered the same thing for her. He and Wilbur asked for whiskey for themselves. Nell didn't care for sherry at all now and would have liked whiskey, but she was afraid the others would disapprove. So instead, she sipped the too-sweet drink.

Helen complimented Nell on her hat and the blue dress, and began talking about her children. Then she confided she was chairwoman of a ball that would be one of the social events of the year. The proceeds would benefit St. Anthony's Home for Infants, Helen explained. She lowered her voice. "I should not tell you this since you will be shocked, but many of those children were born out of wedlock." She leaned back and nodded.

"And you don't approve?" Nell asked.

"Well, I certainly don't approve of their mothers. But the children, they are very sweet."

"The sins of the fathers . . ." Wilbur smiled.

"It is the women who sinned. But I don't believe the children should be blamed. Do you?" Helen asked.

"Certainly not," Nell said.

"The little bastards." Wilbur smirked.

"Wilbur!" his wife said.

"Are they ever adopted?" Nell asked quickly.

"The lucky ones. The others we train, mostly as domestics. They're quite satisfactory," Helen replied.

"Our Helen is quite the organizer. I'm sure she wouldn't mind your help," Wade interjected, and Nell wondered if Wade's wife had been involved in charitable works. Of course she had. It was the proper thing for a banker's wife to do. And then Wade added, "Abigail was good at such things."

"I would indeed like you to help," Helen said, and Nell thought she meant it. "But I doubt you have the time, being a new woman."

"A new woman?"

"Oh, you know, a feminist. I'm told you have a profession."

"Oh," Nell said, relieved. She didn't mind being called a feminist, but Wade frowned at the word.

"She's not a professional. She's just a teacher," he said. "I thoroughly approve. Besides . . ." He stopped. Nell was sure he was going to say that besides, Abby had trained to be a teacher.

"Perhaps you'll be interested later on. After you're married," Helen said, looking pointedly at Wade. Nell reddened and looked down at her sherry glass. After a few minutes, when the men were caught up in a conversation of their own, Helen whispered, "I should apologize for shocking you."

"Oh, but you didn't. I know about illegitimate children. They're not unique to Kansas City."

"No, of course not." Helen glanced at the men, who were still talking, and lowered her voice. "I mean about suggesting you might marry—might marry Mr. Moran, that is. But you see, we've worried about him. It's high time he found someone to replace Abigail. I have introduced him to ever so many lovely young women, but you are the first one he's seen fit to ask out. I hope you like him, as he obviously cares for you."

Nell was saved from answering when Wade turned to her and said, "You lived in New Mexico, didn't you? Wilbur was just telling me about a rancher who has applied to us for a loan for his—what did he call it, Wilbur? His 'outfit'? Funny word, isn't it? We've begun looking at the Southwest. It's quite the coming area. We already have several ranchers as clients. This particular man was a Rough Rider."

Nell hoped the others didn't see her flush. Her hands were damp inside her white gloves, and she picked up the sherry glass and played with it.

"I don't suppose you'd know the man—Oscar Garrison."

Nell shook her head, relieved, for her first thought had been that the rancher might have been Buddy. But that was ridiculous. New Mexico was a big territory with hundreds of ranches. Still, the question made her curious about how Buddy had financed his ranch. Probably with Alice's money. Or rather her father's money. He was a banker. He would have been happy to loan his son-in-law money to buy property.

"You lived in New Mexico? How exciting," Helen said.

"My aunt lived there. I spent almost a year with her."

Wade leaned forward and grinned. "She was a hired girl."

Nell shot back, "And Wade was once my grandparents' hired man." Then she muttered, "We were both 'professionals.'"

"Oh my! I rather like that," Helen said. She glanced at her

husband, who frowned at her and shook his head. She ignored him and said, "And I worked as a waitress."

"Oh, but I did, too," Nell told her.

"That is, before Wilbur rescued me and I became a prim and proper wife," she said, and even Wilbur laughed.

Nell decided that Wilbur might be stiff, but under her banker's-wife demeanor, Helen was still someone she could enjoy. They might even become good friends if she and Wade . . . Nell glanced at her date, who smiled at her with approval.

Later, as they left the hotel, Helen took Nell's arm and said, "Wilbur may be a banker by day, but at night . . . well, he is not always so formal. Perhaps Mr. Moran is not as stuffy as he appears."

Nell hoped she was right.

One Sunday after the school year had started and they had been seeing each other for several weeks, Wade called for Nell in a buggy and took her for a drive through Kansas City. After a time, he stopped at Forest Park, an amusement park that was shuttered for the season. They walked along the tracks of a scenic railroad, and Wade pointed out the monkey house and the laughing gallery. The place reminded Nell of Elitch Gardens, and she remembered the afternoon she had spent there, ducking into the café nearby to get out of the rain. It might have been the nicest time she had had in Denver.

Wade was talking, but Nell didn't hear him, and in a moment he said, "You are far away. What are you thinking about?"

Nell shook her head to rid herself of the memory of that afternoon at Elitch's. "Just thinking of Denver. This reminds me of a park I visited there. It's not important," she said.

Wade studied her for a moment. Then he pointed. "There's the carousel. It's quite the attraction. Have you ridden one?"

"No. What a pity it's not operating. I should like to try it. Have you ridden it?"

"Not yet. It's fun, at least that's what they tell me. When I saw it, I thought how much Margaret would like it. I think she would have chosen to ride the pink horse with the gold mane. The animals go up and down, you know, and there is a giant calliope that plays when the carousel is turning. Abigail loved music."

"You'll always think of your wife and daughter when you see things they'd like, won't you?"

"Wouldn't you?"

"Yes, I suppose." They had walked around the park, and Nell felt tired and climbed onto the carousel and sat down in a carriage that was painted gold with big white feathers on the side. She closed her eyes and raised her face to the afternoon sun.

A caretaker approached and told them the carousel was shut down for the season. Wade slipped him a coin and said the lady was tired and just wanted to sit for a few minutes. The caretaker disappeared, and Wade sat down in the coach beside Nell. "It's a proper coach for a fine lady," he said.

"Well, I'm hardly that."

"You'd have to convince me otherwise."

Nell turned and faced him. "Then perhaps I should. You don't really know me. You told me about yourself, and now it's my time to talk."

"Nell, I hardly think—"

"No, I believe you ought to know certain things, and then perhaps you will not want to see me again." Nell looked away and stared at a blue pig, at its ears where the paint was nicked. "I was going to tell you before, but then, well, I didn't. It's not easy."

"I doubt—"

Nell held up her hand. "Please. This is not easy for me, but I want to tell you now, before we grow fond of each other." She gripped the side of the carriage with one hand and turned to Wade. "You see, I am not so innocent as you might think."

"If you must," he said, "but it's not necessary."

"Yes, it is." Nell leaned back in the carriage and began. She told him about Buddy, about the night in the cabin and then how they had fought and separated. She told how she'd been attacked in Denver and James had rescued her, how he had turned out to be a polygamist and she had almost married him, had almost been poisoned by a jealous wife. It was the first time she had talked about Emily, and she felt a weight lift from her when she was finished. She liked that she could share the story with someone. "So you see, I have something of a past, and I believe you ought to know about it."

The telling had taken a long time. The sun that had been shining when they sat down had gone under the clouds, and the day had turned cool. The wind came up then and swirled discarded newspapers and dead leaves about the carousel. Nell shivered and pulled her coat around her, then removed her gloves from her purse. She started to put them on, but Wade took them away from her and held her hands.

"But I did know about it," he said. "Everything, except for the polygamy and the poisoned cake. Everything. You didn't have to tell me."

Nell looked up at him. "Everything? How could you?"

"Yes, everything. Your grandmother wrote me. She told me

because she did not want me to call on you if I disapproved. She didn't want you to be hurt again. I'm glad you told me, and I believed you would sooner or later. I knew it all before I ever met you, however. Your honesty makes me admire you even more, and I already admired you a great deal."

"You don't think I'm easy, then? I will not make that mistake again. I do not intend to be with a man that way until I am married."

"I approve entirely. I like you awfully well already, Nell." He patted the side of the carousel coach and said, "Perhaps someday we will ride off together in our own golden chariot."

CHAPTER TWENTY-THREE

Wade called on Nell each week. Sometimes he took her for a buggy ride about the city or under the high bluffs or along the Missouri River. Once they went aboard a steamboat and watched the workmen load freight, then rode across the river to the Kansas side and back. Wade took her to museums and the symphony, and often they went for long walks, even after the weather turned cold. Wade gave her a cunning little fur muff for their outings in the snow. He said that when summer came, he would take her to see the Kansas City Blue Stockings play a baseball game. She'd never seen a baseball game; James hadn't been interested in sports, and the cowboys were as likely to run around a bunch of sandbag bases in their boots as they were to tap dance.

Nell suggested they go to one of the music halls where they could hear jazz. She'd been told it was the newest craze, and she'd heard the music being played on the street. But Wade said such places catered to thugs and prostitutes and he wouldn't want to expose Nell to them. She didn't tell him that she had met prostitutes when she was a waitress, and they weren't much different from anyone else, only maybe a little nicer—and certainly better tippers.

Sometimes Claire went on the outings with Nell and Wade, which pleased Nell, because Claire did not have a regular beau. The three of them attended the flickers or walked to the drugstore for ice cream. Claire was discreet and asked Nell once, "Do you really want me tagging along? You can tell me the truth."

"Of course I do," Nell said, and she did. She appreciated Wade's thoughtfulness and his generosity, but the truth was, he bored her a little. He was stiff and too formal and sometimes made suggestions about how Nell should act or dress. At times, she wondered if he was trying to turn her into his first wife. He spoke of Abigail less often when Claire was with them, so Nell sometimes had a better time when the three of them went out.

Then Claire met a young man of her own, Steve Sorel, and on occasion the two of them double-dated with Nell and Wade. While he was funny and self-assured, as handsome as a motion picture actor, Steve was also flashy and too forward. Neither Nell nor Wade cared for him much. Nell believed he thought too highly of himself, and Wade said that Steve lacked decorum, often drinking too much and making loud, sometimes blasphemous remarks. Steve liked to hold Claire's hand or put his arm around her shoulder at the movies. Wade had never done that, and Nell knew he didn't approve. Nell herself thought such gestures were improper, then laughed at herself, wondering if she was getting to be too much like Wade.

Of course, she did not say anything to Claire, because Claire enjoyed Steve, although she seemed uncomfortable when he got too familiar. She laughed at his jokes and loved his gifts of chocolates and perfume. Nell was all too aware that it was difficult to meet eligible young men, although she hoped that Claire didn't have to settle for less than love. But then, Nell asked herself, was she willing to do just that?

The two talked about it one Saturday afternoon as they sat in the front room sewing. Nell was making a quilt while Claire stitched on a shirtwaist.

"Do you think there is such a thing as true love?" Claire asked. "You know, like in the magazine stories or the flickers, a love that makes you give up everything for a man?"

Nell looked up. "Yes."

"You know for sure?"

Nell nodded. "I've loved two men that way. You wake up every morning thinking what a wonderful place the world is. You see him, and it's like the day has dawned on a golden sunrise. You think you'll burst from happiness." She looked down at her sewing. "And when it doesn't work out, you are wretched. You believe you'll die. In fact, you want to."

"That's how it was with you?"

Nell nodded.

"You don't feel that way about Wade, though." It was a statement, not a question.

"I wish I did," Nell replied. She wished her heart caught when she saw Wade or that she got that feeling of wanting when he touched her hand, but she didn't. "Maybe it doesn't matter. It might even be a good thing. I couldn't bear being hurt like that again. I'm very fond of Wade, and I think that might be enough." She gave a wry laugh. "I didn't do so well with true love, as you call it." Then she asked, "How do you feel about Steve?"

"Oh, I like him pretty well. But . . ."

"But what?"

Claire took a final stitch in a seam and snipped off the

thread. "I sure wish we had a sewing machine. Maybe we ought to save up for one. We could buy it together. It would make sewing ever so much easier."

"You're changing the subject. Maybe you ought to tell me why you brought up this true love business."

"Oh, I don't know. Steve is fine, but I just don't get all sticky inside when I think of him."

"I'm glad."

"You don't like him?" Claire asked, pausing with her needle in the air.

Nell was sorry she'd said anything. "I'm not the one going out with him. But he seems awfully fast."

"Yes, I've had to tell him to keep his hands to himself. But I like him because he makes me laugh. And he reads the newspaper—all of it. Do you know how many boys I've gone out with who never get beyond the sports pages? You're lucky that Mr. Moran is so up-to-date on things. I'm tired of dates who think I'm so stupid I don't have opinions of my own. They're surprised I know who the president is. The men I meet don't think much of women," Claire said.

"I am lucky I met Wade," Nell replied, and she knew she was. They often discussed politics and world affairs, although Wade sometimes frowned when her opinions differed from his own. Nell didn't believe Steve was much interested in Claire's mind, however. "Do you think these blues go together, or do they clash?" She held up two scraps of flowered fabric.

"Um, I don't like them," Claire said. "Why don't you try the blue with the green?" She reached into Nell's sewing basked and removed a length of material.

"I wonder if a year from now, we'll be sitting here sewing and talking about men," Nell said with a laugh.

"Me maybe, but not you. You'll be married by then."

"I'm not so sure. Wade's never said anything, and I don't know what I'd reply if he did."

"Of course, you haven't known him very long, but I'm sure he will." Claire laughed as she glanced out of the window. "Maybe today. There he is now."

"Don't bet on it. I never knew of a man who proposed at the movies." Nell set aside her sewing.

Wade knocked on the door just as Nell answered it. As he walked into the room, he took off his hat and glanced at the sewing baskets. "Such a nice scene of domesticity," he said. "Am I early?"

"No, we were talking and forgot the time," Nell said. She reached for her wrap.

Wade invited Claire to go with them, and Nell urged her roommate to say yes, but Claire demurred. "I have an engagement with Steve, although I think I would very much enjoy going out with the two of you."

"Perhaps another time, then," Wade said. He didn't suggest that Steve join them, and Nell wondered if it was as obvious to Claire as to her that Wade didn't like him.

They left just as Steve drove up too fast in his autocar. He slammed on the brakes, sending up a shower of dirt, then revved the motor. "I'm taking Claire for a spin," he said. "Pity this thing has room for only two, or we'd all go together."

"Pity," Wade said.

"Where you going?" Steve asked.

Nell wanted to say it was none of his business, but instead, she replied, "To the pictures."

"Then to dinner," Wade added.

Nell and Wade walked to the corner and took a trolley to the movie palace. The feature was a comedy. Nell didn't care for slapstick. When the film broke and the lights came on while the film was being repaired, she complained of a headache. The flickering of the picture had brought it on, and now the bright lights and the noisy theater made it worse. She asked Wade if she could go home. "I'm awfully sorry, but I'm wretched company tonight. I would like to take a headache powder."

"We could stop at a drugstore on the way and find something to treat you," he suggested. "Abby got headaches, and aspirin and soda water helped."

Nell liked that he was so thoughtful, although she knew his wife's remedy wouldn't do her any good. "No, my grandmother makes up a compound with feverfew in it that works better than anything."

"Then I shall take you home."

He was solicitous as they got off the trolley and walked the block to Nell's house. He held tight to her arm and talked in soft tones, almost whispering, because when they left the theater, she had held her hands over her ears to keep out the noise. He opened the door quietly and held it for Nell.

When they entered the front hall, Nell thought they were alone. Then she heard the sound of something falling and a loud cry. "Stop it. Get off me. You've no right." Claire's voice was high and out of control.

"You want this. You know you do. You girls always say no, but that's not what you mean."

"Stop it!" Claire shouted.

"You're all alike. You let us spend our money on you, and then you won't put out. What's so special about you, anyway?" There was the sound of a slap.

Nell froze. For an instant, she could not move, as the horror of what had happened to her in the restaurant came back to her. "No," she muttered. "Oh no, Wade. Stop him."

She took a step forward, but Wade pushed her aside and rushed past her to the living room. He stood in the doorway a second, letting his eyes adjust to the dark room. Nell was behind him, and she looked past Wade's shoulder. Claire thrashed about on the sofa, Steve on top of her, his hands pinning her shoulders to the back of the couch so that she couldn't get up. "Stop it!" Nell yelled.

Steve heard them and turned and snarled, "Get the hell out of here. Mind your business." His face was twisted with anger, and Nell saw in it the determination of the man who had attacked her. With a cry of fury, Nell took a step toward them, her fingers outstretched, her nails ready to tear into Steve's back. But Wade held out his arm to stop her.

"This *is* my business," Wade said. "Get out!" he told Steve. His voice was strong and steady. Nell had never seen him angry before.

"*You* get out. This is between me and her," Steve shot back.

"I told you to leave." Wade's voice carried a sense of authority.

Steve released his hold on Claire. He turned to Wade and said, "All's I wanted was a little kiss. You're a pious son-of-a-bitch. You don't have the nuts to do this yourself."

Before Nell could think, Wade was at the sofa. He grabbed Steve by the arms and threw him onto the floor. Although it had been years since he'd worked as a hired man, Wade was strong. Steve was younger and fit, and Nell thought he would strike Wade. She looked around the room for something she could use to hit Steve and grasped an umbrella. Wade stood over Steve, his fists up, and said, "If you touch her again, I'll kill you."

Steve got to his feet and started to leave the room, but then he whirled around and struck Wade in the jaw. Wade lurched to one side, and Nell started forward with the umbrella. Before Nell could strike, however, Wade shook his head and punched Steve in the stomach and then in the chest, and finally in the head.

"You bastard!" Steve muttered as he fell to the floor.

Wade might have kicked him, but Wade was like the cowboys, Nell thought. They believed it wasn't fair to strike a man when he was down. "Stand up," Wade ordered.

"Aw, hell. Can't a fellow have a little fun? All I wanted was a kiss," Steve said, then scrambled to his feet and darted out of the room. "I didn't mean nothing by it," he added as he ran out of the house to his horseless carriage.

Nell rushed to Claire, whose clothes were mussed, and put her arms around her roommate. "I'm so sorry. It's awful," Nell murmured. "Go ahead and cry." She held Claire, who began to sob. "It's all right," Nell muttered. "You're safe."

As she rocked Claire, she heard Wade in the front yard. "I know who you are," he called in a measured voice. "You are never to contact Miss Claire again. If you ever so much as drive down this street, I'll have the police on you. And don't think I don't know the chief of police himself." Steve's autocar started up. The engine roared. Then it grew softer and died away as the vehicle sped down the street.

Wade came back into the house. "You will not see him again."

"Do you really know the chief of police?" Nell asked, looking up at him in admiration.

Wade smiled. "No, of course not, but he doesn't know that."

"Should we call the police?" Nell thought of her own ugly incident and how the police had arrested her attacker and thrown him into jail.

"I wouldn't advise it. It would just be her word against his."

Nell glanced at her roommate. Maybe Steve had indeed only intended to kiss Claire. That was what he would claim, anyway. And she hadn't seen anything more than Claire pinned to the sofa, Steve's face against her friend's. Maybe after what had happened to her in Denver, Nell had suspected Steve of trying something more than he'd intended. Nell would never know for sure, and most likely Claire wouldn't either.

"You would not want it to get into the newspapers. Miss Claire's reputation would suffer, and she might lose her job," Wade continued. Nell knew he was right. Even if the incident wasn't Claire's fault, she could get fired. The school board didn't like scandal.

"If you hadn't come . . ." Claire said.

"But we did," Nell told her.

"He thought you wouldn't be back this soon. We went for a drive. He had a flask and was drinking. When we got home . . ." Claire began to cry again.

"You're safe," Nell told her. She handed her roommate a glass of water that Wade had fetched.

"I never should have let him come inside when he was drunk. And I shouldn't have accepted his presents. That seemed to make him think he had the right . . . It's my fault—"

"It's not your fault," Wade broke in, and Nell wondered at his compassion, surprised that he should understand the guilt Claire felt. Maybe he remembered what Nell had told him about the attack in the café and how she had blamed herself.

"Wade's right. You can't blame yourself," Nell repeated. "Steve Sorel is a wicked man. He got what he deserved."

Wade left the room, and Nell heard him moving about the house, checking the doors and windows. When he returned, he said, "He will not be back. You don't have to worry about him. Tomorrow, I'll have my lawyer contact him. When my solicitor is finished, you will not have to worry about Steve ever again." Wade reached for his hat, which had fallen onto the floor. "I'll come by in a day or two to make sure you are all right."

Nell walked him to the front door, saying, "I don't know what she would have done if you hadn't taken charge. I am so grateful."

"I remember what you told me about the man who . . . came into your café," he said. "I was so angry. It was as if I were rescuing you." He took a deep breath, then kissed Nell on the cheek. He'd never done that before.

When Nell returned to the living room, Claire was standing up. "I have to take a bath. I feel so dirty," she said. Nell understood, and she turned on the taps in the tub while her roommate undressed. Claire was in the bath a long time. Nell picked up the living room, then went into the bedroom and turned down the sheets. When Claire emerged from the bathroom, her face was bruised. "I will have to say I fell down the cellar stairs," Claire said with a tiny laugh.

"If you can laugh, you'll be all right," Nell said. Then she told her roommate she would sleep on the couch.

"No!" Claire said. "I would feel so much safer if you were here." So Nell undressed and got into the bed they shared and held her roommate until Claire went to sleep.

Late the next morning, a boy came to the door with a bouquet of red roses for Claire. The note with it was signed simply "Wade."

Nell's headache turned into a bad cold that forced her to stay home from work. She had agreed to go with Wade to Helen's charity event the following Saturday night, but she telephoned him that morning to explain she was still too sick to attend.

"Would Miss Claire care to go in your place?" he asked. "It won't be the same as having you there, but she might enjoy getting out. And I do need to escort someone."

"It's a wonderful idea," Nell said, thinking the outing would take her friend's mind off Steve's attack.

Claire agreed, and put on the blue silk dress that Nell had worn to her first dinner with Wade.

"You look better in it than I did," Nell told her.

Wade arrived with a bouquet of flowers and a bottle of ginger ale for Nell and a corsage of gardenias for Claire. As Nell pinned them on her roommate, Wade said, "I didn't know what to bring, but these were a favorite of my . . ." His voice trailed off.

"They're lovely," Claire replied.

Nell was asleep when her roommate returned, but she woke up as Claire quietly undressed. "How was the evening?" she asked.

"It was fine. If he weren't your beau, I'd go after him myself. He's thoughtful and charming—and he wouldn't stop talking about you. I think you are the luckiest girl in the world, Nell. I'm surprised he hasn't proposed by now. He must be waiting for the right time."

"You mean he didn't talk about his wife?" Nell asked.

"Well . . ." Claire replied, and they both laughed.

CHAPTER TWENTY-FOUR

On a fine Saturday morning in November, Wade knocked on the door of Nell's house. He was dressed in a motoring cap and a duster, and a pair of goggles was perched on his head. Nell looked beyond him to a horseless carriage parked in the street. It had yellow spoke wheels and red trim.

"I'm thinking of buying it, so I'm taking it out for a test," he said. "Want to come along?"

"Of course," Nell said. She had never ridden in a motorcar.

"I've a pair of goggles for you, but you'll need a coat and a hat. The car's an Oldsmobile Curved Dash, and it goes very fast—up to twenty miles an hour. I want to take it out of the city before I make up my mind whether to buy it. I thought we could motor to Liberty and have dinner. I will get you home before evening. The Oldsmobile has lamps, but still, I don't care to drive it after dark."

Nell quickly put on a coat and tied a scarf over her hat so that it wouldn't blow off. She'd seen hats flying down the street behind motorcars and didn't want to lose hers. As she started for the door, she asked Claire, "Want to come?"

"Yes, please do. I think we can fit three on the seat, although it will be crowded," Wade said.

Claire shook her head. "I have papers to grade. You go ahead and have a good time." She walked outside with them to admire the motor.

"Don't expect us until you see us," Wade said as he helped Nell into the auto.

Despite the time of year, the sky was clear with no trace of clouds, and the air crisp. The leaves were turning, and Nell thought it was a glorious day to be riding to Liberty in a new autocar. She smiled at Wade as he climbed into the Oldsmobile beside her. "I'm so glad you invited me to come along."

"I want your approval. I hope we will be riding in this horseless carriage for a long time. I'm told there are even a few women who drive them. Perhaps you will be one." He smiled back at her.

"I wasn't sure you would ever want a motorcar," Nell said.

He thought a moment before he turned to her. "You mean because of Abigail and Margaret?"

Nell nodded.

"It took me a while to make up my mind. But then I realized that it wasn't the car that killed them. It was the driver." He started the engine, and saying "hang on!" he drove slowly along the street. Wade was a cautious driver, not at all like Steve, who had liked to start up quickly and speed away, drawing as much attention to himself as possible. Wade avoided busy streets, driving quietly through neighborhoods, so it took a long time before they were on the Liberty road. He didn't talk but instead concentrated on driving. Once they were out in the country, he relaxed.

"Have you driven before?" Nell asked, above the sound of the engine. She was holding on to her hat so that it wouldn't blow off.

"Not alone. But the salesman showed me how. It's not so hard." He jerked the tiller to avoid a hole in the road, and the Oldsmobile swerved to the left. Nell slid over on the seat until she was next to him. "Well, I haven't quite mastered it yet," he said, laughing, as Nell righted herself.

She liked driving in the country, although at nearly twenty miles an hour, it seemed that they were going so fast she could scarcely see a building or an animal before it was behind them. The farms with their white houses and red barns reminded her of Harveyville. She missed that farm, but she would be there at Christmas. Perhaps she should take Claire with her, but she dismissed that idea. There were things she didn't want Claire to know. Maybe she could invite Wade instead. Her grandparents would like that, but Wade might not think it proper. Perhaps later, if they were engaged. She was sitting closer to him now and wondered if he would put his arm around her. But he kept both hands on the tiller.

"The bank has made a loan on that place," he said, nodding at a yellow farmhouse. "The people there reminded me of your grandparents when I worked for them. They are hardworking folks."

"You handled the loan, then?" Nell asked.

"Yes, I'm making more and more loans on farms and ranches. That seems to be my specialty now. The collateral is good, but I'm betting on the people. I think I'm pretty good at sizing them up." He glanced at Nell, and she wondered if he had sized her up, too.

"Does that mean you'd give me a loan if I had a farm?"

Wade laughed. "You're a woman."

"Oh, you noticed."

"Of course I did. The first time I met you."

A Ford motorcar came up behind them, and Wade pulled off the road to let it pass, and they waved to the driver. Wade glanced over at a farm where children had seen the car and come running to the fence to watch it go by. Wade waved at them, too. "Do you miss the farm?" he asked.

"Sometimes. I miss the quiet and the fresh air and the chickens. Most of all, I miss the people. I like farm people." Ranch people, too, she thought.

"But you don't mind the city?"

"Oh, no," Nell replied quickly. She couldn't tell him that cities made her apprehensive, that she didn't care for the coal smoke that hung in the air or the clatter of the streets, or that she'd never felt altogether safe in either Denver or Kansas City. Still, cities were exciting, with movies and plays, symphonies and art museums—although she still wished Wade would take her to hear jazz. Perhaps one day, she thought, smiling to herself.

"I hope that smile is for me," Wade said as he pulled out onto the dirt road again.

"Naturally," Nell told him. "It's a lovely day, and I am having a grand time." She looked out at the leaves on the trees that had turned yellow and red, at a cow that watched her from over a fence, at a quail that flew up out of a cornfield into the sky. People stopped what they were doing and stared at the car as it flew past. Some of them waved, and one man yelled, "Get a horse." Wade squeezed the horn at him. Nell felt lazy and content, and she could thank Wade for that. She cared a great deal for him. It wasn't true love, as Claire would have put it, but it was a comfortable affection. He was easy to be with, and kind. Wade was a good man, and Nell knew that if she didn't marry him, another woman would snatch him up. Still, she wished Wade made her heart beat faster, made her want him to touch her, to hold her, to make love to her.

They reached Liberty, and Wade drove slowly down the streets. "I was here once before, in a carriage, and there is an acceptable little restaurant. Abby was with me. She liked . . ." Wade stopped. "I liked it very much. We can try it if you like, or perhaps there is someplace you'd rather go."

Nell told him the restaurant was fine, and he stopped the auto in front of a small café with red-checked curtains in the window. As Wade turned off the motor, several little boys ran up to the car.

"Hey, it's a horseless carriage," one of them said.

"Wow, mister, can I touch it?" A boy held his hand next to the black metal fender.

"Can I steer the tiller?" a third boy questioned.

"You bet," Wade told them. He took off his duster and suit coat and rolled up his shirtsleeves. He walked around the car with the boys, pointing to the engine and the oil lamps and the mounted horn. Nell climbed out so that the boys could sit on the seat. One reached over and squeezed the horn, and they all laughed, looking at Wade to see if he was angry. But he laughed, too.

"Want to ride in it?" Wade asked.

"Wow!" the boys said, looking at each other and grinning at their good luck.

While Nell stood on the sidewalk, the children took turns riding up and down the street with Wade. Nell watched them, but mostly, she watched Wade. He was awfully good with boys.

She liked that about him. It was important. He would be a good father.

The boys ran off, yelling, "Thanks, mister," and Wade rolled down his shirtsleeves. He grinned at her sheepishly and said, "I didn't mean to keep you waiting so long."

"I didn't mind at all. I loved seeing you with the children," she said and took his arm. They went inside the restaurant and ordered dinner and sat for a long time, talking. It was one of the best days she'd ever had, Nell decided, certainly the best day since she'd come to Kansas City, and she was in no hurry to end it.

They didn't notice the weather, and when they went outside, late in the afternoon, storm clouds covered the sky, and it had begun to rain. "We can't go home in this weather. We'll be drenched. I should have gotten an auto with a top," Wade said. "I'll park the car under a tree. Then we'd better go back inside and wait it out." They returned to the café and ordered a pot of tea and watched the rain streak the windows. "It's a good thing the Oldsmobile has lamps," he said. "I don't think we'll get home before dark."

They waited a long time, until the rain stopped and the storm clouds blew away, and then Wade went outside and wiped off the seat. Nell came out of the restaurant, and he helped her into the car. "It's going to be a cold ride, I'm afraid," he said as he settled beside her. He tried to switch on the lamps. They flickered and went out. Wade got out the instruction booklet to see what was wrong, but just then, a Ford auto pulled by a mule team passed them.

"Stay off the Kansas City road. It's as muddy as a pigpen," a man wearing goggles called to Wade. "I had to get pulled out."

Wade put down the booklet and turned to Nell. "I don't

know how to say this, but I think it is foolish to try to return this evening. I will if you insist upon it, but we are likely to get stuck out in the open. The mud could cause an accident. I very much think we should find accommodations for the night."

If Wade had not been so honorable, he might have planned this, Nell thought, but there was no way Wade could have known that it would rain and that the roads would be impassable. Still, would Wade . . . would he take advantage of the situation? He knew all about her, so she could hardly act offended if he expected to spend the night with her. But there was no choice. They couldn't go home. Nell didn't want to risk an accident on a muddy road late at night. "Yes, I think that would be wise. I should not like to spend the night lying in the mud," Nell said at last.

Wade shut off the motor and went inside the café to ask about rooms. As he helped Nell out of the Oldsmobile, he said, "We are in luck. There is a hotel just down the street."

Nell wondered what Wade would tell the proprietor. He would see they had no luggage and might realize they were un-married. When they entered the lobby, however, the desk clerk said, "I seen your car and knowed you wasn't going anywhere tonight. Lucky I got a room."

"Two rooms," Wade said.

The clerk smiled and barely raised an eyebrow, "Adjoining, of course."

"Certainly not," Wade said.

The clerk flushed. "No, of course not." He handed Wade two keys. "They're both on the second floor—opposite ends of the hall."

The two were silent as they climbed the stairs. When they were out of view of the clerk, Wade said, "He was fresh. I hope you weren't offended."

"Only amused," Nell said, although the clerk had made her wonder what this would do to her reputation. "Still, I hope no one at the school finds out about it."

"They won't hear about it from me, and we should be home tomorrow. If the roads are wet, I'll find a carriage to hire, or even a farm wagon." He laughed at that. "I'll get you back long before school starts on Monday, and no one will be the wiser."

"I will think of it as an adventure," Nell said.

"You are a good sport. Another girl would be upset."

Another girl, Nell thought, would not already have spent the night with a man—with two men.

They went to supper, then walked around until they found a drugstore that sold tooth powder and toothbrushes and combs. Wade escorted Nell to her room and wished her good night. He didn't kiss her, and Nell waited a long time to see if he would knock on her door after she'd gotten into bed. Would she let him in or pretend she was asleep? She didn't know. But there was no knock until dawn. When Nell peered through a crack in the door, Wade said, "The roads are frozen, and I think we ought to get a start. If it's agreeable, I'll go to the café for rolls to take with us, while you dress."

Nell had slept in her chemise and quickly donned her dress, which was wrinkled but dry, then hurried down the hall to the bathroom to brush her teeth. She was sitting in the Oldsmobile when Wade came out of the café. He handed her a sack of doughnuts and a cup of coffee, telling her he had persuaded the waitress to sell him the china cup so that Nell could take it with her. Then he turned on the engine, and they started off.

The road was bumpy because the ruts were frozen, and it

took twice as long to drive home as to make the trip the day before, but they arrived with no mishap.

"There was a terrible storm," Nell told Claire, after Wade saw her to the door and left. "I was afraid you would worry."

"It stormed here, too. I knew you would have taken refuge somewhere." She studied Nell a moment. "Most men would propose after spending a night with a girl."

"Oh, it wasn't anything like that. There was a hotel. Two rooms. It was perfectly proper."

"He didn't even try—"

Nell shook her head.

"Pity."

"Perhaps." Nell grinned. She wondered again whether she would have answered if he had knocked on her door in the middle of the night.

Nell had hoped to go home to the farm for Christmas, but school did not let out until Christmas Eve, and by then it would be too late to take a train. She didn't want her grandfather to have to drive to Topeka in the dark to pick her up. So she decided to go to Harveyville on Christmas day. That way, she could have Christmas night with her family and stay until New Year's.

It was Claire who came up with the idea for Christmas. "Mr. Moran's been so kind to us that I think we ought to do something for him," she told Nell, who quite agreed. "Let's fix Christmas Eve dinner. We'll make it very special."

"But I had planned to take you out for dinner on Christmas Eve," Wade protested when they told him.

"We won't hear of it," Nell said. "You leave Christmas Eve to us."

She and Claire made a fruitcake with nuts and candied fruit, then poured whiskey over it and wrapped it in cheesecloth and stored it in a tin. They ordered a goose from the butcher, who instructed them on how to prepare it. Nell made grits with cheese and green chili, the way the cowboys at the Rockin' A liked it, while Claire fixed dressing and boiled potatoes. They added stewed tomatoes that they had canned in the fall, and bottled beans, and lettuce with salad cream. And in case Wade didn't like fruitcake, they made a trifle, layering pound cake and boiled custard and blackberry jam that Claire's grandmother had sent. There was enough food to feed her entire school class, Nell announced as they set the table.

Wade arrived with a pound of chocolates and a bottle of sherry and two small boxes wrapped in paper, which Nell and Claire opened. Each contained a watch attached to a pin so that the women could fasten them to their jackets or shirtwaists. Claire's was silver, the watch hanging from a silver bow. Nell's was gold, the back blue enamel with gold fleur-de-lis, and it was attached to a larger gold fleur-de-lis pin.

"We have something for you, too, from both of us," Nell told him, and handed Wade a large box. She and Claire had spent a long time deciding what to give him. Of course, it would be improper to buy him an article of clothing, and Nell had never been to Wade's house, so she didn't know what would be appropriate for it. Then she thought about the playground Wade had established in memory of his wife and daughter, and she suggested to Claire that they buy something for it. Wade had taken her to see the playground once, and she had noticed one of the swings was gone, so she and Claire had purchased a replacement, a wooden seat attached to long chains.

"I'm afraid you can't wear it like a watch," Nell said after

Wade opened the box, which they had wrapped in crepe paper and decorated with colored stars. She felt a little embarrassed then. It wasn't much of a gift. Besides, the playground was a private thing. Wade might feel they were intruding on his grief.

He didn't say anything for a moment, only stared at the swing. Then he announced, "Nothing could have pleased me more." He gripped the women's hands.

After dinner, Wade suggested they attend a midnight church service. Claire begged off. Nell would have, too, but it was Christmas, and she knew Wade would be disappointed, since he'd told her he had always attended Christmas Eve services there with his wife and daughter. So she agreed. Snow had begun to fall, and Nell put her hands into the muff as they walked along, Wade holding her arm.

"That was a fine gift," he said again. "The only thing that would give me as much pleasure is your photograph. Have you one? I should very much like to have it."

Nell thought. The only photograph she had of herself was a Kodak Lucy had taken of her at the Rockin' A. Lucy had had a copy made and given it to Nell. "It's not a very professional likeness. Perhaps I should have one taken in a studio."

"No, I should like the snapshot," he told her, and Nell promised to give it to him when she returned home.

Despite the late hour, the church was filled with families. The sanctuary was decorated with evergreens and lilies, and white candles lined the aisle. The smells and the Christmas carols made Nell nostalgic for the winters she had lived with her grandparents, when they had gone to the tiny country church. "God's in his heaven. All's right with the world," she told Wade as they left the service.

"I feel that way, too," Wade said.

"Did you see all the families there?"

"Yes, Christmas is a time to be together." He stopped, and Nell walked on a little before she realized Wade was not beside her. He did not catch up with her but instead remained where he was, his hand brushing snow from a high iron fence that surrounded a house. He looked at her a long time without saying anything until Nell asked what was wrong.

"Nothing. Nothing at all. I . . . Nell, will you marry me?"

Of course Nell wanted a husband. That was why she had come to Kansas City, and Wade had made it clear he was ready to marry again. But she had not expected a proposal that night.

"I do not mean to shock you. I had planned to ask you on New Year's Eve, but you won't be here, and Christmas seems appropriate. I think we both hoped from the beginning that this would be the result of our friendship. After seeing the families at church, I thought we could be a family, too, the way I used to be. We could add children of our own. I care for you very much."

He didn't say he loved her, Nell thought. Did she love him? She still wasn't sure, but perhaps that wasn't important. She had loved two other men, and they had failed her. Maybe it was better that she marry a man she respected. Wade would be true. He was steady, so steady that Nell could picture what every day would be for the rest of their lives. He had a fine job and might even be president of the bank one day, and he would take care of her. He wasn't balky like Buddy, and he didn't have another wife, at least not one that was alive, although Nell thought she would always live with the ghost of one. But then, he would live with her transgressions. Wade was the kind of man she had come to Kansas City to meet, and she had been fortunate to find one who was so kind and so successful—and one who accepted her with all her missteps. What did it matter that she found him dull at times? Or that this proposal didn't make her feel giddy, as she had been when Buddy and then James had asked her to marry them?

"Of course I will marry you, Wade," she said.

He smiled at her and put his arms around her and kissed her, and if the kiss seemed too chaste, what did that matter either? She felt a swell of emotion, and tears came into her eyes, not tears of love but of relief, of gratitude. She did not feel the surge of excitement she had when she knew she would join her life with Buddy's or with James's, but she was older now, more mature. She felt fortunate she had found a good man, and she knew they would have a good life together.

Wade accompanied Nell to Harveyville on Christmas day. "It is only right I ask your grandfather for permission to marry you," he explained. Nell found that sweet. Neither Buddy nor James had suggested such a thing.

"What do you think he will say?" she teased. "Do you think he will want me to marry the hired man?"

"I shall try very hard to convince him I have come up in the world."

Of course Wade didn't have to convince him at all. When Nell's grandfather saw Wade step down from the train with her, he grinned. He slapped Wade on the back and said, "If I'd knowed you'd be part of the family, I'd have paid you better wages."

It was a fine visit. A storm had blanketed the countryside in white, and they all crowded into a sleigh to attend church and to visit with neighbors. Nell and her grandmother cooked and sewed and gossiped while her grandfather showed Wade about the farm, remarking on changes and improvements he'd made since Wade left. "This will all go to Nell one day," he said. "You didn't know when you was here that you was working for yourself, did you?"

Wade said he wanted to be married in February, when things slowed down at the bank. He brushed aside Nell's suggestion that they wait until the school found someone to replace her. That wasn't important, he said. Besides, it would be easier for her grandparents to get away in the winter, and they both wanted the ceremony to be a family event. They would be married in Wade's church, the one he had attended with Abigail and Margaret, and they would live in Wade's house. It was a perfectly good house in the fashionable Hyde Park neighborhood, and Wade saw no reason for them not to live there. Later, when she saw it, Nell had to admit it was indeed a fine home, although she would have preferred they start out with a place of their own, one that didn't have the ghosts of Wade's first wife and daughter. But she didn't know how to explain that to him.

They talked about their plans on New Year's Eve. Her grandparents already were in bed, and Wade and Nell had gone outside in the snow to look at the stars. He reached into his pocket and took out a leather pouch, then extracted a diamond ring. "I brought this with me. This will seal our engagement," he said and slid it onto her finger.

It didn't fit, and Nell couldn't help but wonder if it had been Abigail's. But she didn't ask. She said only, "It is lovely."

"I think we will have a good marriage," he said, taking her arm.

"Yes, I know it will be." And she did. Marriage to Wade would be good. Not exciting but good. She couldn't ask for more.

As soon as she returned to Kansas City, she purchased fabric and cut out her wedding dress. The gown was finished when, three days before the wedding, Nell ran away.

CHAPTER TWENTY-FIVE

"Again! Why did you run away this time, Granny?" June asked.

"I . . ." Ellen stopped. "That was Nell, not me."

"But you're Nell, aren't you?" June laughed. "I figured that out when you told me how stupid you felt about James. How would you really know unless you were Nell?"

"You're too smart for your own good," Ellen said.

"Not so smart. I thought it was pretty obvious. Were you really called Nell instead of Ellen?"

"In those days, yes. Ellen's my real name, of course. Nell was only a nickname. When I married your grandfather, I thought Ellen sounded more adult. So I asked to be called that. Besides, I was leaving the old days behind. I was starting over with your grandfather."

"I don't get it. Why did you run off the third time? Did Wade do something?"

"He didn't do anything. I came to my senses."

"Did you leave him for Grandpa Ben? Did you know him in

Kansas City? How does he fit into this, anyway? You never mentioned my grandfather in your stories. I don't get it. Was it just love at first sight with him?"

"Almost. You don't know how charming your grandfather could be. Or handsome. He still is." Ellen thought of Ben's clear brown eyes, his thick hair that was white now, and his hands, square and sensual. "I have to say that ever since I lived in New Mexico, I sure did like cowboys." She blushed. It was true. How could Wade Moran compete with a cowpoke like Ben?

The two women looked up when they heard a truck turn off the main road to the ranch. "That'll be Wesley with your grandfather now. I bet Ben remembered you're here and wanted to get back to see you." Ellen folded the quilt, which was finished now. She ran her fingers over the fabrics and stopped on one, pointing at it. That scrap was from the first wedding dress, the one Lucy gave her, she told June. It was a pity to cut it up, but most of the fabric was yellowed and dried out. What was the point in saving it? She moved her finger to a bit of heavy brocade with purple flowers in it. "This was the material James gave me for the second wedding dress. See the violets. They haven't faded."

"Why did you save that one? I'd have tossed it away. Ugh." June shuddered.

"I was in such a hurry to leave Denver that I just packed up everything without thinking about it." There hadn't been any real reason to throw it away, she said, and after a while, she forgot she had it. She came across it when she was looking for material for June's quilt. "It really is quite pretty, isn't it? The purple hasn't faded the least bit."

"Didn't women used to wear purple for mourning?"

"I certainly don't mourn the fact I didn't marry James Hamilton," she said with a laugh, then fingered the scrap. It was the finest material in the quilt. Ellen traced one of the flowers with her fingertip, then studied her hands, which had aged far more than the fabric. But Ben never noticed how old her hands had gotten, and that was all that mattered.

"What about the dress for your marriage to Wade? Which one is that?" June asked.

Ellen looked over the quilt and tapped a yellow silk so pale that it was almost white. "That one."

"You cut up that dress, too?" June asked.

"No, it was just one of the scraps that were left over. I don't know what happened to the dress. I left it behind. There's not much use for a yellow silk dress on a ranch. Besides, I married your grandfather in a hurry and didn't take much with me. Maybe Claire wore it as a wedding dress."

"Claire?"

"She married Wade, of course. I felt pretty bad about what I'd done to him. He was such a decent man, and he had been so good to me. In the end, he did better. Claire made him a much better wife than I would have. She was more . . ." Ellen paused. "More accommodating about his first wife, I guess you'd say. I suspect she was thrilled to marry up, although she really was very fond of him. When I thought about it, I realized she always had been. And Wade, he couldn't have been too hurt that I ran out on him, because he married Claire four months after I left. They were happy." Ellen stood when she heard the truck door slam and watched as Wesley got out, then went around to Ben's side and opened the door for him. Ben waved away the hired man, annoyed that anyone would think he needed help. Still stubborn, Ellen thought.

Ben walked slowly toward the porch. His hat was pulled down over his face, and he was more than a little bowlegged.

He grinned when he saw June and Ellen and touched the brim of his hat. Ellen kept her eyes on her husband when she spoke to June. "I've always kept in touch with Claire and Wade. They visited the ranch a few years ago. He didn't once mention his first wife."

"But who was Grandpa Ben? Is he the reason you ran away from Wade? How did you meet him?" June's voice was insistent. "Tell me, Granny."

"That will have to wait for later." Ellen held out her hand to her husband, who squeezed it.

Ben pecked June's cheek. "I sure am glad you're here, little girl. Your Granny and I have missed you. Seeing you get off that plane last night was as good a sight as I've seen in a long time."

Ellen beamed at her husband, glad that for now, at least, his memory was all right.

Ben turned to Ellen then. He removed his hat and kissed her cheek, and then he took his right hand from behind his back and handed her a stem of chamisa. "I picked this on the road. I remember I gave you a chamisa flower a long time ago, Miss Nellie Blue-Eyes," he said. "You always said chamisa was your favorite."

"Why, thank you, Buddy." Ellen held his hand a little longer than necessary before she threaded the stem of the chamisa in the buttonhole of her shirt.

"You better shake it and make sure there's no bee in it," he said, glancing at her slyly.

"You don't forget everything, do you?"

June's mouth dropped open. "Wait, Granny! You married Buddy? Grandpa Ben is Buddy?"

"You been telling that child tales?" Ben asked. Then he told her, "Doc says Little Texas will be fine. I best put him in the barn and feed him. Then I'll wash up for supper."

"Little Texas was the name of Teddy Roosevelt's horse in Cuba," Ellen explained to June. "Your grandfather always admired the colonel. His horse, too."

June brushed that aside. "I want to know how you met Buddy again. I don't understand."

"What are you two talking about?" Ben asked.

"Granny was telling me how she ran away from getting married three times."

"That so? Well, lucky for me she did," Ben said, his eyes crinkling as he looked at Ellen. "I sure am glad she gave that first fellow another chance."

"How did it happen?" June asked. "How did the two of you meet again?"

"You tell her," Ellen told her husband.

Ben took off his hat and combed his hair with his fingers. His skin was burned to leather by the sun. "It was a stroke of luck. That fellow your grandmother was going to marry, Wade Moran his name was. He was my banker. He financed this ranch when I bought it. I was a pretty good customer and made my payments on time. So when I needed money to buy more cattle, I went to see him in Kansas City."

"And he told you about Granny?"

Ben turned away and stared out across the ranchland for a long time. "What's that?"

"Wade Moran told you he was going to marry Granny?"

"Did he?" Ben turned to his wife.

Ellen closed her eyes for a moment. She had been so glad he was lucid, but it hadn't lasted long. He was confused now. She glanced at June, whose eyes were clouded with tears. "Go take care of Little Texas. We'll wait supper for you."

The two watched Ben make for the barn, and Ellen said,

"You can see how it comes and goes with him. Usually he's better when he's someplace that's familiar, like the ranch. In town, unless he's talking to some of his old friends, he's worse. That's another reason I want to keep him here as long as I can."

"It won't be forever," June said.

"No." Ellen didn't want to think about it anymore.

June waited until her grandfather had disappeared into the barn. "So did Wade Moran tell Grandpa Ben he was going to marry you?"

"Not exactly. Wade didn't know we knew each other. When I told him about your grandfather, I called him Buddy. Wade knew him as Ben. Like your grandfather said, he went to Wade to finance a cattle purchase. Wade agreed to loan your grandfather the money and said he was in a good mood because he was getting married. Then he picked up that picture of me I'd given him, the one that was taken on the old Rockin' A in New Mexico. Wade had put it into a silver frame." Ellen laughed. "He sent it to your grandfather later as a wedding present. Not right away, however. It was after he married Claire.

"When your grandfather saw the picture on Wade's desk, he said, 'Ain't that a dinger?' He never let on that we knew each other, just got Wade to tell him about me. Wade said I was a schoolteacher and even named the school. Ben was so stunned at what Wade told him that instead of going out to dinner, which they usually did when he was in Kansas City, he said he was feeling poorly and wanted to go back to his hotel. Poor Wade— your grandfather told me later, 'If he hadn't had a leaky mouth, he could have married you.'"

"But of course he didn't. And I bet Grandpa Ben didn't go back to his hotel either." June leaned forward in her chair and grinned. "Did he go right to your school?"

"He did. He barged into my schoolroom—well, he barged into half a dozen rooms before he found me—and he grabbed me and said we were getting married that afternoon."

"That must have thrilled your class."

"Fortunately, school was out, and the students were gone," Ellen said.

"Then he hadn't married Alice?" June asked.

"That's what I asked. He told me he'd have gone to Texas before he'd marry her. He'd just said it to make me jealous. He wanted me to think he was the whole herd, and when he thought I didn't, he wanted to hurt me. So he said he was going to marry her. But in truth, I was the only girl he'd ever cared about, and if he couldn't have me, he wouldn't marry at all. He told me that letting me go was the biggest mistake of his life." Ellen reddened and turned away, embarrassed. "That's what he said, at any rate."

"I love it, Granny! So you married him right away."

"That very afternoon. I had on my schoolteacher skirt and white blouse with chalk smears on it and my white apron. I forgot to take it off. I was married in it," Ellen said. She pointed to the white square she had added to the quilt that morning. "That's a piece of the sash."

"Wade must have been furious."

"Oh, I don't know. He gave Ben the loan. He could have canceled it, I suppose, but he was a man of integrity." Ellen glanced at her granddaughter. "He's been loaning us money ever since." Ellen stretched out her hand to indicate the ranch. "We wouldn't have all this without him."

"He's still alive?"

"Yes. Claire died a couple of years ago. He wrote just last week that he'd remarried. The whole letter compared his new wife to Claire. I guess he finally got over the first one. I wish Claire knew that."

June sat for a moment, absently running her hand back and forth over the quilt. "You never stopped loving Grandpa Ben."

"No," her grandmother replied. "I never got over Buddy. Of the three men, I was always best with him. I knew the minute he walked into my classroom and grabbed me up that he was the only one I truly wanted to marry." She blushed a little. "Ben's his real name, of course. Remember I told you that Buddy was the name of his horse."

The screen door slammed, and Maria came outside. "There's somebody on the telephone for Miss June," she said. The two women had been too caught up in their conversation to hear the ring.

After June went inside, Ellen asked, "Her mother again?"

"No, ma'am. A man."

"Dave, the fellow who was here last summer?"

Maria shrugged. "He didn't say."

Maria went back into the kitchen, but Ellen remained outside, watching for Ben to come out of the barn. The sight of him still warmed her heart, just as it had in New Mexico more than fifty years before. She picked up the quilt and ran her hand over it, pulling off a loose thread and tossing it off the porch, watching the wind pick it up. She'd wait outside for June, too. The girl might want to talk to her, out of earshot of Maria.

Ellen was right. June was on the telephone for a long time before she came back outside. "That was Dave. I guess you know that," she said. Her mother hadn't told him where to find her. Dave had figured it out on his own. "He knows this is my favorite place in the whole world, so I guess it wasn't hard," she said.

Ellen waited.

"I was wrong to run off like that." June glanced at her grand-mother. "Running away doesn't solve anything."

"No. I'm proof of that," Ellen said. She patted the seat beside her on the swing. "I'm not a very good example."

June sat down. "Maybe you are, Granny."

"Did you make any decisions?"

"Actually, we did."

"Whatever you decide, it will be the right thing. You can learn from my mistake." She pushed the swing back and forth.

"I don't think it was a mistake, not running away from James and Wade, anyway."

"But it was a mistake running off from Buddy."

"Was it? Maybe losing him made you realize how much you loved him. Buddy sounded pretty stubborn back then."

"He still is."

"You are, too, but you seem to work together all right. I can't help but think maybe he mellowed a little after you left. If you'd married him the first time around, he might never have let you stand up to him. Maybe he learned to value you more and figured he ought to stop telling you what to do."

Ellen hadn't thought of that. "Maybe," she said. She would ponder it later. Right now, she wanted to know about her grand-daughter. "So what did you and Dave decide?"

"A lot." June blew out her breath. "First of all, he agreed we shouldn't get married next month. He goes along with calling off the wedding."

Ellen looked down at the wedding quilt. "I guess I can put this away, then, at least for a little while. It'll be there whenever you marry."

"I'll claim it one day, just not right away," June told her.

"Have you broken up for good?"

"Oh, no." June turned to her grandmother and put her smooth hand over her grandmother's sunburned one. "We're going to wait until Dave's out of the service to decide. He agreed to that. I didn't think he would. He said he's been considering quitting the army ever since that fight."

"So you'll take the bank job in Colorado Springs?" Ellen was pleased. June would be only a few hours away, close enough to drive down for vacations or even long weekends. Ben would like that. The two of them could ride up into the mountains. For the first time Ellen saw that June was wearing blue jeans. She'd been so absorbed in the quilt and in her storytelling that she hadn't noticed. The girl had intended to go riding that day with her grandfather. Ben could still ride even if she couldn't. Now, living so close, June could accompany him.

"No, I'm not going to take it."

"Oh." Ellen tried not to show her disappointment. "Why not?"

"Because I want to move here, to the ranch."

Ellen almost let the quilt slip out of her grip before she realized it was falling to the floor and grabbed for it. "I don't understand."

"That is, if you want me. I can help Grandpa Ben with the cattle and do the ranch work you used to do with him. I could take over some of your chores—keeping the books, for instance. Paying the bills. After all, I took accounting. Dave won't get out of the army for two years, so I'd be here at least that long. Will you think about it, Granny?"

"I don't have to," Ellen said. "You're a godsend. You being here will give your grandfather two years before we have to move."

June reached for the quilt, running her finger over the last patch. "Maybe you won't have to move at all. I told Dave about

Grandpa Ben and how he's failing. Dave said maybe we should think about taking over the ranch and running it for you, maybe buy you out one day. He loved it down here. He said that after he read my note, he got serious about whether he wanted to spend the rest of his life in the military. With his family history, he'd never thought about doing anything else. He got to thinking about it and kind of liked the idea of doing something different. So when his time is up, he's going to ask for a discharge. Of course, he could change his mind again, but I'd be here for two years—time enough for you to pass on more of your stories—that is, if it's okay."

"Okay? Honey, you can stay here the rest of your life. In fact, I hope you do."

"That's what I'm thinking, Granny."

Ellen put her hand to her face and wiped away tears for the second time that day. She was getting to be a foolish old woman. She looked up to see Ben emerge from the barn and walk toward the kitchen. Her eyes followed him until he disappeared around the side of the house. Then she took the quilt from June and put it under her arm and picked up her sewing basket. "You're right to be cautious, Junie. Marriage lasts a long time. Your grandfather and I have been married almost fifty years," she mused.

June reached for the scissors that Ellen had left behind and started to open the screen for her grandmother. Then she stopped and laughed. "More than that, Granny. Dad is over fifty."

Ellen gave an embarrassed smile but didn't reply.

"Isn't that so?"

"I expect it is."

Ellen stared at the scissors a moment. "Wait. You were married, what, in 1902? Dad was born in 1899."

Ellen nodded. "That's about right."

"That means . . . I mean . . ." June said, looking away, too embarrassed to continue. "Did you know when you left the Rockin' A?"

Ellen shook her head. "By the time I knew I was going to have a baby, I thought Buddy had married Alice. I was too proud to let him know about my condition. Lucy might have told me he hadn't married, but she was dead." Ellen smiled at her granddaughter. "Why did you think I was so anxious to find a husband?"

Ellen looked down at the quilt in her arms, then held it to her face, her cheek against the white cotton square. She added, "I have to say those men were awful good about it when they found out I had a son. They wanted me anyway. James"—she shook his head—"I guess he just loved children and didn't care how he got them. And Wade might have needed to replace his daughter. Funny thing is, Wade was the one who told your grandfather about John. He said he was marrying a woman who had a three-year-old boy. He just let it slip out. Buddy always was pretty good at math." Ellen smiled, remembering. "I didn't have to tell Buddy about John at all. He just walked into my classroom and said we were getting married and he was taking his family home to Colorado."

Ben came out of the house onto the porch then and put his arm around Ellen's waist. "Come on, honey. Supper's ready. Maria's got it on the table."

Ellen leaned over to her granddaughter. "Your grandfather was wrong about one thing. I *did* think back then that he was the whole herd. I still do."